THE ANGEL
AND
THE SWORD

THE ANGEL
AND
THE SWORD

Sally Wragg

ROBERT HALE · LONDON

Robert Hale Limited
Clerkenwell House
Clerkenwell Green
London EC1R 0HT

www.halebooks.com

Typeset in Sabon
Printed in the UK by Berforts Information Press Ltd

For Emma and Nick – with love

Chapter One

High above Loxley New Hall, on a grassy hilltop dotted with buttercups and daisies, Henrietta Arabella, second Duchess of Loxley, despised flame-coloured hair flowing in an iridescent cascade behind her slim back, whirled dizzyingly round before finally, and with a cry of deep and utter joy, throwing herself spreadeagled onto the ground, to lie gazing up at a sky cobalt blue with fluffy white clouds. Miraculously, school was finished and much as she was going to miss all the friends she'd made there, she wasn't ever going back, no matter what anyone said, even her grandmother Katherine Loxley, the stern old matriarch who ruled their family with a rod of iron.

The world stopped spinning and Hettie became aware of a bee buzzing dangerously close to her nose which she flapped away, laughing delightfully and looking over to her companion, a good-looking boy of roughly her own age with dark curly hair and a cherubic expression hinting at his personality.

'No more school, Bill. Can you believe it?' she asked, flipping over onto her stomach. Bill threw himself down beside her and grinned.

'You'd better make the most of it, Het. They'll be on at you for something else before you know it,' he advised, as ever the voice of reason.

Aware of the truth of this curb to her freedom, Hettie pulled a face. It was an occupational hazard of being a duchess, she'd discovered. 'They can try,' she replied, levering herself up onto her elbows to cup her head in her hands. Mercurially, her mood had changed though Bill couldn't guess she was thinking of her late and much lamented father and how, school holidays and if only he'd still been here, they would have been off on one of their famous jaunts together. The Lakes, London, once even the giddy delights of Paris where they'd disappeared for a whole, blissful week together. Hettie still missed him; she still looked round for him, desperate to tell him some little happening in her life and then hurt like mad to find he wasn't there. Grandmother said life went on and time was a great healer but, for the moment, her pain was still too raw. Worse, she couldn't speak about it to anyone, not even Bill. But wasn't she too young to know that life could be so cruel?

Intuitively sensing more than she realized, Bill squeezed her hand, looking gratified when she didn't pull free. He wanted to kiss her and Hettie felt relieved when he decided against it. Reluctantly he let go, pulling at a blade of grass and chewing it meditatively.

'Mother's having another baby,' he blurted out.

She sat up quickly, suppressing her first and unforgive- able desire to laugh. Following the loss in the Great War of the father he was named for, Lizzie, Bill's mother, had married Sam Tennant, a Londoner, injured in the same war and who'd arrived in Loxley for what had been meant as a short spell of recupera- tion. Instead, he'd fallen in love with the place and with Lizzie Walker too, so he'd settled here for good, industriously building up the thriving little garage business in which Bill was currently employed. Poor Bill! However would they fit another child into that cramped little cottage next door to the garage? Hettie hardly knew what to say. But was it so very terrible? Her gaze slid towards him and she saw by his expression that it was. What an embarrassment parents were! 'At least you'll always have someone to talk to,' she soothed. 'Father always used to worry about me being an only . . .'

'But that'll make seven of us,' Bill groaned and, woes accumulating, revealed the rest of it. 'Mother's on about me going to college again,' he said.

This was more serious. Hettie frowned. 'But we'll never see each other!' she complained.

'Suppose,' he said, sounding uncertain.

Hopefully that meant he didn't want to go? 'At least your parents are happy,' she wheedled, quickly changing the subject onto safer ground. She was too happy; her spirits were too high to think about anything so unpalatable as Bill not being here, exactly where she wanted him. The summer stretched before them invitingly to do with as they would.

'What are you doing next, Het?' he asked.

'Having some tea, I expect,' she answered cheerfully and deliberately misunderstanding.

'I meant with the rest of your life.'

'Oh that. . . .'

'Yes, that!'

Why did he always have to be so serious? Feeling defensive and not sure why, she folded her arms around her knees and gave it some thought. 'Well, there's the estate,' she answered. Though given the mess affairs had been left in following her father's death and the swingeing taxes levied by Her Majesty's Government, she was more than a little relieved even her grandmother agreed she wasn't to trouble herself about that just yet.

'And . . . and marriage . . . children. Stuff like that?' Bill asked, colouring up but something – a death wish, he expected – driving him to ask. Some of Hettie's joy in the day evaporated.

'Someday, I'll get married. I suppose I'll have to, though thank goodness that day's a long way off yet,' she replied evasively.

Irritatingly, even then he refused to take the hint and let the matter drop.

'Hettie, you . . . you do know what I'm trying to say?'

Hettie did and in the typically awkward manner she usually

found so endearing. She scowled. She was so much more grown up than Bill, she mused, partly, she presumed, because of the serious business of being a duchess and partly because, well, girls simply were more mature than boys, weren't they? Everyone said so! This time her hand sought his, lacing her fingers through his so his blush deepened delightfully. 'If we want to be together then we will,' she told him with a quiet authority unusual in one so young. 'I won't let them force us apart if that's what you're worrying over. Just let's not . . . go too fast?'

'If you say so, Het,' he answered and a slow smile spread across his face, illumining it delightfully. 'I still can't believe you're here.'

'Nope, me neither.'

'Oh, Het,' he groaned, reaching towards her.

He'd changed his mind again and now he really did want to kiss her. He'd have to catch her first! Laughing, she sprang up, neatly evading him. 'Catch me!' she hooted and was off like a young gazelle, running down the slope and taking no heed as Bill sprang up and, with a warlike cry, bounded after her.

Watching the pair through the sitting room window stood a tall, fine-boned woman with a straight back and a remarkably forthright gaze telling any who cared to see it that this was a woman to be crossed at their peril. Katherine Loxley, Dowager Duchess of Loxley, frowned gloomily. With Hettie at boarding school and only home for the holidays; her grandmother had been praying she'd got young Bill Tennant out of her system long before now. With a rush of irritation, Katherine realized, since her son Harry had died, she'd let things slide, allowing situations to develop that once upon a time she'd have put a stop to long before now. Banging her stick to the floor, harrumphing quietly to herself, she swung away from the window, her gloom only deepening at the sight of her daughter-in-law, Bronwyn, entering the room, who, unforgivably to Katherine's view, given the statutory year's mourning was not yet out, had appeared at breakfast that morning dressed shockingly in a lilac skirt barely reaching her knees. There'd been words already. Quite frankly, Katherine hardly knew what society was coming to. Her brows rose, her gaze raking her unfortunate daughter-in-law from top to toe.

'Harry wouldn't have wanted me dressed in black forever,' Bronwyn murmured complacently, withstanding both look and frown with a fortitude brought about by long practice. She put down on the table a book of Katherine's she'd borrowed and was returning and which, in reality, was only an excuse to see her. As if she needed one! She smiled firmly. Shocked as they all were over Harry's death, Bronwyn could no longer avoid the fact, if this most pleasant part of England was not to fall into rack and ruin, economies would have to be made. Unpalatable as it was, it was time Katherine was made aware of it, too. 'I think we should sell one or two of the paintings,' she ventured, unsurprisingly nervous over the response.

Katherine was genuinely shocked. 'But things aren't so bad, surely?' she demanded, sharply.

'I'm afraid they are,' Bronwyn admitted quietly. 'If only we'd known beforehand, made some contingency plans, we could have avoided the worst of the death duties. . . .' Her voice trailed away. If only they'd known the fragment of shrapnel lodged in Harry's brain would move, thereby putting an end to the years of suffering he'd endured and which had been so dreadfully upsetting to everyone and to Bronwyn especially, who'd borne the brunt of it. Headaches, mood swings, the feeling no matter how hard she tried nothing was ever quite right. The last years of their married life had hardly been easy and she was only relieved she'd managed to shield Hettie from the worst of it. Hettie had adored her father and he'd adored her, too. Katherine's hand brushed hers, but so lightly she wondered if she'd imagined it. Despite the antagonism between them, she smiled gratefully.

'We must do what's needed,' Katherine agreed quickly and, as ever, resolutely refusing to give in to her own grief. What an iron-force the woman was!

'What are your plans for Hettie over the summer?' she asked, abruptly.

'Why . . . nothing in particular!' Bronwyn smiled. 'It'll just feel good to spend some time together. The theatre, shopping, that sort of thing?' Her face, largely untouched by the passing of the years, lit up happily at the thought.

'And long-term?' Katherine persisted.

'Something worthwhile – just until she's old enough to manage the estate. It is her birthright, remember?' she added teasingly and taken aback that Katherine, who was such a stickler that Loxley's numerous and occasionally irritating traditions must always be observed, had to be reminded of the fact. More sanguine as their relationship had been since the terrible fire, years since, when Loxley had nearly burnt down to the ground, Bronwyn sensed trouble. 'Feel free to join us, if you like?' she offered, wondering if, with Hettie having been away so much at school, Katherine had felt left out and that this was the problem.

'Better my company than her idling about with young Bill!' came the forthright reply, instantly making everything so much clearer.

Bronwyn frowned. 'Bill's a lovely young man,' she answered quietly.

Katherine's brows rose. 'You can't mean to say you haven't noticed how close they've grown of late? It simply won't do, Bronwyn! We don't want any unnecessary attachments forming. You know how headstrong the child is.'

Pots and kettles sprang to mind if she'd ever dare to express the thought. Bronwyn suppressed a smile. 'And if they have formed an attachment?' she demanded obtusely, deep down not wanting to understand.

Katherine's ire was stirred. 'You surely want more for her than the chauffeur's son? Think of her position, Bronwyn, for

Heaven's sake!' she barked.

'The chauffeur's grandson,' Bronwyn corrected bravely, taking pleasure in putting the old curmudgeon right. As soon as he'd returned from the Front, thankfully in remarkably good shape, Alf Walker, Lizzie's father, had resumed the reins of his old employment on the estate. Lizzie had only been guarding the position for him. Chauffeur he'd been before the war and chauffeur he would remain. But no matter how delicately Bronwyn put it, young Bill came from a working-class family and as far as Katherine was concerned, it simply wouldn't do. 'In any case, she's still only seventeen and that's far too young to be making any kind of an attachment yet, Bill or otherwise,' she persisted.

Katherine's eyes gleamed, leaving Bronwyn with the vague impression she'd been misunderstood and bringing to her mind the time when Harry had first introduced her as his prospective wife and new Duchess of Loxley. Daughter of a simple country doctor, she hadn't been considered good enough and it had taken the fire some several years later for Katherine to realize exactly where her true values lay. She couldn't have forgotten already, surely?

'Better nip it in the bud all the same. She should go away a while, see something of the world,' came the swift reply, so swift it was obvious she'd been mulling over the idea. Unfortunately, she'd forgotten the salient point and it was up to Bronwyn to put her right.

'Katherine, we simply can't afford for Hettie to go gadding about,' she reminded her.

Katherine shook her head pityingly. 'I have some money put by,' she persisted. 'She should travel. Paris, Venice, Rome. . . . It won't put you out, Bronwyn, if that's what you're thinking. Miss Pettigrew must be brought out of retirement. Blessed woman's nothing else to do other than to sit twiddling her thumbs.'

Dolores Pettigrew, known fondly by all as Dizzy, had been Hettie's governess before she'd been sent away to school. So neatly outmanoeuvred, Bronwyn bowed her head. Bang went her plans for the summer! Clearly irritated, she subsided into a silence fuelled by the thought that no matter how much Katherine desired it, the plan was doomed. The simple fact was if it meant she had to leave Bill behind, Hettie wouldn't want to go. Knowing how stubborn her young daughter could be once her mind was set, Bronwyn also knew, much as Katherine might wish it, there was no way she could force her.

It wouldn't stop her trying, she conceded, wearily. Battle, it appeared, was about to commence.

'I'm not going!' Hettie's voice brimmed with resentment and if she hadn't, at that moment, looked the very spit of Nell Loxley, her high-spirited ancestor, the first Duchess of Loxley, whose portrait hung in the great hall, Bronwyn would have said the one person her daughter most resembled was her formidable grand-mother. What a pair they were, the one so stubborn, the other so set in her ways and poor Bronwyn as usual caught in the middle, so whatever she did was wrong.

It was breakfast the following morning and Soames, their elderly butler, was refilling the coffee cups when Katherine first mooted the idea of Europe. Sensing trouble, Soames did as he always did at such times and discreetly withdrew, pulling the baize double doors quietly to behind him.

'Nonsense, child! It's just what you need,' Katherine answered, sanguinely.

'But I have plans!' came the indignant response. Hettie glared at her grandmother. Like spending as much time as she could with Bill, for one, though she'd no intention of telling her for-midable relative so. In desperation, she turned to her mother. 'You can't want to send me away again already? I've only just got home!' she wailed.

Bronwyn sipped her tea, answering with as much calmness as she could muster. 'I can't deny your grandmother has a point, darling. Think how marvellous it would be – all those wonderful places. You might never get another chance!'

They were ganging up on her and it wasn't fair but the situation could still be turned to her advantage. Hettie smiled sweetly. 'I thought you said we needed to economize?' she pointed out, unable to hide her triumph at stating this one, undeniable fact.

'I'll take care of the cost,' Katherine said, at once.

But if she went away now, she'd never be able to see Bill! This thought was hotly followed by the next, which was that somewhere here was the real reason for this wretched plan. Exactly what she might have expected from her grandmother but her mother, too? How could she! Hettie set down her cup with a clatter. She was furious with them both and not afraid to show it.

'They're trying to split us up,' she burst out crossly to Bill as soon after breakfast as she could decently get away. They stood together on the garage forecourt beside the battered old Ford motor which, with Sam's blessing, Bill was in the process of doing up. He stood, running a hand through his hair, leaving a smudge of oil on his cheek that instantly Hettie longed to smooth away. Events were moving too fast, even for her, leaving her emotions all over the place so she scarcely knew what she wanted any more. She frowned, looking past Bill and into the garage where Sam Tennant lay flat on his back under a motor's exhaust pipe which, given the fact he'd lost the biggest part of his left hand when the Boche had tried to blow up the bus he'd driven transporting troops along the front line, he was fixing with remarkable dexterity. In the garden of the cottage next door, numerous children of varying sizes were playing happily whilst Lizzie, their mother, grown comfortably plump over the years and already filling out with her pregnancy, hung the washing out. She saw Hettie and waved happily.

Hettie waved back. 'What are we going to do?' she demanded, if having no expectation of an answer.

Bill was at a loss too. 'I knew this would happen,' he grumbled miserably, looking young and confused and something else now too, forbidden fruit when Hettie wouldn't be forbidden anything, not now, not ever and certainly not when she was nearly eighteen and already a duchess. Not for the first time, Hettie considered the power of her position. She would have what she wanted and no one was going to stop her, not even her grandmother, well-intentioned as she might be. Uncaring that Lizzie might see and perhaps unforgivably considering the way she knew Bill felt about her, she reached up and dropped a light kiss on the young man's cheek, gratified when at once he attempted to pull her into his arms. Teasingly, she sprang away and, experiencing one of her abrupt mood changes, laughed happily up at him.

'Sorry, Bill, I shall have to go. . . .'

'Hettie, don't. . . . Stay a while!' She shook her head. It was tempting but she really did need to get back. 'I'll be back. And don't worry,' she encouraged him. 'They'll send me away from Loxley over my dead body. . . .'

Basking in the warmth of the light reflected from the church's great west window, Ursula Hamilton, née Compton, knelt to settle sweet williams on her grandfather's grave. Ned Compton had loved sweet williams. She liked to think of his old bones at rest here in the churchyard, companion to Loxley's other favoured servants who'd finally thrown off the shackles of life. If Ned was here now, he'd tell her to pull herself together, Ursula mused, fretfully.

'I wish you were here, Grandpa,' she murmured, rocking back on her heels and thinking of the dear old man whose passing had left such a void in her life.

The morning was rushing on. Regretfully she stood up, dusting down her knees and reclaiming her shopping, at her feet, not having to think far why she'd so impulsively slipped into the churchyard. She often did when she'd anything of importance to tell him. And now there was nothing for it but that she must tell the living too. Starting not where she ought, with her husband Freddie, who she somehow couldn't yet face, but with her mother, an interview bad enough as it was. . . .

'Are you alright, our Ursula?' Mary Compton asked, knowing as soon as Ursula walked through the door, looking as if she'd the cares of the world on her slim shoulders, that something was up.

'Why shouldn't I be alright?' Ursula retorted flatly, only deepening her mother's concern. Wearily, she dropped her bag to the floor before sinking thankfully into one of the chairs at the table where her mother stood, making the pastry for a pie.

'Your dad's out. . . .'

'I saw him talking to one of the helpers in Freddie's field, on the way up here,' Ursula agreed but so listlessly, Mary knew wherever her thoughts were, they certainly weren't with Tom, her father nor with anyone belonging to the camping trip from the boys' home who'd rented one of the Hamiltons' fields for the week.

'I'll make tea,' she said, wiping flour from her hands and crossing the kitchen to lift the kettle.

Seeing her disinclined to talk, whilst she made the tea, Mary kept up a ceaseless chatter, full of all the things she'd been wanting to tell her but hadn't, as yet, had chance. She'd seen so little of her daughter of late, unsurprisingly, given this time of year and the fact all the farms roundabout, Freddie's included, were busy with hay-making. Her thoughts emerged randomly. The honey harvest from the bees in the back garden, so satisfyingly good, Hettie Loxley back from school and causing trouble already from what she'd heard, the village cricket match and fancy them asking Tom to open the batting at his age and when he had a bad knee to boot. . . .

'Ursula, have you heard a word I've said?' she demanded, finished at last.

'I've been to the doctor's,' Ursula answered quietly and so shockingly unexpectedly, Mary knew she wasn't about to hear the news she and Tom had been so longing to hear. She sank back into her chair, her face instantly fretted and worried.

'You're not ill, our Ursula? Please tell me you're not ill!' she demanded urgently.

Aware there was no easy way to say this, Ursula did her best to compose herself. 'I'm afraid I've had some bad news, Mother. News that I don't quite know how to tell you . . . but . . . oh dear . . . I can't have children!' she blurted out, her own pain in giving air to such a horrible truth completely overriding her mother's gasp of dismay.

Typically, Mary's first thoughts were for Ursula.

'Oh my darling. . . . I am sorry! But . . . but you mustn't fret. It's really not the end of the world.'

'Just feels like it?' Ursula answered drily, wishing desperately that ever since she and Freddie had wed, she hadn't so desperately pinned her hopes on their having children, a force of nature she'd always taken for granted. Freddie she knew had always longed for children. 'It's my fault,' she added bitterly, wanting there to be no illusions and wondering if she should have made this clear from the start. It was all her fault, nothing to do with Freddie and for the moment she wasn't sure if this made things better or worse.

'It's no one's fault. These things happen,' Mary hastened to assure her, trying to soften the blow.

'You think I don't know it?' her daughter demanded scathingly, too late biting her lip. Dimly she was aware, and ashamed of herself for it, that she was lashing out and at her mother, of all people, who only ever wanted the best for her. But she needed to rail at someone and who better than her mother? Freddie would be upset enough as it was. Thoughts she'd yet to tell Freddie only deepened her gloom.

'It wouldn't be the first time doctors have got things wrong, our Ursula,' Mary pointed out.

'I've been for the tests and had the results. There's no mistake,' she murmured, miserably. There was no point leaving any false hope. Sorrowfully, she remembered the kindly doctor who'd patted her shoulder in a fatherly manner, telling her meanwhile there was more to life than having children and she wasn't to treat it like a calamity. Ursula shook her head. If only he'd had the slightest idea how much she longed to hold a baby in her arms, the likeness of Freddie who she loved more than life itself.

Mary, meanwhile, farmer's daughter and pragmatist, upset as she was by the news, was already coming to terms with it. 'What's Freddie had to say?' she asked, going straight to the heart of the matter.

Ursula took a gulp of tea with a hand that wasn't quite steady.

'Freddie doesn't know. I haven't told him yet,' she said.

Her mother was scandalized. 'Darling, I really think you ought!'

'You think I don't know?' Ursula's voice was shaking, the despair she'd hugged so helplessly to herself finally bubbling over, almost overwhelming her. 'He wants children more than anything, Mother! How can I tell him? He only got through the war thinking of the family he'd have when he got home. And now I've failed him even in this!'

Mary came round the table and hugged her, not letting go until she saw she had her feelings back under control. 'You'll get through this,' she said firmly, willing her to believe it.

Ursula shook her head. Her mother hardly knew the half of it, yet.

Katherine Loxley sat stiffly upright in a hard-backed chair, directly across from the little man with the unassuming face and yet surprisingly sharp, intelligent eyes, owner of a set of shabby rooms over the haberdasheries in Derby's Sadler Gate. A man discreet enough to hide his surprise at the intended sale of the bracelet she'd just taken from her bag and handed across the desk.

'It's a fine piece, Your Grace,' he murmured quietly, relinquishing the magnifying glass through which he'd been perusing it and going on to name a sum happily surprising to her. Trust George, her late lamented husband, old rogue that he'd been! But she'd always known he would never have given her anything of inferior quality. George had always wanted the best, especially when it had come to his marriage. She'd been a good wife to him and if he, at times, had behaved badly towards her, she'd loved him all the same.

'You're a good man, Gideon,' she answered, reaching across to shake his hand and seal the bargain. Selling the bracelet left her curiously unaffected, she realized as, transaction complete, she slipped back down the narrow staircase, re-emerging into the bright sunshine full of the promise of a long and lazy summer to come. The morning was rushing on and yet, the finance for Hettie's proposed venture happily secured, still Katherine lingered, musing over her reflection in the shop window and remembering the evening many years since when George had given her the bracelet, peace offering for all that business over the girl he'd got into trouble and the baby laid at their door. Blood money, she grimaced – no wonder she'd been glad to see the back of it. It was release to think some good should finally come of such wrong. Mollified by the thought, she walked on, quickly regaining the cathedral, by which the Daimler was parked. Seeing her, Alf Walker hurried to open the door.

'There you are, ma'am. . . .'

'Home,' she ordered, before thankfully sliding onto the back seat and, as the familiar countryside flashed smoothly by, giving her thoughts once more to Hettie's trip to Europe and how she was best able to bring it about. Hettie was so stubborn, her mind so unfortunately set on a boy who if likeable, to put it bluntly, simply wouldn't do. A boy who happened to be her driver's grandson, she realized, with a start, frowning at the back of his head and the neatly cropped grey hair showing under his driver's cap. She leaned forwards, tapping sharply on the glass partition with the handle of her walking stick. 'You must be pleased to see Lizzie so settled, Alf,' she began pleasantly as his head craned round towards her.

'I am that, ma'am,' he agreed, sounding surprised.

'And young Bill provided with a father?'

Eyes firmly fixed on the road now, his head nodded rapidly. 'Aye. He's a bright lad, Your Grace. His mother wants him to go to college.' The old war veteran sighed, a note of frustration entering his voice of which Katherine was instantly and hearteningly aware.

'But that's good, Alf, surely?' she probed.

'Hah! Stupid young fool won't go. . . . Says he's more important things on his mind!' he retorted, for a moment forgetting to whom he addressed himself. Suddenly he did remember and his neck flushed a dull shade of red. Aware of it, Katherine leaned back, shocked into doing what she hadn't done for many a long while which was to consider the situation from another's point of view.

'You mean Hettie's on his mind?' she asked quietly.

Alf Walker was obviously mortified. 'I didn't mean 'owt by it, Your Grace,' he blustered.

'Quiet, man,' she said, not unkindly, her mind working overtime and wondering how best to turn the information to all their advantages. 'Would you like me to talk to him?' she asked abruptly.

Alf glanced quickly over his shoulder. 'But we couldn't possibly trouble you, Your Grace!'

Couldn't they indeed? His employer smiled. 'Consider it done,' she said.

Back at Loxley and deciding there was no time like the present, first calling to the two dogs, a black and a golden Labrador, lounging in the sunshine pooling through her sitting room window, she returned quickly outside, heading in determined fashion back towards the village and Sam Tennant's garage where once again she discovered luck was on her side. It gave her heart, should she have required it, assuring her her actions were right. The young lad in question was seeing off a customer, standing back as the motor drove away and wiping his hands on a cloth as Katherine appeared on his horizon. He frowned in obvious surprise.

'Um . . . can I help you, Your Grace?'

'Bill, isn't it?' Katherine smiled, seeing at once what Hettie saw in him. A fresh-faced young boy with an air of honesty about him but one, as she'd thought, totally lacking in the social graces. Thoughts of her precious Hettie making any such disastrous attachment drove her on. 'Could you spare me a moment, Bill? I promise I won't keep you long.' Without waiting for answer, she called to the dogs, presently receiving a gratifying fuss from any number of children playing in the garden next door, and began to walk back the way she'd come. Clearly perplexed as to her business, Bill hurried after her.

Katherine's sideways glance slid over him. There was no way other than to come right out with it. 'You and Hettie seem very close,' she said.

'She's a grand girl, Your Grace,' he answered, far too vehemently for Katherine's liking.

They were at the top of the road leading out from the village.

'She most certainly is,' she agreed, treating him to the kind of look which had made many a lesser man quail. This young man, however, was made of stronger stuff and stood his ground admirably. 'She also happens to be the Duchess of Loxley,' Katherine persisted, despite it, a glint of steel springing into her eyes. 'Free as she might appear now, with regards to her future, well. . . . Clearly her future is already marked. As yours is too, I believe? Your grandfather was only telling me this morning, college has been mentioned?'

The young man frowned. 'It has but. . . .'

'I can't believe you wouldn't want to go. You must want to

make the best of yourself?' Katherine's voice drove on remorselessly; carrying all before it, even Bill. 'Just as it's important that Hettie be allowed to spread her wings and travel Europe as we'd planned. Of course, on her return, we'll need to find her a suitable husband.' She paused, sweeping her hand towards Loxley, shimmering and twinkling before them in the warmth of the midday sun. 'Someone of . . . equivalent social standing, shall we say?' Did he understand her? She saw by his quick frown that he did and unexpectedly she discovered she felt sorry for him. Her voice softened and if only she could have softened the import of her words. 'You have to let her go, Bill. Before you hurt her irreparably,' she said softly.

'But I love her!' he burst out heatedly.

'You only think you do,' she answered sharply. 'You'll move on, find someone else.'

'I won't! I'll never love anyone else!'

The vehemence of his reply took her aback but Katherine wasn't about to put up with such defiance from anyone, least of all this young pup. And yet still, oddly, she found herself wishing there was some way these two young people could be together. She shook her head, as if to clear it from such a preposterous notion. Her darling girl was heir to Loxley and this young man must be made to understand it. 'You have to be strong . . . for the both of you,' she urged, her hand brushing his arm gently, before calling to the dogs and walking briskly away.

Bill stood, staring balefully after her, a great well of protest rising up inside him. He couldn't give Hettie up and how the blazes could anyone expect him to? He loved her; he'd always loved her, a situation unspoken between them though she knew it as perfectly well as he. They were meant for each other. Surely life couldn't be so cruel. . . .

Dressed in riding habit, Hettie was returning from the stables where she'd taken upon herself the task, whenever she was home, of exercising her father's hunter, Tallow. The euphoria of leaving school had already and annoyingly vanished. Two whole days had passed since she'd last spent meaningful time with Bill, time in which despite all her best efforts, he'd proved frustratingly evasive, unbelievably pleading he'd altogether too much on at the garage to spare any time to see her; worse, capping it all this afternoon by bolting into his house as she'd ridden by when she knew he must have seen her. She was beginning to think she'd upset him. How crazy to have imagined, now school was over, they'd have spent every spare moment they could together.

Walking through the great hall, she made straight for the sitting room where Soames was dispensing afternoon tea to her grandmother. 'Mother not here?' she asked, throwing herself disconsolately down into an armchair.

'She's gone into the village.' Katherine passed her a cup of tea, failing to add it was to see Dizzy Pettigrew to test the waters with regard to the proposed trip to Europe. There was no point causing further upset when, going by the look on Hettie's face, there was trouble enough. 'No need to ask if you've had a good day,' she added drily, taking her own tea and going to stand with her back to the empty fireplace to drink it.

Soames departed. Hettie drank her tea moodily. It wasn't just Bill. She was only too aware it had all gone suspiciously quiet about the Europe trip, leading her to believe things were happening she wasn't, as yet, a party to. Her grandmother didn't usually give in so easily. 'I'm not going on that trip,' she said defiantly, raising the matter herself.

Katherine drank her tea calmly. 'Aren't you, dear?'

'I mean it!'

'Child, you're seventeen,' the old woman scoffed gently, still yet something inside warming at such an uncommon show of spirit. The chit was a Loxley after all and Katherine wouldn't have it any other way. 'We'll see,' was all she said. She finished her tea, regarding her granddaughter's glowering countenance with affection which, in anyone else, might have been described as doting. 'Is there anything else troubling you?' she enquired innocently. Hettie's slim shoulders lifted. 'It's Bill if you must know, Grandmamma. He's avoiding me and I've no idea why.'

'Oh I see,' said Katherine, who had every idea and perversely, was very sorry for it. She was getting soft in her old age! 'But he must be busy, darling,' she encouraged. 'I was talking to Alf Walker, his grandfather, only the other morning. He told me his family want him to go to college.'

'Hah!' Hettie exploded.

'But important at his age, don't you agree?' Katherine persisted, for her, surprisingly gently. Really, she considered, the child was being ridiculously obtuse. 'My dear girl, you're both so young. I know right now Bill seems the most important person in the world to you. . . .'

Hettie's features sprang to vivid and over-emotional life. 'Oh but Grandmamma, we really like each other! I mean being with each other so much, I've even wondered – oh, if it might not be something more!' It had gone deeper than she'd hoped. Katherine shook her head sadly. 'Believe me, darling, you'll grow out of it. You mustn't set such store by your feelings!'

'We're old enough to make up our own minds,' Hettie retorted, suddenly aware, dearly as she loved her grandmother, that as far as Bill was concerned, she was talking to the enemy. Opposition was coming from all quarters, she and Bill frowned upon as if they had no right to be together and it simply wasn't fair! Worried she'd said too much already and worse, to her grandmother who was in any case only intent on packing her off to Europe, she sprang up and, first throwing the old woman a look full of reproach, departed the room, going quickly upstairs to change before heading outside.

'Whatever's got into you, Bill? That's the monkey wrench, not the spanner!' Sam Tennant poked his head out from under the bonnet of the motor occupying space in his garage, his quick frown sitting uneasily on his lean, good-natured face. The years had been good to Sam Tennant, the happiness of his marriage and his family life, and the thriving little garage business he'd built up during the intervening years, doing much to help wash away so many of the bad memories left over from the war. Bill retrieved the spanner from the workbench, passing it into his stepfather's good hand. Seeing the young lad's crestfallen demeanour, Sam's expression softened. 'Are you still fretting over college?' he asked.

'Yes . . . no . . . sort of. . . .' came the garbled reply as, at that moment, the slim figure of a young girl appeared at the entrance to the garage. It was Hettie. Having a strong suspicion that here, more than anywhere else, was the cause of Bill's erratic behaviour, Sam nodded towards her. 'Looks like you've a visitor,' he said.

Bill spun round, blushing miserably when he saw who it was. 'Hettie. . . .'

'Bill. . . .' she responded so awkwardly, instantly Sam wondered if they'd had a falling-out. What a pair!

'Why don't you go for a walk,' he suggested, scrambling up and reaching for a cloth from the bench to wipe his hands. 'It's near enough teatime and you're no good to me as you are, lad. A little fresh air will happen clear your head.'

Miracles might happen! Hettie threw him a grateful look before following Bill outside into the warmth of the afternoon, by common consent, turning away from the village and back towards Loxley, which even now, mixed up as she was, seemed to draw her from all points of the compass.

He might look pleased to see her. 'What's wrong?' she asked.

Bill plunged his hands into the pockets of his overalls. 'Must there be anything?' He scowled.

'Oh . . . I wondered, that was all, only you seem in a bad mood.'

26

'Do I? I can assure you, I'm not.'

'They're still on at me about Europe,' she said, puzzled by his obvious animosity.

'What a surprise,' he responded, shooting her an enigmatic glance that only made the situation worse.

They'd reached the top of the lane. Nimbly, he vaulted the dry stone wall shielding the lane from the meadow beyond, turning to help her over, piqued when she ignored him, preferring to scramble over herself. 'You might look as if you're bothered,' she said, feeling hurt and confused and only too horribly aware that her temper was stirring. Whatever could have happened between now and their last meeting when he'd been so happy to see her? Was he having second thoughts? Heaven forbid if he'd decided he didn't care for her after all!

'Hettie, I'm going to college!' he burst out, shocking her, the last thing she'd expected.

They'd begun to walk down the meadow towards the hall but, at this, she cannoned to a halt, staring up at him in consternation.

'I thought you'd decided against it,' she wailed.

Bill's gaze, normally such a steady one, was curiously evasive. 'I . . . I hadn't really thought about it but. . . . Now I've decided I want to go!'

'But why . . . I don't understand!'

'I have to, Hettie, can't you see?'

She could see and part of her accepted it made sense. But equally she was sure there was something else he wasn't telling her. 'But we'll never get the chance to see each other,' she said, slowly, the reality of it hitting her as hard as if he'd dealt her a physical blow. 'What about us, Bill?' she asked quietly, aware now of her heart thundering in her ears, like she'd just asked the most important question she'd ever asked anyone ever and worse, knew that the answer was going to be one she didn't want to hear. It was there, plain on his face. He was going to college where he'd forget all about her. He didn't care about her at all.

'There'll be evenings, weekends,' he pleaded.

'You'll have homework . . . college work!'

'There's that, of course. . . .'

'So you'll see me when and if you can manage to fit me in?' She fired up indignantly and yet, part of her was aware she was being unfair. Why shouldn't he go to college and make the best of himself? She'd gone away to school, much as she'd hated it. 'I might as well go to Europe. There's nothing to keep me here,' she muttered, disconsolately.

Bill stood, running his hand through his hair. It was obvious she knew nothing of her grandmother's visit and he realized now there was no way he could tell her. The old woman had stitched him up good and proper; knowing full well he was bound to put Hettie's needs first. He swallowed miserably. How could he give her up given the way he felt?

'It . . . it might not be a bad thing, Het. It won't be forever after all,' he said.

It would just feel like forever. If this was love, you could keep it! Hettie's pride stifled her instant heartfelt retort that she loved him, that she never ever wanted them to be parted. She couldn't believe he was doing this to them. She wouldn't give him satisfaction! He could do whatever he wanted without her! 'It will be forever, Bill,' she uttered fiercely, even though her voice was trembling and she hated with a passion the fact they were falling out. Her grandmother was right after all. She was too young to fall in love properly and especially with someone like Bill who didn't even appear to know his own mind any more. So saying, without giving him another glance, she walked smartly away, knowing instinctively that he stood watching her until she was out of sight.

Chapter Two

'The post, Your Grace,' Soames murmured, proffering the silver salver bearing the morning's post to Bronwyn, who sat drinking coffee in Katherine's sitting room. Her face broke into a wide smile of approval.

'Another card from Hettie!'

'Where's she got to now?' Katherine demanded but only after their old family retainer had retired. This was family business. She stood by the empty fireplace, fingering an exquisitely carved bird; one of several similar woodland creatures discovered in the cottage last inhabited by Reuben Fairfax, their ex-gamekeeper, whom Katherine still hated to think of as her husband's by-blow. She returned the bird, a kestrel, wings outstretched, to its resting place. News of Hettie, on whom she doted, had at least snapped her out of her reverie.

'They've reached Venice,' Bronwyn replied, reading out loud, 'Dizzy has a cold. The hotel summoned the doctor, who confined her to her room . . . Heavens – but in summer? "Please tell Bill I miss him."' She paused, wishing, too late, she'd kept this last to herself. Inwardly cringing, she waited for the inevitable outburst.

'We'll tell him no such thing – she's being deliberately provocative, of course!' Katherine snorted, clearly irritated and right on cue.

'Bill is her best friend,' Bronwyn protested at once, ignoring her mother-in-law's small moue of disapproval which, for once, left her unperturbed. Delighted as Bronwyn was that Hettie was taking the chance to travel around Europe and at an age when she was most likely to reap its benefits, she still felt uneasy about the way Katherine had so successfully engineered events. Worryingly, after her initial refusal to countenance the trip, Hettie had been too compliant by far for her mother's liking, setting off with Dolores, her ex-governess, without a whimper of protest, so unlike her when, more usually, she had an opinion on everything, no matter how minute. Pig-headed some would say, Bronwyn conceded, knowing who to blame for it too and throwing Katherine a glance touched by a surprising fondness. But some altercation had occurred between Hettie and young Bill, Lizzie's eldest, before her daughter had left. Bronwyn treated Katherine to another, this time uneasier, glance. 'I saw Lizzie the other day,' she added belatedly, remembering the news that had brought her hurrying up here. 'Isn't it wonderful about the baby?'

Katherine frowned. 'Another baby on the way? For heaven's sake! But where on earth will they put it? The house is crammed enough already!'

Inadvertently, it appeared poor Bronwyn had only wandered from one thorny subject to the next. But if that was how Lizzie liked it? Imagining if she tried hard enough, she might even manage to find a subject upon which they both agreed, the younger woman subsided back into her chair. 'At least she thinks Bill's settled at college,' she murmured, wise enough now to refrain from telling this overbearing woman what Lizzie had added, that her dear son had spent so much time moping around the house of late, she'd been glad to get him out from under her feet. There'd been no need to ask why and a good part of Bronwyn felt sorry for it. She was sorry for Hettie too, if she'd never dare to admit it to Katherine.

'You shouldn't concern yourself so with the servants,' Katherine pointed out sharply.

She meant not to lower herself by engaging in conversation with a woman whom Katherine considered working class. But what if Lizzie *was* working class! Bronwyn happened to be inordinately fond of Lizzie Tennant even if, for now, expediency made her bite her tongue. She was tired of arguing. 'I wonder what Reuben's up to nowadays?' she asked, trying fresh tack and remembering the way Katherine's expression had softened when she'd held Reuben's carving. If she'd never admit it, Katherine missed him as much as everyone else. Once upon a time, Reuben Fairfax had been a fixture around this place. But he'd gone, disappeared as if he'd never existed, and there was no way to find out where he'd hidden himself. Katherine stiffened visibly. 'I'm afraid I've no idea where Reuben is and that's just the way I'd like it to stay,' she added, as if she felt she needed to.

'He was Harry's brother,' Bronwyn answered quietly, aware she was taking a chance in rattling this particular skeleton in the Loxley cabinet. But Katherine must have feelings on the subject and it didn't do her any good to keep her emotions so consistently in check. A stiff upper lip was one thing but, as usual, she took it too far. There was something else Bronwyn needed to mention and this was altogether too good an opportunity to miss. 'I was surprised he didn't come to the funeral. It was in all the papers. Surely he must have seen it?'

Her mother-in-law's response was unexpected. 'Mayhap he did,' she murmured, enigmatically. 'Mary Compton thought she saw him during the service or, at least, someone very much like him but he'd left before she had chance to find out for sure. I'd have told you at the time but. . . . Well, my dear, you were grieving for Harry. I didn't want to upset you when there was perfectly no need.'

Such an unwarranted show of sensitivity, and from Katherine, of all people, was surprising but the news itself was encouraging. Perhaps Reuben had cared about Harry after all? Somehow it mattered that he had. 'But I wonder why he didn't stay on?' Still digesting the news, Bronwyn frowned. It wouldn't have hurt him, surely? He surely could have waited to see them if only to check that they were alright? Temporarily, the discussion was halted as the door opened and Soames reappeared.

'A visitor, Your Grace. A Mr Roland . . . de Loxley?' he intoned and with only the barest of tremors in his voice to indicate the news distressed him. The name made both women start.

'De Loxley?' Katherine demanded.

Wondering what further surprises the day was likely to bring, Bronwyn put down her coffee cup and stood up. 'You'd better show him in,' she said, throwing Katherine an uneasy glance.

Moments later, the old man returned to usher in their visitor, a man in the prime of middle age, his dark hair, greying at the temple, worn short and neatly cut. He was wearing a tweed jacket and jumper over casual trousers, the whole effect understated and yet obviously expensive. Bronwyn found her hand enveloped in a cool, firm grip.

'Please forgive the intrusion,' he murmured in a voice bearing only the faintest of accents. 'But I was over in England on business and this seemed altogether too good a chance to miss. . . .'

Bronwyn was charmed. He turned to Katherine, who took his hand frostily, her gaze sweeping over him from head to foot.

'I'm afraid you have us at a loss . . . Mr de Loxley. . . ?' she exclaimed stiffly.

'Please, let me tell you why I'm here,' he returned, standing up to the scrutiny remarkably well. His explanation was both swift and succinct. He wondered if they might be related, he told them, to their general astonishment. His family were wine-makers, settled in the Loire valley for generations reaching back to the Civil War when, Royalists to a man, his ancestors had fled from Cromwell's England to a France which had apparently welcomed them with open arms. He smiled, his eyes twinkling. 'Our connection goes back to a younger brother of the fourth Duke. . . . Tenuous, I know but a link for all that!' he finished warmly. 'Nell Loxley's uncle?' Bronwyn frowned though thinking, on reflection, that the story their visitor had just imparted was not so very outlandish. From all she knew of Nell Loxley's immediate family, during the time of the Civil War, they were scattered all around Europe.

'How did you come across this information?' Katherine demanded, sounding put out.

Roland de Loxley sat down, looking towards her eagerly. 'It was something rather mundane, I'm afraid, a series of articles on English stately homes published in one of our qualities, one in particular focusing on Loxley and the discovery of some remains, several years ago, by the vicar here, a Mr Lawrence Payne. I understand it led to a clearer understanding of your family's ancestry?'

'I might have known,' Katherine muttered crossly. Bronwyn meanwhile, merely looked worried. Whilst her redoubtable mother-in-law had to admit the truth of all that had been uncovered those years since concerning Nell Loxley and the two local brothers, one of whom she'd married, the other with whom she'd fallen in love, she hardly liked to be reminded of the fact that generations of staid and, in the main, eminently respectable Loxlians issued from an illegitimate line. If he did but know it, their visitor was skating on extremely thin ice. 'It was only hearsay. . . .' Katherine's tone was icy.

Belatedly Roland de Loxley became aware that he might have caused offence. 'I do hope I haven't spoken out of turn? Our connection is very well known to the rest of our family. I'm only surprised . . . you've never heard of us?'

Katherine drew herself up to her full height. A powerful and intimidating woman, unused to being baited and worse, in her own lair. 'You'd be amazed how many folk would like to lay claim to our family, Monsieur de Loxley!' she answered haughtily.

For the first time during the interview, Roland de Loxley appeared uneasy. 'Well, there it is. I can only reiterate that I hope you don't mind I've looked you up? If I've inadvertently caused any offence, I do apologize. . . .'

One of them at least remembered their manners. 'Of course

you haven't,' Bronwyn interceded pleasantly. 'Why on earth should we be offended? We're delighted to see you. Are you here for long?'

He flashed her a grateful look. 'Roland, please,' he countered, all smiles again, the most amiable of men, moreover one refusing to be riled even by Katherine. 'A few days,' he answered quickly. 'Though I was hoping I might be able to stretch it to longer. I'm put up at The Oak in the village. I'd take it as a huge compliment if you would allow me to get to know you both a little better? My mother will be absolutely delighted when I tell her we've been in touch. . . .'

'Look at this – best we've had this month!' Holding a tray full of eggs, the day's quota, Pru Flite shook off her wellington boots and hurried into the kitchen of Merry Weather farm where Ursula Hamilton stood at the table making up a flask for Freddie, who'd been up in the fields since daybreak, giving the distinct impression he was avoiding her. Since she'd told him about the baby, or the lack of one, things had been difficult between them to say the least. She looked up and, despite her uneasiness, still managed to find a smile. Ursula had always got on well with Pru, who'd been with them for years, first arriving at the farm as a young land girl and then, discovering she liked the life so much, seeing no reason since to leave. She rented a cottage from Freddie on the land bordering Loxley and had made herself so useful they couldn't do without her now.

'You must have hexed the hens,' Ursula joked, surprised at a little, rising stab of resentment at the thought. She'd looked after the hens herself during old Raith Hamilton's time and had been lucky if there'd been eggs enough for the farmhouse's needs, never mind the ever growing number of villagers they now supplied. Raith had used to tease Ursula remorselessly at the birds' lack of productivity, as had Freddie. It had been a brainwave on her part to let Pru take over.

'Wise birds, hens. They sense when they've met their match!' Pru returned swiftly, depositing the tray on the table and sitting down to cup her capable hands around the mug of tea Ursula poured and pushed across the table. Her gaze grew suddenly serious. 'Are you alright, Ursula?' she asked. 'Only . . . you have been rather quiet of late.'

That was Pru, always spoke her mind. It was on the tip of Ursula's tongue to tell this pleasant and still attractive woman exactly what was wrong. The baby that wasn't and never would be, her aching sense of loss and, worse, her inability to share her feelings with Freddie. All they'd succeeded in doing so far was to skirt around the problem, both apparently too concerned with their own loss to cope with the other's misery as well. It might even do her good to talk to Pru and yet inhibition – or pride, she wasn't sure which – held her back. It didn't feel right talking to anyone else about something so personal, even Pru, especially when she and Freddie had yet to resolve the issue themselves.

'Oh, you know how it is – too much work, not enough time,' she said and, well intentioned as it was, passed off the enquiry before moving the conversation to other, less important matters: the weather, Freddie's plans for winter planting, the butter in the dairy that refused to turn. Pru was no fool and Ursula had the uneasy feeling she hadn't fooled her in the slightest.

On the excuse of taking Freddie his flask, she finished her tea and removed herself outside, away from her employee's too penetrating gaze, into the remains of the summer and a welcome cool breeze which fanned her overheated cheeks. As she walked, still with the lithe and easy steps of a girl, into the scene of her childhood, centring her no matter what problems life threw her way, Ursula began at last to relax. Behind lay Loxley, golden in the sunshine, and beyond, the Old Hall, raising its broken turrets into a bright blue sky dappled with fluffy, cotton-wool balls of scudding cloud. Hurrying now, suddenly longing to see Freddie, she pressed on towards the meadow, her spirits lifting when she saw it dotted with canvas tents, colourful strips of bright blue and green. This week the field had been rented by a troop of Venture Scouts, the scheme Ursula's own, putting to good use an otherwise unproductive pastureland and bringing in a steady and surprisingly lucrative income to the farm. It was a relief to know she could still get some things right.

She could see Freddie, kneeling by the wall at the bottom end of a field where he'd just herded the sheep out to pasture. Once upon a time, the sight of her husband going about his tasks around the farm would have had her taking to her heels, a giddy young girl again, nothing in her head but flying into his open arms. And what would happen if she did that now, she wondered and, imagining his surprise, shock even, restraining the impulse; sorry then that she did, thus denying them a moment of happiness when there'd been so little in their lives of late. At her approach, Freddie stood up, brushing the dirt from his knees and frowning.

'I've brought your tea,' she began, handing him the flask sedately and as befitting a matron of her advanced years. She smiled up at him. The years had been kind to Freddie Hamilton; his thick, curly hair still without a trace of grey, the craggy features below it, filled with the same restless energy which had seen him through both the war and all the trials and tribulations of farming life.

'Thanks, love,' he said but his voice so low and devoid of emotion, once again she was left wondering how this constraint had happened between them and, worse, how she was ever going to break through it.

They loved each other. There must be a way.

'Freddie, we need to talk!' she blurted out.

Not even bothering to argue with her, he nodded uneasily, his gaze sliding past her to the wall he was in the process of rebuilding. Good Derbyshire stone of varying sizes and heaviness which he was fitting together with the skill he brought to all the tasks around the farm. Ordered things he knew how to manage as, of late, Ursula sensed he'd known so little what to do with his wife.

'You mean about the baby. . . .' he muttered, frowning.

'I mean about the baby,' she agreed, as if it had once been a living, breathing entity when the reality was, other than in leaving a heart still recoiling and arms aching its loss, it had never existed at all.

'You think I blame you?'

'But you must, a little,' she argued, amazed and a little angry he was even trying to deny it.

'I don't blame you, Ursula,' he returned. 'I never have. If you really want to know, despite what the doctors say, I happen to think it's my fault. And . . . and in any case. . . . It doesn't matter! It doesn't matter whose fault it is. . . .'

'We still have to live with it!' she finished fiercely, wondering next what difference this made to the equation. A lot, she guessed. There was a gap in their lives; a gaping hole neither had the slightest idea how to fill. Hopes, plans for the future, all turned to ashes.

'It isn't easy,' he muttered, stating the obvious.

'But I never said it was!' she wailed, wretchedly aware that this was what always happened. Round and round they went in ever decreasing circles, never seeming to reach a point where they were any further forward. Wouldn't it be better to say nothing, to put it behind them and concentrate instead on all the good things they had going, like each other and the life they'd built together at the farm?

'If the war hadn't happened, perhaps it wouldn't matter so much,' she said, her face glowing with the earnestness that once he'd said he loved her for. 'Or, at least, not as much as it did?' she added, seeing now the dark circles shadowing his eyes. He looked tired, worn out in fact and she chastized herself that she'd only just noticed.

'The war was a long time ago.'

'Father says there'll be another before the decade's out.'

He winced as if she'd struck him. 'There you go, then,' he answered sharply. 'What a good job we're not bringing any bairns into the world. . . .'

'Is that what you really think?'

'Yes . . . no . . . . Oh Lord, I don't know, Ursula.'

He stood running a hand through his hair but then, taking her by surprise and before she could stop him, he pulled her into his arms. As if he thought that way he could settle their problems and if only it was so simple! Relieved to give in, she leaned in, resting her head against his chest and absorbing the peace that always came when he held her this way. A comforting aroma of smoke still clung to his clothes from burning the stubble earlier that morning, reminding her of the passing seasons, with better days surely bound to return.

'We have each other,' he soothed her, stroking her hair, kissing the top of her head, tricking her there was nothing wrong after all, and that they'd only to work through this as they had everything else in their married life.

Thankful to be out of the wall of heat generated by what had proved a day's relentless sunshine, Hettie Loxley slipped into Venice's Basilica only to discover that she'd merely exchanged one extraordinary set of circumstances for another. Her gasp of pleasure was involuntary. Where she'd expected coolness and darkness, she was met instead with a wall of shimmering light, a glittering, shifting mosaic almost blinding her, trammelling her senses and stamping on them the indelible impression that she'd inadvertently stumbled into another, and impossibly even more overpowering sun. She stood, craning her head upwards towards the glittering gold of the high-domed ceiling, making a mental note meanwhile to remember every detail to tell Bill when she got home, surely the highlight of this tour so far. Unexpectedly, she found herself blessing her grandmother Katherine for forcing her to leave Loxley, particularly when she so much hadn't wanted to go.

She was mortified Bill wasn't here to share it with her and when she had so much to tell him. The thought brought the first cloud scudding into the sunshine of the young girl's so unexpected happiness. Since she'd left for this tour, she'd never heard a word from Bill, though she'd written several times and left a forwarding address, even in desperation writing to her mother and grandmother, hinting one or the other might jog the young man's mind to write and at least tell her what was going on in his life. What could she conclude other than he didn't care, that he'd gone to college only to forget her, precisely as she'd always known he would! Curiously deflated at the thought, she slipped upstairs to the Basilica's famous bronze horses, as much a symbol of Venice as the winged lion of St Mark's, so overcome by their power and antiquity, she stood looking as if mesmerized and could hardly bear to drag herself away.

Still, drag herself away she must and if only because time was passing. Outside, it was still too hot, like walking through thick, golden honey. With a happily vague sense of direction, she set off back towards the Hotel Duono Palace where she and Dizzy had booked for three nights, plunging into the labyrinth of narrow streets she'd already discovered full of enticing little shops and cafés, whose owners always had a ready smile for the young English girl, so cheerfully passing through.

Unforgivably perhaps when she knew Dizzy would be waiting, she gave in to her impulses, taking the time to browse lazily in and out of the shops, all too quickly losing track of the time and, worse, when at last, belatedly, she did realize it, finding she didn't have the slightest idea where she was. It didn't seem to matter. Venice, she was discovering, had precisely that effect, her only concern being a particularly beautiful glass shoe she'd admired in a poky little shop a few streets back and considered buying for her mother. Too late to wish she had bought it now. Frowning, she turned off into a tiny square and a narrow street leading from it, standing to look around her and finding, surprisingly, the shops had disappeared to be replaced by villas and private dwelling houses, shuttered up in the main and so crowded in, one upon another, the place was cast in shadow, lending to it a surprisingly bleak and desolate air. Gone were the crowds of jostling tourists trooping wearily, if happily, back to their hotels. Here, nothing looked familiar. Hettie shivered, realizing, with a little quickening sense of apprehension, she really was lost. Vaguely worried by it, she turned and tried to retrace her steps only to discover, several hot and dusty minutes later, she was no further forwards; indeed, perplexingly, she appeared to have returned to the same wretched spot. If only the streets and alleyways weren't so empty, so closed in upon themselves, so each looking exactly the same! The joy of the Basilica seemed a lifetime ago. Doggedly, refusing to give in to the twist of fear plucking at her insides, Hettie plunged off in another direction, into more narrow and mean-looking streets, all intersected by Venice's intricate network of canals, which here, in this poor place, seemed deep and stagnant pools of brooding, sullen water with who knew what lurking beneath. And always the presence of the gaunt and shuttered villas, giving the insidious feeling that behind their windows, she was watched and not with benign intent.

Her nerves were on edge. She walked on, seeming now in her growing fear to hear footsteps behind her, drawing closer though there was a singular and unnerving lack of people around. She stopped, listening carefully, greeted only by an eerie silence interspersed by the soft lap of water and the croak of a bullfrog from the canal. There was no mistaking the footsteps had stopped too. Hettie swung round, wondering if that really was a man's figure she saw, slinking behind the shadowed recess of a wall or merely a trick of the worryingly fading light. Crazy to think anyone meant to do her harm but she'd no intention of stopping to find out. She hurried on, instantly and horrifyingly aware of the sound of swift and stealthy feet padding behind her, leaving her without the slightest doubt that she really was being followed and with what intent, she could only dread – a thief or worse and it was no good now to remember all Dizzy's ceaseless warnings to have a care. She hurried on, the footsteps behind hurrying too, so at last, she gave in to her rising panic and broke into a headlong and reckless run. Instantly, the footsteps began to run too, leaving her all too horribly aware that they were eating up the steadily narrowing gap between them with long and easy strides.

Her pursuer was all but upon her. Hettie's breathing grew ragged; her heart thudded against its ribcage. Suddenly, a hand reached out, grabbing her shoulder and spinning her round, halting her progress so abruptly that she stumbled; nearly fell, only miraculously righting herself. Tensing to face her attacker, she steadied herself, surprised then in a sudden and overwhelming anger. A man dressed in a dirty shirt and greasy canvas trousers, his thin face scarred by pock-marks, stood before her. But whoever was he and how dare he frighten her like this! Her anger, written so clearly on her face, had surprised him too, his gloating expression instantly and satisfyingly changing to one of uncertainty.

'Hey! You! Leave her alone. . . .'

The voice, wonderfully English and emerging from the alleyway behind them, startled Hettie nearly as much as it did her attacker. Miraculously, aggressor was now victim. A hand grabbed a hold of his shirt, pulling him round to deliver a well-aimed punch so there was the satisfying sound of knuckles smacking against jaw. Cursing out loud, the man staggered, was lucky to recover before taking to his heels and running off, like a startled hare, back down the street. Hettie's liberator started after him but then, evidently thinking better of it, returned so she could see now that it was a boy of roughly her own age, dressed in shorts and a white collarless shirt. He was scowling. A pair of deep-set and brooding eyes stared down at her from under a mop of dark and unruly hair.

'Are you alright?' he demanded.

'I . . . I think so,' she said, deciding quickly and thankfully that she was. 'I was looking for my hotel, the Duono Palace. I'm lost, I'm afraid,' she confessed.

The news seemed to startle him. 'I've no idea how you've managed to end up here, then,' he replied, looking at her as if she'd lost possession of her wits. His gaze was tinged with mockery so she blushed furiously. 'Rum-coloured hair,' he said at last, with the ghost of a smile.

Hettie's hair had been called many things but never that. How rude he was! Some of her gratitude towards him for saving her began to disappear. There was no time to remonstrate.

'You'd best follow me back,' he muttered and, at which words, he spun abruptly on his heels and, without waiting for answer, or even more worryingly, stopping to see if she followed or not, walked quickly away. Not of a mind to stay here a moment longer than was necessary, Hettie was left with no option but to follow him, on an endless trek taking them through even more sunless and convoluted corridors so that soon, unbelievably, she was more lost than ever and worse, beginning to dread she'd merely exchanged one set of dangerous circumstances for another.

All at once they plunged into a widening alleyway, the end of which catapulted them into a busy little sunlit square that she instantly and thankfully recognized.

'Your hotel's down there,' the boy muttered, nodding towards it and then, maddeningly before she'd even chance to thank him for saving her, walking quickly away in the opposite direction. He never even bothered to look back. Some knight in shining armour she thought, sorrowfully. And yet, rude as he'd been, he had saved her. Perplexed, thankful, still in some state of shock, Hettie stood frowning after him, only the lateness of the hour and the likelihood of Dizzy raising the heavens if she didn't make haste recollecting her to the present. Luck was with her. Back at the hotel and making her way upstairs to their suite, she discovered her former governess was only now, thankfully, rousing herself from a deep and refreshing sleep miraculously rendering her unaware of all that had befallen her young charge, rushing so guiltily into their rooms. She sat up on the bed, patting her sadly greying hair, a bony, highly strung woman, her features saved from plainness by her kind and benign expression.

'There you are, my dear! Have you been enjoying yourself? But goodness! Look at the time; why didn't you call me? I think I could manage a little dinner today. We'd better get a move on if we aren't to be late. . . .' she finished, gingerly easing her legs to the floor.

It was good to see her more her usual self and Hettie felt a surprising rush of affection. Glad to put the afternoon's business behind her, obediently she washed and changed, following her mentor downstairs, meanwhile allowing the older woman's usual and ceaseless prattle to drift gently and harmlessly over her head. They ate in the elegant and high-ceilinged dining room of the hotel and after their meal, plain food cooked deliciously, took their coffee outside onto a small terrace leading from it, dripping with bougainvillea and overlooking the canal and where the warm and rapidly falling darkness was punctuated by the bright lights of the gondolas reflecting on the glittering water like stars. A heady atmosphere, oddly engendering the sense something was missing if only Hettie had the slightest idea what that was.

It had been that sort of a day. Thinking of Bill, she frowned.

'You'll allow me to join you, please?' Though the voice was English, its heavy accent determined it as belonging to one of the many German residents staying in their hotel. Startled from her reverie, Hettie looked up to see a thick-set, middle-aged man hovering by their table, his iron-grey hair swept back from a high forehead. Above average height, tall in fact, an intimidating man she sensed, his smile not quite meeting his eyes, which were of a pale, Teutonic blue and presently looking straight at her. Without waiting for answer, he called to a waiter for coffee and sat down at their table, proceeding then to introduce himself. His name was Count Charles Dresler, a dealer in fine art from Berlin, here in Venice on pressing business. How could he help but notice two such elegant and beautiful young ladies dining here alone and . . . well . . . here he was!

Poor Dizzy was as putty in his hands. Hettie looked on amused. Hettie, he hardly paid attention to and yet, now and then and when, she suspected, he thought she wasn't looking, she felt his eyes move lazily over her, as if he was summing her up. A man who said one thing and thought much else, she sensed, wondering if he was all that he appeared.

The afternoon's adventure had set her nerves on edge.

'But we mean to visit Berlin too,' Dolores told him excitedly, explaining about Hettie's grand tour and her position as her chaperone. Her blush deepened so Hettie guessed, shy person that she was, her former governess was worried she'd been too forward. The Count reached inside his jacket pocket and produced a card, pressing it upon her.

'Please take it. . . .' he murmured. 'I own a fairly prestigious art gallery in Berlin. Whilst you're there, I'd take it as the greatest of honours if you'd call and allow me to show you around.'

'But what a delightful man,' Dizzy murmured when, coffee drunk, finally, he departed but only after he'd assured himself they would take him up on his offer. She tucked the card away in her handbag and smiled dreamily. Hettie smothered a laugh.

'Wasn't he just,' she said, yet not sure if she really agreed and relieved when Dizzy, still weak from her illness, began to yawn and suggested they retire. Upstairs in her room, an annexe leading from Dizzy's, she threw her clothes into an untidy heap on the floor and fell into bed, thankfully drifting at once into a deep and dreamless sleep and not waking until the early morning sunshine flooded her room, dappling her face in shades of a warm and golden, yellow-greenish light.

She stretched, yawned sleepily, lying quietly awhile to think. Her itinerary, chosen by her grandmother, was a crowded one and hardly gave the travellers chance to draw breath. But now they'd actually embarked on the adventure, even Hettie had to agree, it seemed only expedient to cram in as much sightseeing as possible. Tomorrow they were travelling to Vienna for a two-day stay, followed by a further two days in Prague. Today, the morning was to spent exploring the Doge's Palace and the afternoon filled with an excursion to one of Venice's more prestigious glass factories. She was looking forward to both visits, she discovered, happily. Jumping out of bed, she dressed quickly, waiting impatiently for Dizzy to complete her toilet before hustling them downstairs to the dining room and the breakfast table where she couldn't help but notice that Dizzy kept her gaze glued firmly to the door.

'I do believe you're on the lookout for your Count,' she teased.

'I was doing no such thing!' the older woman bridled, affronted, so, rather ashamed of herself, Hettie apologized at once. She was relieved when breakfast was over but emerging from the dining room into the hotel foyer, as luck would have it, at once they spied their Count, the suitcases piled around his well-shod feet suggesting his departure was imminent. Poor Dizzy and when she'd only just met him, Hettie thought, glancing at her companion's stricken face and pleased for her that at least, after his offer to visit him in Berlin, there would be opportunity to see him further along the tour. And then her heart skipped a beat. She saw now that the Count was talking to a young man who stood with his back towards them. Spending so long in its proximity, Hettie would have recognized that back anywhere. The Count saw them and smiled, causing the young man to turn around, revealing thereby his handsome if still scowling face. Wondering if that was his natural expression and, if so, why so, she fixed a smile on her face and made her way towards him.

Her rescuer and now, at last, she had the chance to discover exactly who he was. . . .

Chapter Three

The dawn chorus had subsided, drawn into the low mist that lay blanketing the ground and shrouding the low-roofed farm, which loomed behind the slim, energetic-looking woman walking briskly up the lane. A cow bellowed. It was too early to be up. Calling to the brindle bitch with the short, stumpy tail, snuffling in the hedgerow, Ursula walked on, deep in thought, mulling over her argument with Freddie last night, every single, uncomfortable word of it, the cause of her sleeplessness and early rising, too early even for the farm and its myriad of chores. Freddie had argued it was unfair of her to neglect her duties when there was so much needed doing about the place. Ursula's indignation grew. As if he thought she didn't realize, with the harvest on top of the usual chores, she'd had no business swanning off to Derby and, worse, forgetting all about her promise to lend a hand getting in the potatoes.

Well, she had forgotten and part of her ill humour now, and thus the need to walk it off, was the fact that her husband had a right to be angry with her. She'd been selfish and seeing him so bewildered had only made her long to throw her arms around him and tell him she'd never be so thoughtless again. Pride had stopped her – that and his plain speaking, putting her so firmly in her place it had only made the situation a whole sight worse.

'We can't afford to carry passengers, Ursy. Not even you. . . .'

'But surely, your wife. . . .'

'Don't tell me you don't know exactly what I mean.'

She did know. Running a farm, a successful farm, meant giving in to it heart and soul so there was never to be room for anything else – as if she hadn't known right from the start, when Freddie had been so insistent on their getting married, on and on until he'd worn her down. They must marry. She couldn't leave him now! She should forget her reservation because it was being together that mattered and, that being the case, everything else would fall into place. Even now, even given the baby – or lack of a baby. Perhaps if things had worked out with the baby, she wouldn't feel as bad as she did now. Hemmed in, trapped, like being a farmer's wife was the last thing she was cut out to be or wanted to do with the rest of her life. It wasn't Freddie's fault, Ursula conceded but, there again, neither was it totally hers.

She'd reached the brow of the hill leading down to the pasture. With a start of surprise, she pulled up short, to stare in some perplexity at the plot of land more normally hired out to campers and today, supposedly untenanted, ready for the party of hill walkers due at the weekend and using Loxley for their base. At first, the cluster of gaily decorated vardoes she saw there now failed to register, crouching as they were at the top end of the field like a colony of giant and gaudy insects, the horses that had brought them here contentedly cropping the grass around. As Ursula stood watching, the door to the nearest caravan opened and a man emerged, owner to a head of startlingly white, shoulder-length hair, swept back from his face, and dressed in an open-necked shirt, his trousers held up by a length of string. Holding his face up to the sun, he stretched and yawned, an action which startled Ursula's little dog, Fern, who jumped down from the low stone wall marking the boundary of the field and barked, the hair on her neck bristling.

'It's alright, girl,' her mistress murmured soothingly, yet not quite sure if it was. Gypsies! And what right had they taking ownership of this land, ruining all her carefully thought-out plans! Full of righteous indignation, Ursula let herself through the gate and marched down the field towards him. Close up, he was older than she'd thought, yet his face, tanned by his outdoor life, was curiously unwrinkled, dominated by an imposing, aquiline nose. But it was his eyes immediately catching her attention, so deep set and penetrating, and of such a startling blue, that they seemed to see more than what was before him which, for the moment, was her.

'I'm sorry but this is private property. I shall have to ask you to move on,' she began, curtly.

Apparently unfazed, he stooped to fondle Fern's rough head. 'As you see, we do no harm,' he murmured, straightening up.

Ursula's smile grew more fixed. 'That may very well be but. . . .'

'We're peaceful people. You won't even know we're here.'

'You don't understand. I hire the field out,' she persisted patiently. 'It might be empty now but I have a party of hill walkers booked for this weekend.'

The gypsy's gaze swept the length of the field. 'There's plenty of room,' he observed.

'I'm fairly sure the party concerned won't wish to share.'

And certainly not with gypsies, Ursula thought, though not wanting to be rude, not saying as much. There was no point goading him. He smiled, not one whit put out.

'Then it appears we have a problem,' he replied, evenly.

Before she could answer, there was a movement in the caravan behind and a small child emerged, still in her nightdress, a little girl of some two or three years of age, knuckling her eyes and stumbling down the steps towards them. Something about her eyes, which were large and thick-lashed and of a bright and dazzling blue, staring from her small, sharp face, framed by its mass of dark curls, stamped it as belonging in some way to this man. At the sight of her, the gypsy man's smile deepened. 'Maisie May! It's early for you, child,' he said, sweeping her up into his arms.

'Gwamps,' she lisped, still half asleep, snuggling contentedly into his chest.

Ursula's swift retort died on her lips. That there was going to be trouble over the gypsies' presence here was only too clear but to argue the point and in front of such a little one was patently not on. For the moment, any enmity she had with Freddie was forgotten. She'd go straight home and tell him what had happened so, between them, they could decide what should be done.

'I'll be back later,' she said, her tone striking a warning note.

Nodding curtly, calling to Fern, she made her way from the field to regain the lane and struck out, back towards the farm, aware of the gypsy man standing, straight as a die, the child still clutched to his breast, watching her out of sight.

Hettie had seen so many sights, this holiday was beginning to feel a trial of endurance; so much so, this morning at breakfast in the hotel, bleary-eyed after the previous day spent investigating seemingly every brick and stone of the pastel-yellow facade of Berlin's Charlottenburg Palace, she'd found herself thinking longingly of home. Vienna had passed by in a blur of elaborate palaces and coffee houses; Prague, the city of a hundred spires, all medieval cobbled streets and ancient squares, so many, she'd lost count. Hardly a chance to draw breath, this morning they'd spent in Spandau Old Town, lunching briefly in a little cafe in the Schlosspark before Dizzy had returned to their hotel. Ostensibly this was to make the final arrangements for their journey to Bruges tomorrow but more, to Hettie's mind, to allow her chaperone time to put the final touches to a toilette designed to make good impression on Count Charles Dresler. They were meeting him this afternoon, taking him up on his offer to visit his gallery whilst they were in Berlin and which, according to directions given by their efficiently brisk hotel receptionist, was a five-minute stroll from the Palace gardens. Hettie herself had spent the last hour drifting happily in and out of the shops along the Kurfürstendamm, arranging to meet Dizzy outside Count Dresler's. Hettie wasn't sure what she thought of Berlin so far, a beautiful city, no doubt, but she was shocked by the air of menace she'd discovered, amazingly to her who'd paid such scant attention to politics, foreign or otherwise. Here, it was hard to ignore, buildings draped with the flags and swastikas of the National Socialist Party, pavements ringing to the sound of marching boots which seemed to Hettie so ominous and automated. Evil was stirring and, for the moment, she didn't want to think what that might be.

Making the last of her few small purchases, she consulted her street map before setting off, relieved, finally, a few minutes later to turn into the quietly affluent and leafy little street she discovered housed Count Dresler's gallery; an elaborate frontage sandwiched between two large, private residences, where she saw Dizzy hovering nervously by. Here, at least, the hustle and bustle of the Kurfürstendamm was left behind.

It would be a relief to move on to Bruges, Hettie thought, waving happily to her former governess, though she had to admit, if Dizzy was keen on reacquainting herself with the Count, she, Hettie, couldn't deny an interest in the Count's young companion, Lewis Steed. Her pace quickened, thinking now of their unexpected encounter in the foyer of Venice's Duono Palace Hotel, the morning after he'd rescued her from the city's myriad complexities of streets. At least she'd managed to get a name from him, indeed, she'd even managed to worm herself into his confidence enough to learn that he was apprenticed to the Count and had been accompanying him on his trip to Venice to gain insight into the art world in which he was employed. He'd been reluctant to impart even this small nugget of information. But if their meeting had been brief, it had still been enough to whet Hettie's appetite. She smiled inwardly. Oh yes, there was no doubt she was looking forward to reacquainting herself with Lewis Steed, if only to see if his scowling face was every bit as disconcerting as she remembered it!

'There you are!' Dizzy beamed before leading the way into the gallery.

As chance would have it, they entered the thickly carpeted and hushed atmosphere of the entrance hall as the Count himself emerged down the broad sweep of stairs directly across from the door. At first sight, the German appeared bulkier and more imposing than Hettie remembered, his heavy features breaking into a smile as he hurried towards them, holding out a surprisingly elegant hand. Of Lewis, there was disappointingly no sign.

'But how wonderful to see you again!' he murmured gallantly. 'You've had a good journey, I hope? Let me show you round the gallery and you must tell me, truly, exactly what you think!' Hardly pausing to draw breath, giving every indication that he was pleased to see them, he conducted his two visitors upstairs and along an ornate balcony which overlooked the well of the hall, whilst in his effortless and near perfect English, he extracted from a becomingly flushed Dizzy their itinerary since they'd first arrived here in Berlin. That Hettie's former governess was susceptible to the Count's obvious charms was only too clear, even to Hettie, watching on in delight. But why shouldn't the old fusspot be allowed her dreams over her undeniably handsome Count?

The following hour passed too quickly, reeling them from one anteroom to the next, each containing a blur of paintings and sculptures by artists most of whom, Hettie, in her ignorance, had never even heard.

'Are these all German works of art?' she asked, a little shamefaced.

'We do our best to support German talent – as this artist here – a Hamburg man,' the Count agreed, positioning them in front of a particularly striking etching of a lake at night, the moon shining down from a brooding sky illustrated in all its depths and shadows.

'But you exhibit foreign artists, too?' Dizzy ventured, nervously.

'But of course! Alex Windrow has an exhibition here shortly,' their companion returned quickly. 'You'll have heard of him, no doubt? A compatriot of yours, a fellow Englishman settled here in Berlin! Assessing the market, what's back in fashion, what's most likely to sell is what I most enjoy!' His gaze moved questioningly towards Hettie. 'But growing up amongst such exquisite works of art, you'll know this already, Your Grace?'

So he'd done his homework, Hettie thought, the knowledge jarring with her in what was proving to be an otherwise surprisingly enjoyable afternoon. It was too easy to forget this man was first and foremost a businessman and, oddly, the realization brought with it the first inklings of an idea. Hettie frowned. Despite her mother's attempts to keep it from her, she was only too well aware of the colossal tax duties that had resulted from her father's death. The bills back home were piling up. Her face lit up, more with eagerness than thought.

'You must pay us a visit, Count. I may even be able to put some business your way,' she answered eagerly and at once deliciously aware of how grown up this made her sound, a heady, intoxicating feeling, convincing her, as nothing else, she was taking her first, tentative steps towards her adult self. This grand tour of Europe had made her grow up quickly and no wonder her grandmother had been so keen that she should come!

'Oh, but my dear, you mustn't waste the Count's time!' Dizzy protested at once, if with her customary gentleness of manner, appearing perplexingly disconcerted. Hettie frowned. Whatever was the matter with her now?

'But I'm not wasting the Count's time – I meant it, every word!' she retorted, indignantly. 'Even you must know how we're fixed, Miss Pettigrew! Why, I overheard Grandmamma telling Mother that she'd had to sell some jewellery even to finance this trip. There's absolutely loads of paintings at home no one's the slightest bothered about and I'm jolly sure Mother would like to get shot of at least one or two!'

That her enthusiasm had led her to unforgiveable indiscretion was proved both by Dizzy's shocked expression and the acquisital gleam shining, if only momentarily, in the Count's pale, blue eyes.

'I'm sure something could be arranged, my dear,' he murmured. 'I could at least proffer opinion on what might sell or otherwise?'

'But that would be wonderful!' Hettie responded enthusiastically, refusing to be put out by her companion's odd behaviour. She beamed happily. 'That's settled, then! We must fix something up?'

'Indeed and before you leave.' The Count smiled, once again the perfect host. 'Now, if you'll allow me to offer you some refreshment? Please. . . . We'll make our way through to my private rooms. . . .'

Hettie shook her head. It would be good for the Count and Dizzy to have time alone together, she considered. It might at least put a smile back on Dizzy's face! 'I'll join you shortly,' she told them airily, her attention already caught by a movement in a small anteroom directly across from Alex Windrow's painting. 'I'd love a little look round on my own if you wouldn't mind. . . .'

Matters arranged to her satisfaction, whilst the Count ushered Dizzy away, Hettie headed firmly towards the anteroom, as she'd hoped, discovering a familiar figure inside it, balanced precariously at the top of a ladder and in the process of hanging a painting. Engrossed in the task, he hit his thumb with the hammer and thus, she was happily a party to his oath, soft and succinct, in English. Suddenly aware of her presence, he craned his head and saw her.

'We're not open to the public yet,' he muttered, frowning.

Their paths met again. Lewis Steed hadn't changed one iota. Delighted, Hettie smiled.

'Hello, Lewis.'

'Oh, it's you,' he returned, ungraciously.

'It's nice to see you too,' she replied, discovering she meant it. 'You really do work here?' she enquired, coming closer and gazing up at him.

'Didn't you believe me?' He climbed down to stand beside her, gazing with obvious pride at the paintings adorning the wall before them, numbering some dozen in all. Scenes of Berlin skyscapes in the main, rooftops and spires, illumined by light or in darkness and shadow, the skies above filled with wild, storm-tossed weather, all depicted with an artistry which, little as Hettie knew, she guessed belonged to a master craftsman. They were suggestive of some danger lurking and she wondered if the artist saw the peril lurking in modern Germany too.

'Alex Windrow,' she murmured, guessing this was the exhibition to which the Count had referred.

'Alex Windrow is my uncle – well, adopted uncle to tell the truth,' Lewis agreed, still sounding proud. 'He's my stepmother's nephew.'

'Sounds complicated.'

'Don't ask!'

'I wouldn't dream! But these are wonderful paintings,' she enthused.

The young man's features softened. 'Aren't they just! Charles Dresler doesn't usually take clients but he's made exception for Alex,' he proffered without further prompting on her part. He'd mellowed since last she'd seen him, Hettie mused, attractively so, she considered, when, as now, he was regarding her with such a decided interest. He was good-looking, she decided quickly, his mobile features full of light and shadows of their own, lending to his face a vivid and vibrant life. 'But I thought you worked for Charles Dresler?' she asked curiously.

He shrugged. 'In a way but really, I work for Alex, arranging his exhibits and writing up the sales and accounts, that sort of thing.'

'You must be a huge help.'

A broad smile chased the shadows from the young man's face.

'He couldn't manage without me,' he bragged. 'Dresler . . . the Count needed me to help him out too. I'm in demand.'

'And you're learning as you go along?'

'Alex reckons I'll take in more that way,' he muttered, begrudgingly.

'I don't pay you to stand here gossiping, Lewis!' came a sudden, authoritative and distinctly English voice. Hettie swung round to see a middle-aged man making his way towards them, dressed casually in corduroys and an open-necked shirt, the features above his thick neck ruggedly rather than convention-ally handsome and dominated by dark and angry-looking eyes. They were surprisingly like Lewis's eyes, considering their lack of natural kinship if, as Hettie assumed, this was Alex Windrow. He walked with a pronounced limp, so she wondered at once if it was some wound left over from the war that her father had always been talking about. As if talking about it had helped him.

'I need those letters taking round to the post,' the man barked to Lewis but his gaze settled on Hettie so at once she felt herself scrutinized. Scrutinized and causing consternation, she realized, aware of the newcomer's start of surprise, leaving her with the distinct impression something about her had shocked him though she couldn't, for the life of her, think what that might be. Lewis looked cross and she sensed that despite all his bragging, there were problems between the pair, Lewis not liking to be told what to do, for one. The familiar scowl settled across the young man's face and yet he moved away obediently enough before apparently and belatedly remembering her and turning back.

'I'll show you round Berlin tomorrow . . . if you want?' he added, sounding surprisingly hopeful.

What a contrary young man he was and, for a fleeting moment, Hettie felt sorry to disappoint him, a feeling quickly replaced by one of annoyance that it looked like she'd lost an opportunity to find out more about him. She'd never known anyone like him, never having known many boys at all, she conceded, only Bill.

'We're moving onto Bruges tomorrow, I'm afraid, then Paris and home. But I could write . . . if you'd like?' she proffered, by way of an olive branch.

He nodded briefly and departed, so she didn't know then if he was pleased about the offer or not.

'Do I know you?' Alex Windrow demanded sharply, making her jump. He was watching her through narrowed eyes, still summing her up, she thought. Summing her up and not sure what to make of her, as she was unsure what to make of him. She stood her ground admirably.

'I doubt it,' she answered him coolly, not sure that she liked him. He was alarming and she could understand why Lewis hadn't stayed around to argue. She stared back at him with an equal intensity, fairly certain if she had ever been unfortunate to meet him before, he'd have remained firmly stamped on her mind.

'You put me in mind of someone,' he said unexpectedly.

'I do?' Hettie muttered awkwardly, wondering what else he expected her to say.

'You couldn't be! . . . Though there is something . . . Your hair, perhaps . . . Where have you got hair like that, I wonder?' he murmured, almost to himself.

He wasn't making much sense. She frowned up at him, it being on the point of her tongue to pull rank and tell him exactly who she was. Henrietta Arabella, Duchess of Loxley, and he had no right to treat her as if she were someone who'd just wandered in from the street. An unusual reticence held her back but this was, she was very quickly deciding, a very unusual man.

'You're a friend of Lewis's?' he demanded.

She nodded, uneasily. 'We met in Venice. . . . The Count invited us here. He's told us about your exhibition. Your paint-ings are wonderful, so . . . so full of life,' she said, struggling for the right words with which to praise them. Happily, it at least seemed to recall Alex Windrow to his senses.

'Are they indeed! Well. . . . I've no time to stop here chatting,' he muttered rudely and as if what she thought was of little consequence. Whatever interest she'd aroused in him, clearly he'd mastered it. Abruptly he turned and limped away and Hettie had to admit to feeling relieved. She stood, staring after him, feeling oddly deserted, both by Lewis and by this man who, after all, was nothing to her. Dizzy would be waiting and yet, instead of making for the Count's private rooms, instinctively, she headed towards the door at the far end of the room. Through it, she discovered another and smaller anteroom, bare and stark, with an odd atmosphere of reverence. A single painting in an ornate, gilt frame, hung on the farthest wall, nearly covering it in its entirety. A stunning piece of work, placed to captivate the attention of whosoever entered the room. Hettie had always wondered what it would feel like for the hairs to stand up on the back of her neck and now she knew, exactly. She stood, hovering just inside the entrance and staring at the portrait as if transfixed. A young woman, dressed in the fashion of a couple of decades since. Large, luminous eyes stared pensively back at her and into the room.

Involuntarily, she gasped out loud. It couldn't be, it really couldn't be and yet. . . . How could she deny it? The very last person she'd expected to see depicted here, in an upmarket gallery, in the heart of Berlin. It was her mother or someone so very much like her. It simply couldn't be true.

'Monsieur de Loxley, Your Grace.' Standing back to allow their visitor entry, Soames bowed and retired, closing the sitting room doors softly behind him. Springing up from the writing desk where she'd been working, head bent in concentration, Bronwyn smiled and held out her hand, finding it quickly enveloped in Roland's large and curiously comforting grasp.

'But what a surprise,' she murmured happily. Over the last few days, she'd got to know him well. Despite Katherine's insistence on making discreet enquiries into his background, the old battleaxe had been unable to uncover a single troubling fact about him, so that even she had to agree, albeit begrudgingly, to the plan that one or the other of them should show him over the estate. Yesterday, they'd spent a happy hour in the library, poring over the vast archives of manuscripts and letters, some dating back to the Civil War and Nell Loxley's time as Duchess, in whom Roland had taken a long and protracted interest. As far as Bronwyn was concerned, the visit had turned out to be surprisingly good fun. He was good company and made her laugh, something of which, unsurprisingly, she'd done so little of late.

'I'm disturbing you,' he murmured, apologetically.

'Please, don't worry; I was only catching up on a little correspondence. . . .' She faltered, wondering, belatedly, the reason for the visit when, as far as she could remember, the arrangement had been for lunch tomorrow followed by another stint in the library. 'If there's anything I can do?' she prompted gently.

He pulled a face. 'I'm sorry. I wanted to tell you myself but I'm afraid I shall have to cancel tomorrow. I have to return home. Business calls, unfortunately.'

'Oh, but that's a shame,' she burst out, her words as heartfelt as they were sincere.

Roland smiled gratifyingly. 'But I was hoping. . . . That is, if you and Katherine would allow and it's not too much of an imposition, I could return next week? Mother has some papers, dating back from the time when our family first settled in France. I'll bring them with me, if you'd like?'

'But Roland, that would be fascinating! That is. . . .' Bronwyn flapped a hand vaguely towards her writing desk, her warm, openly good-natured face suddenly clouded. 'There's a meeting of the War Cabinet here next week, Wednesday through Friday, a regular arrangement dating from my husband's service years, I'm afraid. I was just writing to confirm it.' The realization brought with it the reminder that already she'd had blows with Katherine over the plan, the grant they received from the War Office, of such importance to Loxley funds, only being a part of it. Bronwyn still couldn't get to the bottom of why Harry's mother should be so dead set against a practice that Harry had initiated so wholeheartedly. The War Office needed a quiet retreat and where better than here at Loxley had always been his view. Katherine was getting old, Bronwyn conceded and, much as she'd never admit it, hated strangers rattling about the place. But at last, despite such perverse opposition, Bronwyn had her own way and the event looked set to continue, it seeming to her such a huge shame should it not.

She sensed Roland's disappointment at the news and felt satisfyingly gratified.

'Oh well, it can't be helped,' he murmured, gamely, 'some other time, perhaps?'

His disappointment helped to make up her mind. 'I can't see what difference it's going to make to the war committee whether you're here or not,' she said, at once. 'So long as I'm within reach, improbable as it is they'll have a need of me. Why don't you take pot luck and come anyway and we'll take it from there?'

Roland's face lit up. 'That would be wonderful,' he said. 'Hettie should be back this time next week. I know she'll be longing to meet you. You will join us for lunch today. . . ?'

Everything was falling neatly into place. Roland agreed only too readily.

Allowing him a pleasant hour in the library whilst she finished up her paperwork, after it they ate a light luncheon together in the morning room; both more relieved than they cared to admit to discover that Katherine, having a prior luncheon engagement with the local hospital board of which she was chair, wouldn't be joining them.

'Why don't we go for a walk?' Bronwyn suggested, after they'd eaten.

He agreed eagerly. Calling to the two dogs lounging under the table they set off at once, walking at a steady pace through the wood behind the hall, to the massive stone hunting tower at its summit, a building erected by Nell Loxley, shortly after she'd completed the New Hall. The round, four-storey edifice, built out of local stone, towered out of the ground and Roland had already expressed an interest in seeing it up close.

'I've always felt that it somehow stands sentinel over the estate, guarding us, if you like, if that doesn't sound too fanciful?' Bronwyn murmured, as they drew nearer, imparting information she'd never yet told anyone. Roland was beginning to have that effect on her; she felt she could tell him anything. Ducking inside the low doorway, she led the way up the winding and worn, narrow stone steps, to the highest room, empty now, bar a few odd bits of Reuben's old gamekeeping equipment and where the view from the window was breathtaking. Loxley, both new and old, reduced to miniature, surrounded by the purple-mauve hills and rugged crags of Derbyshire, cut through by the thin blue ribbon of the River Lox.

'She was some kind of a woman, your Nell,' Roland said, coming to stand beside her. He was slightly out of breath.

'Given your family connections, don't you mean our Nell?' she teased.

He turned towards her and then said something rather shocking. 'Given Nell's son was born the wrong side of the blanket, some would say our branch of the family has more legitimate claim to this estate than yours.'

Bronwyn glanced at him uneasily; relieved to see that he was smiling, signalling he'd made a joke. Despite it, the observation still jarred. 'You mustn't let Katherine hear you say that,' she warned.

'A bit of a tartar, your mother-in-law!' he answered her so, yet again, she wasn't sure if he was joking. The assertion rang too true but it was hardly expedient to agree.

'You've only just realized?' she responded, in similar vein and trying to keep the conversation light. It was clear Roland de Loxley was a man who, if charming, still spoke his mind. But

Loxley men were charming and, for all the distance between their respective homes, she mustn't forget from whence his family originally hailed. 'You ought to meet our vicar, Lawrence Payne, a wealth of knowledge on all things Loxley,' she said, more seriously. 'Why don't I fix up a meeting next time you're over?'

'I'd like that, Bronwyn, thank you.'

They returned downstairs, walking companionably round to the rear of the tower and along the dusty track which led to an area of flat ground and a large, oval-shaped, man-made lake that Bronwyn, feeling more like a guidebook by the moment, informed her guest serviced the fountain in the gardens below. The afternoon sun winked lazily on the water, rippling in the breeze, upon which ducks and moorhens bobbed, dipping their heads in search of food. A place of peace to which Harry had first brought her and which now Bronwyn often visited alone. Here, more than anywhere, she felt close to Harry. A small frisson of pain crossed her face.

'Are you alright?' Roland asked softly.

'I was thinking about Harry,' she answered, truthfully and finding no reason not to tell him.

'You must miss him. . . ?' His face fell. 'Sorry, stupid question, of course you miss him. You lost him so young. Life's not fair.'

'It's not,' she agreed flatly. 'And you?' she asked, swiftly changing subject and acknowledging, if only to herself, that she was curious and simply hadn't liked to ask, nevertheless assuming a wife, children, and commitments, like most people their age.

'I never married,' he answered her shortly, an edge entering his voice that hadn't been there before. She'd entered dangerous territory, asking a question he hadn't wanted to answer, so much was clear. Bronwyn's gaze grew troubled. He was hardly likely to have reached middle age and not have some kind of a history but, after all, it was none of her business. The moment could, should have been awkward but somehow it wasn't. He stopped, pulling a leaf from the copper beech overhanging the lake and twisting it between his fingers. 'Footloose and fancy free as you see me,' he murmured, making an attempt at a smile and smoothing things over, more for her sake, she suspected.

They'd followed the path round to a pretty little Swiss cottage nestling along the shores of the water, which belonged to one of the estate workers. A thin curl of smoke issued from the chimney. A little wizened figure with a humped back was letting herself through the wicker gate leading into the small front garden, a tangle of fading summer flowers, a shawl pulled over her shoulders, her wrinkled face made alive by her sharp, dark eyes which fastened hungrily on the pair walking towards her. An old gypsy woman, carrying a basket of wares; and Bronwyn remembered now Tom Compton telling her about the gypsies who'd taken up residence on Hamilton land.

'You do realize this is private land, Mother?' she asked, feeling duty-bound to point it out.

'Ain't doing no harm, lady!' the old woman cackled, revealing a few brown stumps of teeth. A plaintive, wheedling note entered her voice. 'Sure but you'll want to buy a bit o' summat off an old woman. Mayhap a few pegs or a length of lace?'

'Be on your way, there's a good woman,' Roland interceded.

'A lucky charm, then? I'll tell your fortune, if you like?' She was nothing if not persistent but Bronwyn had no money on her. She shrugged her shoulders, turning to Roland, who pulled some loose change from his pocket, pressing it into the claw-like hand. 'Here, take it and be off,' he muttered but not unkindly.

She turned from him, peering thoughtfully into Bronwyn's face. 'You've had some sorrow in your life, poor lass,' she mumbled. 'Aye and more to come! But mayhap you'll find a little love to soften the load? You and this fine figure of a man, old Rosa reckons.'

It was a statement of fact and the old woman finished with high, cackling laughter. Embarrassed at her outpouring, Bronwyn would have moved quickly on but it was too late. A bony hand plucked at the sleeve of her dress, catching at the material.

'Or is there someone else? Someone old Rosa don't know about? There's no denying, you're still a young woman, there's plenty of life in you yet, I'll be bound!'

That she knew exactly to whom she was talking had become increasingly clear. The Duchess who'd so tragically lost her husband and had somehow lost her way in life. Bronwyn frowned.

'I hardly think that's any of your business. . . .' she began, meanwhile struggling vainly to free herself. The birdlike hand was stronger than it looked, refusing to loosen its grip.

'Lofty as you think yourself, you're only the same underneath as us Romani folk,' she whispered, with a malicious gleam springing into her eyes. 'You remember where Old Rosa is. . . . You might have a need of her one of these fine days, you see if you don't. . . .'

'I'm sure I never shall. . . .'

'Think I'm mad, do you?'

'Why, no, of course not,' Bronwyn murmured helplessly, thinking precisely that. Still she was sorry for her if thankful when, head bent and muttering to herself, she released her grip and shuffled away.

'Crazy old woman,' Roland murmured, frowning.

He was right. A poor, crazed old woman and one, for whatever odd reasoning of her own, who had been intent on embarrassing her. Jealousy, subterfuge, pretending to a second sight she had no claim to. Such was the way with gypsy folk and vaguely Bronwyn wondered if she ought to have a word with Freddie Hamilton about moving the encampment on. Making a mental note to at least talk to him about the situation, she took hold of Roland's arm.

'Tea . . . we'll have some tea,' she said brightly, more unsettled by the incident than she cared to admit. Calling to the two dogs snuffling down by the lake, she headed them back towards the hall.

Chapter Four

It wasn't the most welcoming of weather for a homecoming. The sky was dark and angry-looking with storm clouds gathering over Loxley, their magnificent and much-loved ancestral seat. Surprised by the day's warmth when she'd been sure she'd notice a difference from the interminable heat she'd left behind in Paris, Hettie jumped down from the Daimler and ran up the front steps.

'There you are, Your Grace! A good journey, I hope?' Beaming, Soames threw open the doors.

'Good afternoon, Soames. . . . It certainly was!' she replied, bounding past him to rush inside to throw herself into her mother's arms, leaving poor Dizzy meanwhile to struggle out, unaided, to see to the luggage. 'Have I heaps to tell you! Have you missed me? Where's Grandmamma?' she cried.

'I can't wait. More than I can say and she's in the sitting room!' Bronwyn called to her retreating back as she extracted herself to run into the sitting room to her grandmother, who'd been on the lookout for her since lunch. Not one for overly demonstrative displays of affection, the old woman held her arms wide, unable to disguise her pleasure as Hettie ran into them.

'Grandmamma!' Hettie murmured, suddenly and overwhelmingly glad to be home. Only now did she realize how much she'd missed the old place, proof of the maxim she was only now achieving wisdom enough to realize that it was wonderful to travel but, surely, so much nicer to return home. Shortly, tea was ordered, Dizzy ushered inside and comfortably ensconced in an armchair whilst Hettie, having so much to tell everybody, held forth. 'We've had a simply brilliant time, haven't we, Miss Pettigrew? We've covered every inch of Europe, I should think. And, oh, Venice was wonderful, an absolute dream! I wouldn't have missed it for anything!'

Slightly bemused, Katherine took her tea and sat down. 'I told you you'd enjoy yourself, darling. If only you'd believed me!'

'You certainly did, Grandmamma!' Hettie agreed happily, finding, for once, she was happy to agree with anybody, even her grandmother. 'You'll never guess what?' she went on, excitedly.

Bronwyn took Dizzy's cup and refilled it. 'What's that, dear?' she asked.

'I've seen a picture of you,' Hettie gushed. 'A simply wonderful painting, in an art gallery in Berlin. I couldn't actually believe it was you because you were so much younger but it was you, Mother, it really was. . . .'

Bronwyn frowned, turning back towards her and only now paying attention to what she'd said.

'I'm sorry, darling, but I've no idea what you're talking about.'

Hettie nodded, happily. 'It perplexed us too, didn't it, Miss Pettigrew? It was a painting of you, Mother, done by a man called Alex Windrow. He's a simply wonderful painter according to the Count and he should know because he owns the art gallery where it hangs. . . .'

'The Count?' demanded Bronwyn, none the wiser.

Seeing she'd only confused things further, patiently, Hettie began again. Their meeting with Count Charles Dresler in Venice, the invitation to his art gallery in Berlin and the German's assertion Bronwyn's painting was by Alex Windrow, an English artist living in Berlin. How afterwards, Hettie had searched for Alex Windrow and his adopted nephew Lewis – who helped him with his work – to know the painting's history, only to discover, frustratingly, both men had left for home. Given the travellers' early departure for Bruges the following morning, there'd been no further opportunity to find them. 'I managed to get their address from the Count and I'm going to write to Lewis as soon as I've chance. He did say I could,' she finished, excitedly.

'The boy who works for this Alex Windrow?' Bronwyn demanded, still struggling to keep up.

'A man who's seen your picture in *Tatler* and taken advantage! I wouldn't give it a second thought,' Katherine observed, summing it up in the way only she could.

'And who exactly is this Count?' Bronwyn asked.

'A highly respectable man. You mustn't think anything else, Mother. Miss Pettigrew certainly took a shine to him!' Hettie concluded, impishly. Dizzy coloured up.

'Henrietta! I most certainly did not take a shine to him as you choose to call it!'

'You'll have a chance to make your own mind up, Mother,' her charge responded carelessly and apparently heartlessly oblivious to the embarrassment she'd just caused. 'I've asked him to visit, sometime within the next couple of weeks!'

Bronwyn was horrified. 'Hettie! I sincerely hope you haven't! We already have a guest, due to arrive any moment, never mind the war committee meeting here this week!'

'Child! What were you thinking?' Katherine joined in.

Some of Hettie's infectious enthusiasm disappeared. 'But there's plenty of room! I thought he could have a look round at the paintings and give us some idea as to their value. There's bound to be some worth a bob or two,' she responded, looking crestfallen and too belatedly aware she'd been tactless to boot.

'A bob or two!' Her grandmother's face had gone so deeply mottled at this sacrilege, it seemed expedient to Hettie, at this point, to beat a hasty retreat. The day was still young and, already recovered from the journey, begun at daylight with the ferry from Sables D'Olonne, she had other and more important fish to fry. Hastily she swallowed the last of her tea.

'Perhaps he won't bother to visit after all. It wasn't as if we fixed an exact date.'

'Hettie. . . .'

'Sorry, Grandmamma! I hate to dash but I really have to go.'

'But you've only just got home,' Bronwyn wailed.

'I won't be long, I promise.'

'Bill's at college,' Katherine boomed after her, guessing correctly where she was headed.

Her words fell on empty air. Hettie had already disappeared into the hall, letting herself quickly through the front doors to run down the steps and into the gardens, waving to one of the gardener's lads on the way and quickly reaching the meadows where she headed swiftly for the village and Sam Tennant's garage. Her grandmother was wrong, she thought, rebelliously. It was Saturday and wherever Bill was likely to be, it certainly wouldn't be at college.

She was still upset Bill hadn't written, not once, in the whole of the time she'd been away; worse still, the thought he hadn't even been here to greet her when she'd been so certain that he would. Perhaps he hadn't realized she was back today? She was desperate to see him even if, wretched thought, he couldn't care less she was home.

On the brow of the hill, she cannoned to a halt, lingering momentarily to look back towards Loxley, her home, standing so proudly, as if its turrets were holding up the sky, she mused fancifully, disbelieving quite how much she'd missed it whilst she'd been away. She'd no clear idea why, only that it belonged to her and that now she was the sole custodian of its dusty portals, she was only just beginning to realize the responsibility that brought. One day, she'd make her mark upon this place, she decided impulsively, so that people would talk of her, just as they talked of Nell, the first Duchess. The trip to Europe had made her more aware, she realized, continuing on her way and wondering now how an ancient pile of dilapidated Derbyshire stone had somehow so wrapped itself around her heart she couldn't forget it; nor ever, she thought, vehemently and with a little thrill of ownership, be able to leave it for long.

'Why, Your Grace, what a wonderful surprise!' Lizzie Tennant exclaimed, coming to the door of the little cottage next to the garage where, on the forecourt, her husband Sam was stretched out under one of the two cars wanting attention. She smiled, looking content and incredibly pregnant. Of Bill there was no sign.

'Is Bill in?' Hettie asked, trying and failing not to sound too eager.

Happily, Lizzie nodded. 'He's just finishing his college work. Would you like to come in, Your Grace? You must have had a long day travelling. You're bound to be tired. Have you had a good holiday? Your mother said she was so looking forward to your homecoming!'

If Lizzie was aware she was due back today, then so must Bill know it too. Something inside Hettie curled up and died at the thought. If Bill knew, why hadn't he been there to greet her? Whatever the reason, his excuse had better be good! 'She is pleased and yes, thank you, I've had a wonderful time,' she responded mechanically as she followed the older woman into the cluttered little house and through the dark lobby into the back room where a number of children of varying ages and sizes were playing, making such a crowd, for a moment it deflected Hettie's attention from the young man sitting at the table, head bent so assiduously over his books. He looked up quickly, the joy he was unable to disguise at the sight of his visitor leaping up into his face but so quickly gone that, frustratingly, Hettie wasn't sure then if she hadn't imagined it.

'You're back, then,' he said ungraciously.

'This afternoon,' she agreed, wondering if that was all he was going to say and in such a subdued manner, she might as well have been any old acquaintance wandering in from the village. They were like strangers, not the old and inseparable friends they'd once been. Friends who'd grown up together, what's more, telling each other every mortal thing with nothing spared.

An awkward silence developed, which neither seemed able to break, the situation not helped by any number of inquisitive eyes watching their every move with undisguised amusement.

'Aren't you going to ask Her Grace to sit down, Bill? Now. . . . Who's for the post office and some sweeties?' Lizzie enquired tactfully, her words working as if by magic. Within a short space of time and to the accompaniment of much stamping of feet and shouts of glee, there was a mass exodus as the brood, mother in tow, departed the house. The front door slammed behind them. At last they were alone. Hettie looked at Bill longingly.

'Oh Bill, it is good to see you,' she enthused, pleased for the moment, at least, to find matters so satisfactorily arranged. Unasked, she sat down at the table, across from him. 'You look busy.'

'Only college work,' he muttered. Quickly gathering together his papers and books, he stuffed them into a leather case on the table, snapping the lock shut and yet, all the while, his gaze still, curiously, avoiding hers. Bill, who was so open and honest, she knew exactly what he was thinking, sometimes even before he knew it himself. The fact she'd no idea now was disconcerting.

'Aren't you going to ask me how I got on?' she demanded, stifling a growing feeling of resentment.

'How did you get on?' he asked, his clipped tone bringing with it the thought that, if she'd imagined their enforced separation might miraculously have improved matters between them, wretchedly, it appeared to have done the reverse.

'Wonderfully,' she answered, coldly. 'Why didn't you write?' she blurted out, at once.

He stood up, pushing his chair under the table and positioning himself defensively behind it.

'I dunno, Het. I meant too. It was just. . . .' His voice trailed away awkwardly.

Hettie had no idea what was the matter with him, only that something clearly was.

'What's wrong?' she asked bluntly.

'I've been busy. College work and stuff.'

'Oh, that.'

'Yes, that,' he admitted quietly and with an immense dignity that should have been funny and yet somehow wasn't. 'It's easy for you to say, Het, but homework's important if I want to get on.'

'I see. . . .'

'So you jolly well ought.'

'I do see!' she retorted, indignantly. However she'd imagined the conversation, this wasn't it. 'Bill, I hate it when we fall out.'

'I'm sorry, Het. I don't want us to fall out either,' he responded, at last and thankfully, for the first time since she'd got here, sounding more himself.

'Friends?' she asked, eagerly.

'We'll always be friends,' he replied, but so seriously, it only worried her all over again. But why would he think they might not always be friends? Friends who'd grown up together, been like brother and sister to each other! Deflated, Hettie pushed back her chair and stood up.

'I'd better get back. They'll be expecting me,' she said, miserably, and still with the same curious little ache inside.

'I'll see you round, then?' he asked but looking like he didn't care if he did or didn't or, at least, that was how it appeared to Hettie. Was that it, then? She'd travelled all this way, every moment of her journey spent longing to see him, dying to tell him about all her wonderful experiences, and he'd only . . . see her round? She'd see him round first!

'I expect so,' she told him coldly, only the hurt in her eyes giving away how much his words had stung her. There was no point staying, she decided quickly. Without another glance, she walked out, even, with admirable restraint, resisting the impulse to slam the door.

The air was sultry and heavy, pressing down on her and fuelling her misery. If she'd been home, she would have slammed the door and no doubt got a ticking off from Grandmamma for her pains! She walked on quickly, up the sloping path away from the village towards Loxley, half-hoping to hear Bill tearing after her and yet resigned when he didn't. He really didn't care whether he saw her again or not, she thought miserably. The best, the only real friend she'd ever had, the one person to whom she could tell anything, and he couldn't care less about her. He'd moved on, somewhere far away from her, become unobtainable, confirming her every worse fear before she'd gone away. But hadn't she known that would happen? Her frustration grew. He'd been beguiled by his new life and all the exciting new friends he'd made at college and that was why he didn't want anything else to do with her.

The strident, jarring clang of a police bell disturbed her thoughts as below, on the northbound road snaking the perimeter of the estate, two police cars sped past, heading, it appeared, towards Freddie Hamilton's land. For the moment, if nothing else, it took Hettie's mind from her painful thoughts of Bill and she was grateful for it. She didn't want to think about him! Something must have brought the police out here and, given both cars were crammed full of policemen, in fairly large numbers too. Her first thought was for the huddle of gaily coloured vardoes they'd passed on the way in that afternoon and that she'd meant to ask her mother about but in all the fuss of homecoming had forgotten. Forgetful too of the promise to her grandmother that she wouldn't be long, she hurried eagerly after them.

Easing his boots off at the door, Freddie Hamilton entered the kitchen of Merry Weather Farm. It was earlier that same day and he'd just returned from Bristol where he'd taken the cart to pick up some feed for the cattle. 'I did warn you I was going to take action over the gypsies,' he said to Ursula, who stood at the rough deal table, pummelling the dough for the day's bread, with more force, he discerned, than was strictly necessary. 'The wholesaler is right across from the police station and it was too good an opportunity to miss,' he went on, speaking conversationally and as if dealing with the local constabulary was something he did every day of his life. Ursula frowned.

'But we agreed when we talked yesterday, we wouldn't involve the police,' she observed crossly.

'I don't think we did, love. Anyway, it's too late. I've done it now. Is there a cup of tea on the go? I'm parched. . . .'

Shooting him a look of vexation, Ursula dusted her hands over the bowl before reaching for the kettle and lifting it onto the stove. 'They're only gypsies,' she murmured, taking a grip on her temper. 'They don't mean any real harm.'

'Their presence leaves no room for the Girl Guides you had rented the field to,' he pointed out but this time with an edge to his voice. 'That's the trouble with gypsies; they don't give a thought to anyone else. . . .'

It was turning into an argument and there'd been too many of those of late but Ursula was too fired up by now to pay heed. 'Bronwyn's been kind enough to allow the girls the use of one of her fields. It was fallow anyway, no one minds in the slightest. . . .'

'We shouldn't be putting on our neighbours like this. . . .'

'We haven't. Bronwyn volunteered.' At least Bronwyn Loxley had seen the fix she was in, Ursula fumed, making her more than kind offer despite the fact that, many years ago, it was a gypsy woman who had once tried to burn Loxley down to the ground. Bronwyn said Katherine, her mother-in-law, had taken against the whole clan of gypsy folk because of it, so much so, it was a wonder she hadn't called in the police herself and armed them with shotguns whilst she was about it, too! Sighing, she poured a mug of tea and pushed it across the table. But then, given Hettie was returning home today from her jaunt abroad, thankfully Katherine Loxley had other and more important matters on her mind.

Freddie took his tea and drank it gratefully. 'You do know there were a couple of extra caravans turned up this morning? Talk about taking a liberty! On top of the two that arrived yesterday and the one the day before. . . .'

Even Ursula was unhappy to hear this state of affairs detailed so plainly. Her husband was watching her over the rim of his mug, aware of her little start of annoyance.

'Love, I don't understand you,' he said.

Ursula's gaze fell away, hardly able to blame him when she wasn't sure she understood herself. She felt sorry for the gypsies, that was the truth of it, and in particular, for their children, who, to her mind, didn't seem to have any kind of a life that normal children might have. She'd hate to see them frightened and that was precisely what they would be when a bunch of heavy-handed policemen turned up at the site. 'What did the police say they'd do?' she asked, flatly.

'I don't know. Move them on, I expect.'

'When?'

'When they've manpower enough.'

She needed fresh air. 'I'd better go and warn them,' she retorted.

Ignoring his snort of exasperation, calling to Fern, lolling at her feet, Ursula went outside into the warmth, glancing up into a sky so overcast, she wondered if a storm was brewing, indeed half hoped that it was, if only for the comfort of existing in elements so in tune with her feelings. She walked briskly, glad to let off steam, her footsteps guiding her over the brow of the hill so, in a very short time, she'd arrived at the meadows with their tumble of gaily decorated vardoes and horses tethered on land which, this week, should have been dotted with tents holding the party of Girl Guides who'd booked it. Freddie was right, there were more caravans now than when first they'd appeared and, if she'd never have dreamed of admitting it, a little part of her couldn't help but think this was taking advantage of her good nature. From the communal fire from which plumes of greyish-blue smoke wisped upwards, a large cooking pot hung, attended to by an old woman with a wrinkled, wizened face and a crooked back. Nearby, a little knot of women stood chatting whilst they kept an eye on the group of children of varying ages, playing at their feet. Dirty and unkempt the children might be, they looked happy enough. It was a peaceful scene and again Ursula couldn't help but wonder at Freddie going to the police when, surely, merely the threat of forceful eviction would have been enough?

The gypsy leader she now knew as Leon was sitting on the top step of his caravan, which was lavishly painted in an extravaganza of reds, yellows and greens and decorated with elaborate carvings of lions and horses. He was whittling a piece of wood, Maisie May snuggled up beside him. A proud man who saw much and said little and yet, what he did say would be good, sound common sense, Ursula hazarded, letting herself into the field and making her way towards him, wishing forlornly, meanwhile, she had something to say other than what she'd come to tell him. She was acutely aware of the women watching her and that she was the centre of a not altogether welcoming attention.

'We meet again,' Leon murmured, dropping his clasp knife into his pocket and getting to his feet, his keen, dark eyes, so incongruous under his mane of snow-white hair, scrutinizing her face though not in an unkindly way, she thought. 'You have a problem?' he asked, unnervingly as if he'd read her thoughts.

There was no way to say this, other than to come right out with it. 'Not me, exactly,' she replied, awkwardly. 'I'm afraid my husband's been to the police about your presence here and they're coming to move you on. I thought I ought to warn you. I am sorry,' she finished, truthfully.

The old man's shoulders lifted. 'A gypsy's lot, I'm afraid.'

'I wish there was something I could do.'

'It's hardly your fault, child. What will be, will be. Please, come inside; let me make you some tea.' The invitation surprised her. Not waiting for an answer, he stooped, swinging Maisie May up into his arms and retreating inside so it seemed churlish not to follow him. Intrigued, despite the troubling news which had brought her out here, and keen now to be away from a distinct hostility emanating from the other gypsies, Ursula bid Fern sit and quickly followed him into the caravan. Inside, she was amazed to find herself in a bright and neat living area, partitioned by a gaily coloured curtain at one end with a wooden seat running the length of both walls. A little wooden table was placed centrally, covered with a lace cloth on which stood a vase filled with wild flowers, which greeted her with their faint perfume. Gleaming crockery and utensils hung on the walls.

'But this is delightful!' she exclaimed and then blushed, in case he should guess the truth. It had been the last thing she'd expected, exposing her prejudice for exactly what it was. Whilst she sat with Maisie May on her knee, Leon busied himself with a small primus stove on which a kettle was soon bubbling away merrily.

The child was sleepy, leaning in against her trustfully.

'She's lovely,' Ursula murmured, glancing down and experiencing the usual and by now expected stab of pain that she got whenever she had anything to do with children, something to which she'd had to get used but still tugged at her heartstrings horribly.

Leon poured tea and pushed a cup across the table towards her.

'Children are a great solace,' he said.

'You have full care of her?' she asked, sipping the tea, which was hot and sweet, calming the nerves which had seen her hurrying over here. Vaguely, she wondered what Freddie would think if he could see her now, fraternizing with the so-called enemy. She was at once aware of the spasm of pain crossing the gypsy leader's still handsome face.

'Her mother, Riah, my daughter, died when she was born,' he said, explaining all.

'Oh . . . I see . . . I am sorry. There's no father on the scene?' He shook his head regretfully. 'Not one of any use, I'm afraid.'

'I'm sorry,' she repeated, feeling again the inadequacy of her words. She wished she could have found something more consoling to say but there was nothing. They all had their troubles, this man included, it appeared.

'We get by,' he replied, his gaze falling to Maisie May and with such warmth of affection, Ursula knew whatever else she might be missing in her life, the little girl didn't lack love.

The thought was troubling. As if Leon hadn't enough on with the care of such a little one without Freddie sending for the police. It wasn't right and now Ursula was here, and saw for herself how the gypsies lived, she felt worse than ever. Lost revenue apart, could she really say the gypsies' presence here was doing harm?

The sounds of angry shouts drew Hettie down towards the caravans, proving her suppositions correct. Several burly police constables had emerged from the two cars parked up on the verge, and were already heading for the caravans as Ursula Hamilton appeared from the top of the lane leading down to Merry Weather Farm. That she was upset was also clear.

'What's wrong?' Hettie called, running down the road towards her.

Ursula swung round, waiting impatiently for Hettie to draw level. 'My husband's called the police, that's what. They're here to move the gypsies on,' she said.

Knowing what her grandmother thought of the gypsies, Hettie assumed this was all to the good. 'You don't look too pleased,' she hazarded.

'But where will they go? There are children involved. They'll be so afraid!' came the alarmed and alarming response. Not waiting to see if Hettie followed, her neighbour swung away and started to run down the road towards the policeman who, by now, had let themselves into the field and had come up against a straggly line of gypsy folk, arms linked, barring their way to the caravans. If their biggest number comprised women, it was still an explosive, volatile situation. Hettie saw an old man with a shock of white hair emerge from the nearest caravan and hurry across the meadow to put himself at the head of the protesters.

Obeying her every instinct, Hettie charged after Ursula and down towards the policemen, crashing to a halt in front of them, where she was surprised to discover that she knew the officer in charge, a man from one of her grandmother's myriad of committee meetings, often held at the hall.

'Please. . . . This really isn't necessary!' Ursula began, waving her arms ineffectually. The officer in charge stared at her in surprise.

'Don't you go worrying yourself, ma'am. We have the situation in hand,' he replied.

It didn't look to be in hand. Under their tanned, weather-beaten faces, the gypsy women were tense and determined, making it perfectly clear if they were to be moved, it would have to be by force. As if in proof of it, stern-faced and resolute, the old man with the white hair sat down, cross-legged on the ground, folding his arms defensively across his chest. Seeing it, his followers adopted suit to form an immoveable human barrier so Hettie dreaded what might happen next, it flashing into her mind then that, whatever her grandmother might think, gypsies were only folk with the urge to roam, after all.

'I'm sorry but I've changed my mind. I'd really rather you left these people alone!' Ursula muttered belligerently.

'With all due respect, ma'am, I'm acting under orders from your husband.'

'My husband's gone to market.'

'And these itinerants are trespassing.'

'But not if I say not, surely?'

'That's not what your husband says, ma'am.'

It seemed impasse was reached but meanwhile, Hettie's

indignation was growing. It wasn't just what Ursula had said; Hettie knew it wasn't right either. Gypsies or not, people deserved to be treated with respect, not bundled off as if they were so many cattle on their way to market. Her gaze wandered to the old man, sitting so straight-backed, so determined and somehow regal, she couldn't help but feel an admiration for him. It helped to make up her mind.

'Surely Mrs Hamilton has the right to say what goes? This is her land, after all!' she joined in, shocked to discover her voice ringing with an authority she hadn't the slightest idea she possessed.

Everyone stopped and looked around. The officer touched his cap. 'Your Grace. . . . I didn't see you there,' he murmured but his tone was pleasingly mollified.

Hettie took advantage, smiling disarmingly. 'But you could leave things awhile, I'm sure? I'm certain my grandmother wouldn't care to hear that there's been . . . any kind of an unpleasantness.'

Mention of the formidable Katherine Loxley hung in the air, the pivot on which this whole unpleasant situation might turn. All at once, the tension in the air relaxed. The officer nodded curtly, turning abruptly back to address the gypsy leader. 'I'll allow you a few days' grace, no more. We'll be back . . . so watch yourselves!'

Having fired this volley, relieving some of his ire thereby, his gaze flickered towards Hettie, his eyes narrowing, so she knew then that he would have liked to say more but that something restrained him, a respect for her position, she realized, with a little thrill of triumph. She had a voice, one that could make people do things they didn't want to do, even someone in the exalted position of this man here. Her eyes gleamed. It was with some satisfaction that she stood back and watched the police depart, leaving the field to the victors. Shortly, the two cars were speeding back up the lane. As the gypsies scrambled to their feet and began to drift back to their caravans, their leader came towards them.

'You changed your mind, Mrs Compton,' he said, calmly.

Ursula nodded uneasily and Hettie wondered what Freddie Hamilton would have to say when he discovered that not only had his wife defied him but in such a public manner, too.

'I couldn't stand back and see you badly treated,' she answered. 'Though what we'd have done without Hettie here, I really don't know. . . .'

The gypsy's gaze moved to Hettie and she found her hand enveloped in a warm, firm handshake.

'We owe you our thanks, too, Your Grace.'

'Oh, it was nothing, really. . . .'

'It's not the first time Loxleys have had to do with Romani folk. We go back a long way. . . .'

'Do we? Oh, gosh! But I didn't know!'

Amusement sprang into the man's face, a fine face she thought, with much going on behind his keen, dark eyes. He nodded. 'Centuries ago to the time of the Civil War when our people had only just arrived in this land and could be hanged for simply being a gypsy.'

It sounded barbaric. Hettie shivered. 'Do you mean whilst Nell Loxley was alive?' she asked, having been well schooled by Dizzy concerning Loxley's redoubtable first Duchess and her Royalist sympathies, a woman of spirit and fire with whom she felt great empathy and whom she would love to emulate. As if he guessed her thoughts, the gypsy leader smiled.

'Indeed, Your Grace. Nell Loxley knew we gypsies could well keep a secret. We were once able to do her a great service. Just as you have done for us! We're grateful to you and if there's ever anything we can do for you. . . ?'

Hettie smiled and shook her head, unsure what to say. But there was nothing! How could there be? She was suddenly aware that time was passing and she wasn't where she was supposed to be.

'I'd better go,' she muttered, now all the excitement was over, feeling slightly embarrassed. Refusing Ursula's offer of a cup of tea back at the farm, she said her goodbyes and hurried away; letting herself from the field and walking, head bowed and deep in thought, back up the lane towards Loxley. Her trip around Europe already seemed a lifetime away, and yet, she'd only just got back home. Such a lot had happened, not the least of it Bill's upsetting attitude towards her.

At the head of the lane, another shock awaited her. At once, she was aware of a man leaning with his foot on the low stone wall and staring down the meadow towards Loxley. Something about his stance drew her gaze so it stuck there. Hettie's footsteps slowed. But, surely, she knew this man, indeed had seen him only far too recently! She hurried closer. 'But you're Alex Windrow!' she said.

Alex Windrow straightened up, tipping his cap to the back of his head with a thumb.

'Your Grace,' he responded, seeming not one whit surprised to see her.

So, he knew who she was too when she was sure he hadn't, when they'd first met in Berlin.

Eager questions tumbled from her lips. 'You painted that portrait of my mother!' she said accusingly.

'So I did.'

'Why did you?'

'Why not?'

'You do know her, then?'

'In a fashion.'

'What are you doing here?'

His smile, tenuous as it had been, instantly disappeared. 'Why I'm here is my business. . . . But better I hadn't returned. Better I'd never set foot in this place again!' he muttered, his voice throbbing with some inner and disturbing tension. An odd, strange man, Hettie surmised, feeling the first, faint stirrings of unease.

Though she'd thought about the painting of her mother often, she never thought she'd see its creator again. Something about him unnerved her.

'Shall you come back to the hall?' she enquired haughtily, not even sure if she ought to ask him. It was with a certain relief she saw him shake his head.

'I think not . . . yet.' His lips curled into the semblance of a smile. It appeared their conversation was over. 'Good day, to you, then,' he snapped. And that was it, she was dismissed and when she'd never even had chance to ask him about Lewis! Touching his cap, he limped quickly away, back down the road to leave her staring balefully after him. What did he mean in saying he shouldn't have come back? Why shouldn't he? Had he then visited Loxley before? Was that when he'd been so captivated by her mother he'd been urged to paint a picture of her – and such a picture! Wait until they heard of this back at the hall! Forgetful of both dignity and authority, so newly and pleasingly discovered, Hettie tore away, scrambling quickly over the wall to run, whooping with glee, pell-mell down the hill towards the bridge, arriving home red-faced and out of breath and bursting through the front doors just as her grandmother emerged from the sitting room from her afternoon nap.

'There you are, child,' Katherine retorted icily, out of sorts because she'd slept too long and woken with a start. Her disapproval deepened. 'Look at the state of you! Whatever have you been up to?'

If Hettie had been at all inclined to discuss the sensitive subject of the police trying to evict the gypsies from Ursula Hamilton's field and the unwitting part she'd played in dispelling them, the meeting with Alex Windrow had quite driven it from her head.

'Grandmamma, you'll never guess who I've just seen outside in the lane? Alex Windrow! You know, the painter I told you about who did that portrait of Mother hanging in the art gallery in Berlin. . . .'

'No, I don't know! Why should I?'

'Whatever is he doing here at Loxley? I must go and find Mother. . . .'

As was her want, Katherine Loxley summed up the situation quickly. 'You'll do no such thing, my girl! Your mother has quite enough on her plate as it is! You leave this with me. I'll find out exactly who the man is and whatever he imagines he's up to following you here. . . .'

Yawning heavily, Tom Compton plumped himself down at the kitchen table.

'Here, tuck into this, lad,' Mary, his wife, encouraged, plonking his supper down in front of him. 'You look all in. You do know you're doing too much?'

'Someone has to make a start of winter planting, my love,' he pointed out patiently and in a vain attempt to placate her. Mary was a grand lass but she had a sharp tongue on occasion, particularly when she imagined her husband wasn't taking good care of himself.

'The old skinflint ought to take on more staff,' she retorted.

'Don't start, my love. You know how things are. . . .' he responded, glancing across the comfy little kitchen to his wife's unnaturally serious face. 'Are you alright, Mary?' he enquired uneasily.

She sat down at the table, resting her chin on her hands. 'I am worried, I have to admit.'

'Not our Ursula again.'

'Things aren't going well with Freddie. I just know it.'

'Has she said as much?' Tom asked, sharply for him, the most amiable of men.

She shook her head. 'I'm her mother. She doesn't need to say.'

They'd had this conversation many times already. Even if he knew he might as well bang his head against a brick wall as repeat words he'd uttered so many times already, Tom did his best to soothe the situation. 'I've told you already, Mother,' he chided. 'You leave our Ursula alone. The young folk'll sort things out if you'll only let 'em. . . .'

At that moment, there came a sharp rap at the door, making both old folk jump. It was late for callers and, in any case, none were expected.

'Who's that now?' Mary grumbled, nevertheless getting up to answer it.

At once, she gasped and flung the door wide, allowing her visitor to limp past her and into the room, where he stood, looking around him as if he owned the place.

'Good evening, Tom, Mary. You might look pleased to see me,' he muttered, smiling coldly.

Tom Compton half rose from his chair and then, as if in shock, plumped back down again. The last person he'd expected to see here, the one place on earth he'd hate to be!

'Hello, Reuben,' he responded, heavily.

Chapter Five

Her arms full of the threadbare sheets she'd just taken from the ottoman in the State Bedroom where they were stored, Bronwyn emerged into the Long Corridor just as Mary Compton's comfortable frame appeared from the direction of the Blue Bedroom. Given that both the war committee and Roland de Loxley were due that afternoon and that there were more beds to make up than they had decent sheets to go round, both women were flustered.

'Any more left?' Bronwyn enquired, glancing down fretfully at the sad bundle she carried and praying she wasn't meant to use these.

Mary frowned. She'd looked worried all morning, Bronwyn realized, assuming Loxley's lack of adequate bedlinen wasn't the sole cause of it. She'd no idea what the problem could be.

'Indeed there isn't, Your Grace,' Mary answered, with that touch of deference Bronwyn should have been used to by now and yet somehow wasn't. 'Why don't I fetch more from home? They'll tide us over, if nothing else,' she suggested practically.

It had come to something, Loxley depending on linen from the estate manager's cottage but it appeared there was no alternative.

'It's good of you to help out, Mary, without having to provide decent sheets on top!' Bronwyn complained, giving in with good grace.

'Your Grace, you know I'd do anything to help. . . .'

'I know you would, and believe me, we're more than grateful!'

Bronwyn smiled, wondering meanwhile where the estate would be without these faithful servants to whom Loxley represented so much more than mere employment. Loxley was a way of life, the place where they lived their lives and where their forebears had lived their lives too, enabling the sense of continuity.

'We put on you too much,' she muttered. 'You should have more help. According to Katherine, the time was, this house was full of servants!'

For the first time that morning, Mary returned her smile. 'Aye and I can remember it too, just!'

She would have gone, bent on her mission, but determined to find out if there was any kind of a problem, Bronwyn delayed her.

'Mary, are you sure there's nothing wrong? Only you do seem rather . . . worried. . . . If there's anything at all I can do to help, you only have to say!'

Mary shook her head. 'It's only tiredness, I expect, Your Grace. I have to admit, these old legs aren't as young as they used to be,' she answered quietly, though the rising tide of colour flushing her homely cheeks told her employer otherwise.

With these far from reassuring words, Mary hurried away downstairs. Bronwyn returned to the State Bedroom where her frustration only deepened, fuelled by her awareness that here was a room with possibilities if only there'd been money to spare to spend on it. She stood looking around her, frowning at the Utrecht velvet on the walls, such a delicate shade of pink, and the matching draperies and bedspread and satin curtains, all in a sad state of disintegration. No one could deny the view from the large bay window was magnificent. The room was said to have been occupied by Charles II, who, in dire need of some home comforts, had begged Loxley hospitality overnight when he'd broken off from one of his infrequent journeys up north. Katherine scoffed at the tale but, romantic at heart, Bronwyn loved to believe it was true and moreover, thought that it was a crying shame that Nell Loxley, ardent Royalist as they now knew her to have been, hadn't been alive to see it too.

Considering it, she decided at once that Roland should be installed in here, rather than in the Blue Bedroom as she'd originally intended. For that Roland was a Loxley, at heart as well as by name, couldn't be denied. More importantly, she knew him well enough by now to know he'd understand the dilapidated state of the furnishings.

As if on cue, the bell over the front door clanged. Moments later, she heard Soames' calm tones ushering a visitor inside, gladly recognizing the response as belonging to Roland. Better still, he was earlier than expected. Suddenly, inexplicably happy, she hastened away downstairs, discovering her distant relative looking remarkably happy to have arrived, a man at ease with himself and his surroundings. At the sight of her, his face broke into a warm smile of approval.

'There you are, Bron. . . .' he murmured, hurrying forward.

'It's good to see you again, Roland!' she responded warmly. 'Soames, take Monsieur de Loxley's cases upstairs to the State Room if you would and then bring coffee to the morning room. Your mother's keeping well, I hope? She really must pay us a visit one of these days. . . .' Keeping up such a steady stream of pleasantries, she led the way into the pretty, south-facing room, where the little sunlight the morning had brought spilled through the French windows in shafts of sifting liquid gold. Shortly, they were comfortably settled in armchairs and drinking piping hot coffee from the best china cups Soames had seen fit to bring out for such a happy occasion. Even the downstairs staff approved of Roland. Bronwyn hid a smile. After all the hurly-burly of her morning, she was relieved to take a break.

'Oh, Roland, it's truly good to see you,' she reiterated. She stopped, as a thought rose, disturbing the calm of her happiness. Unnerved by it, she took refuge in the depths of her coffee cup, well aware that though on the surface, her life here at Loxley was a full one, she'd long felt there was something missing from it too. Warmth, fulfilment, the close physical contact only a man could bring. . . . She missed Harry and always would and with an ache like a bodily pain, often keeping her awake at night. She was lonely, hating with a passion the thought that she'd most likely spend the rest of her life alone. And yet, she was still young . . . ish, she knew she had much to offer a man; why should she entirely give up hope of married happiness?

'You've had a good journey, I hope?' she asked, looking up to discover, disconcertingly, her visitor had been watching her meanwhile and worse, with a worryingly thoughtful expression on his face. What must he think of her! He appeared what he was; a man who'd arrived from an arduous journey and considered every mile of it well worth the effort spent. He smiled easily.

'I've had an excellent journey, thank you,' he replied, his gaze lingering on her far longer than with which Bronwyn was comfortable. She sat up primly and finished her coffee. Her imagination was running away with itself again and if this was what her lonely state had brought her to, she should pull herself together! She put down her cup and, fully in control of herself by now, or so she soothed herself, she smiled benignly.

'I was so pleased you said you were going to stay here despite the war committee's presence. It was ridiculous to imagine you putting up in the village when we have so much room here. . . .' she said, referring to the arrangements conducted by telephone between them. Even Katherine when consulted had been in agreement; there was perfectly no need for Roland to incur the cost of the single inn which the village boasted when he would be more comfortable here at Loxley.

'It's good of you to put me up. . . .'

Bronwyn's eyes twinkled mischievously. 'We're hosting the war committee welcome dinner tonight. I did warn you about it, remember? It's rather a stuffy affair, I'm afraid. You'd be doing me a huge favour if you'd attend.'

'I'd be delighted, if you think it will help.' He smiled his acquiescence.

His response was typical – a kind man always ready to do a good turn. She liked him tremendously. Another, even happier thought, darted into her head. 'It'll be a good opportunity to meet Hettie, too. She's out at the moment, exercising Tallow, her father's hunter. Katherine rides him now and again, of course, but I'm afraid arthritis forbids her as often as she'd like.'

'I shall look forward to it.'

'You'll like Hettie, Roland, I'm sure. The trip abroad's done her so much good.' Delighted to find matters so satisfactorily arranged, Bronwyn settled back in her chair, aware she was repeating Katherine's mantra that the Europe trip must mean some good had rubbed off on Hettie. Would it really have done her as much good as Katherine assumed? To Bronwyn's mind, nothing was more certain than Hettie had been in a dire need of direction before she'd set off. If more than once over the last few days, her mother had happened to think her daughter's extensive and expensive tour had made not the slightest jot of difference to her waywardness, unlike Katherine, she was determined not to make an issue of it.

A gust of wind whistled across the meadows, whipping the bright red hair Hettie so abhorred back across her face. Impatiently, she brushed it away, leaning forwards to murmur encouragement to her mount Tallow, a dappled grey, before spurring him on and taking the high hedge before her at a gallop, sailing over it with a whoop of glee. Pulling up, waiting for her heart to resume its normal pattern, she was only glad her grandmother hadn't been around to see it. Grandmamma would have boxed her ears and given her a ticking-off into the bargain!

'Well done, boy,' she whispered into the horse's ear. Unsure whether to go on or to return to Loxley, in time for lunch, a movement in the hedgerow at the far end of the field caught her attention. To her astonishment, Hettie saw that it was a small child who sat on the ground, pulling at a few late, straggly flowers and babbling happily to herself. Watching her curiously, Hettie walked Tallow nearer. A heart-shaped face framed by a shock of dark, unruly hair. She was adorable. Hettie sat up in the saddle. Gypsy caravans apart, in the meadow below she could see nothing and no one, so to whom else could this child possibly belong other than the gypsies? She wasn't old enough to be out unaccompanied. Not wishing to startle her, she dismounted and leading Tallow by his rein walked him down towards her.

'Have you come from the caravans, poppet?' she asked.

The child looked up and smiled and evidently liking what she saw, held out her little arms. There was no help for it. She couldn't leave her here. Talking soothingly the while, Hettie scooped her up, manoeuvring them both back onto Tallow, who stood patiently by and, by dint of clasping her small charge carefully in front of her, walked them sedately through a gap in the hedgerow and down towards the caravans.

As chance would have it, the first of these they arrived at belonged to the white-haired old man she now knew as Leon, the leader of these people. He was asleep, dozing gently on the steps, but woke at their approach, his expression changing to one of alarm when he saw who it was and, moreover, who was with her. 'Maisie May!' he cried, jumping up and hurrying over. Instantly, the little girl reached towards him, allowing him to catch hold of her and swing her down.

'I found her in the field up top. She must have wandered off,' Hettie exclaimed, jumping neatly down. 'She does belong to you, I take it?'

'My granddaughter, Maisie May,' Leon agreed, clutching the child fiercely to him. 'It appears I'm indebted to you yet again, Your Grace. I didn't even know she'd wandered off.'

He was distressed, feeling guilty he'd been so negligent and, sensitively aware of it, Hettie did her best to comfort him. 'There's no real harm done,' she soothed and yet inwardly acknowledging he'd had a lucky escape. There was no getting away from the fact: the child was very young and he was very old to have a care of her. It was none of her business, of course.

'You must let me repay you,' he murmured, gathering his composure. His eyes, so dark and deep set, so uniquely alive for a man of his age, began to twinkle. 'At least let me make you some tea?'

Hettie was surprised to find herself accepting and yet the truth was, Bill in the kind of mood he was nowadays, she'd been at a loose end all morning, hence the ride on Tallow. She nodded happily and, as Leon disappeared inside his caravan, sat down next to Maisie May, on the steps, lolling in a way that would have sent her grandmother apoplectic if she'd been around to see it and entertaining the little girl by pulling faces, encouraged to more and grotesque distortions by her giggles of delight.

'She likes you,' Leon remarked, returning from his caravan with a mug of tea in either hand and holding one out towards her.

'I've always wanted a little sister,' Hettie agreed, only just now realizing it.

She took her tea, sipping it gratefully.

'We have to make the best of what we have.' Leon smiled and sat down beside her, making himself comfortable. A man who seemed to have an opinion on most things, Hettie surmised, wondering if he really were as wise as he appeared. Abruptly, she remembered what he'd told her a few days ago, after the business with the police threatening to move them on and concerning the gypsies' connections to Loxley.

'You mentioned your people once had cause to do Nell Loxley a good turn?' she prompted, suddenly wanting to find out more.

'Romanies guard their secrets well,' he murmured, enigmatically.

'I'm sure they do,' Hettie agreed earnestly, not sure what else to say.

He drank his tea, his gaze settling on his granddaughter and

instantly softening. 'Knowledge passes from generation to generation amongst our people, from the Civil War when first we came
to this land and even before that time. There's much we could tell
concerning Nell Loxley. She was well known amongst us.'

Hettie smiled. 'Because of her secret love child, you mean?'

'More than that,' he answered and so seriously, instantly her
levity disappeared, replaced by a quickening interest.

'Please won't you tell me?' she wheedled. 'I'm Nell's descend-
ant, after all! Surely, I have a right to know?'

Leon nodded thoughtfully. 'It's common knowledge amongst
us that Alexander Hyssop and not his brother, Rufus, was father
to Nell's child,' he said.

'Oh, but we found Alexander's tomb in a secret passageway
in the ruins of Loxley Old Hall,' Hettie agreed, eagerly. 'It's a
simply wonderful story even if Grandmamma wanted us to keep
it secret. . . .' She ground to a halt, wondering now if she'd said
too much. But, after all, given the publicity following their discovery of Alexander Hyssop's mortal remains, everyone knew the
tale well enough by now. It was spellbinding and romantic and
she loved it.

Leon frowned. 'Many think, mortally wounded as he was,
it was some kind of a miracle Alexander Hyssop found his way
from the battlefields of Naseby to the safety of Loxley Old Hall.
Legend has it it was only with the Romanies' help.' He glanced
back towards the crumbling ruins, his gaze far away, as if he saw
before him the magnificent old edifice still in its prime, massive-
stoned and forbidding, springing up from the rock from which
it was hewn. And Nell Loxley triumphant atop its battlements!
Hettie sat with her arms wrapped around her knees, enthralled.

'Oh, but you have to tell me now, Leon, please!' she implored.

He smiled gently. 'There are secrets that, as Duchess of Loxley,
perhaps you ought to know. Events that happened long ago when
England was a wild and lawless place so different from the land
we now know. . . .'

Hettie opened her mouth to beg him to tell her more but frustratingly, pre-empting her, he stood up, shaking the dregs from his tea out onto the grass.

'Mayhap I'll tell you sometime but not now,' he murmured thoughtfully.

He was a strong-minded man and, she knew him well enough already to know that once he'd made up his mind that was it. The interlude was over and even she could see it was futile to argue. Maisie May was lolling propped against her and had dropped to sleep. Seeing it, her grandfather scooped her up into his arms, cradling her against him.

'Please come again,' he invited, before returning inside the caravan.

The door closed firmly behind him.

It should have been rude but somehow it wasn't. He was a strange man and yet Hettie liked and trusted him. Gypsies were gypsies and had manners and rules of their own, she mused, if inside bubbling over with excitement. Wait until she told Grandmamma! With one thought only now, to get back to Loxley as quickly as possible and to tell her grandmother all that had happened, she jumped up and ran over to Tallow, leaping up onto his back and heading them straight for home.

It was playtime at Loxley village school. A blur of happy, shouting faces, the sight of which winged Ursula swiftly back to the childhood she'd shared with Freddie. She could still picture them now, a pair of tousle-haired scamps, taking it in turns to swing on this same rope ladder hanging from a tree whose thick greenery in so short a time would be a mass of glistening chestnut cobs.

'As I was saying, Mrs Hamilton. . .?' The voice breaking into her thoughts, scattering them to the four ends of the playground, belonged to Cynthia Bardwell, head teacher of the cheerful little stone school building outside which the two women stood, once belonging to the church and now serving the village for the education of its youngest children. 'There's no point finding places for the gypsy children,' she insisted, smiling to soften the impact of her words. 'I'd no sooner have them settled than they'd be off again. I've seen it too often, I'm afraid.'

'But surely even a little education would be better than none at all?' Ursula argued, wondering the while why it should mean so much to her. It was none of her business whether the Romani children were educated or not but something during her last visit to the site, on impulse, to take some cakes she'd baked to Leon, with whom she'd struck up an unexpected friendship, had stirred her into action. The sight of those grubby, happy little faces, she expected, running harum-scarum, in and out of the caravans, unchecked and apparently uncared for and yet, conversely, so obviously loved and nurtured, it had made her all the more keen to ensure they were allowed the same opportunities as children from more conventional homes.

'And then there's general hygiene. . . .' Cynthia Bardwell shuddered visibly, continuing as if Ursula had never spoken. 'My mothers would be up in arms. No! It would never do, I'm afraid.'

Something about her complacency was beginning to annoy Ursula. 'It's only surface grime,' she insisted. 'If you're talking about the way the children are dressed, well. . . . Surely you, of all people, Miss Bardwell, must believe the old adage, clothes never maketh the man?'

She'd gone too far. Miss Bardwell bridled. 'I never suggested that for one moment!'

'But you're prepared to ignore potential?'

'Not that, exactly. . . .'

The tenacity at the heart of Ursula's being, the refusal to give in, no matter what obstacles were flung in her way, sprang to the fore. 'And what if I undertook to bring them here, clean and well presented?' she demanded, her mind already working furiously as how best to effect this miracle. But approached in the right way, she knew plenty of women who would be willing to donate clothing their own children no longer had use for. Earnestness illumined her face. 'Please, Miss Bardwell. . . . Cynthia! You must give these children a chance. It would make all the difference.' She was weakening, she could see. In a nervous anticipation, Ursula waited.

'Oh, for goodness' sake! Very well, then!' she uttered at last, the magic words Ursula had longed to hear. Her face broke into a wide smile of approval.

'Oh but thank you. . . . Thank you, Miss Bardwell! That's simply wonderful. I'll make sure you won't regret it!'

'A trial period only, mind,' Cynthia Bardwell warned. 'Shall we say . . . three afternoons a week?'

She could have named any number of mornings, afternoons, evenings even, Ursula was so delighted. A few moments later found her unhitching their shire Clover from the railings outside and climbing back up onto the cart for home, having achieved far more than she would ever have believed possible when she'd set off, earlier that morning. Inside, her heart was singing. Bad as things were with Freddie, she was desperate now to share her success with him.

The short distance to the farm was completed in double-quick time. Throwing down the reins, Ursula jumped down quickly, heading straight for the kitchen where, as she'd expected this time of a morning, Freddie sat drinking coffee with Pru, their farm-hand, the biscuit tin open on the table between them.

He looked up sharply. 'There you are,' he said, for some reason sounding angry. 'I thought you were waiting in for the vet?' For a moment, Ursula had no idea what he was talking about. And then she remembered, something had been mentioned at breakfast that the vet might, conceivably, call to give the herd the once-over before the winter set in. Freddie and Pru both having their hands tied with the winter planting, it had been made clear it was incumbent on Ursula to keep an eye open for his arrival. She'd taken a chance to go out because, at the time, it hadn't seemed likely he'd turn up before his morning surgery. Instantly, all her pleasure in her achievement vanished. He might as well have thrown cold water in her face.

'Have I missed him?' she asked, sounding subdued.

'He's long gone,' he snapped.

'I see.'

'Is that all you have to say? I see? Can't I trust you for anything any more, Ursula?'

Pru jumped up. 'I'll get back to work,' she muttered awkwardly, throwing Ursula a look of commiseration before hurrying out. Trouble between man and wife, and she had no business with it. Ursula came into the kitchen, lifting the kettle onto the hob, spooning coffee into a cup, finding occupation for her hands because she was in the wrong again and didn't know what to say.

Only when her emotions were back under control did she turn back towards him.

'I'm sorry,' she said. 'I didn't think. Just my luck I missed him.'

Freddie stood up and ran his hand through his hair and she realized now how tired he looked. He worked too hard and she hated the truth that she didn't pull her weight about the place. It was true, though. She was a millstone around his neck instead of the help she'd always meant to be.

'Where were you, exactly?' he asked.

At once, her exuberance returned and her tale spilled out. She couldn't help it but he had to know how important this was. The battle she'd had, her success, the fact children with so little chance in life would now, miraculously, get one and all the while her gaze was fastened on his face, praying he'd understand. She ran out of steam. There was an odd, tense little silence.

'Are you quite mad, Ursula?' he asked, at last.

Her face crumpled. All her hopes and dreams and he hadn't understood one iota. However far apart they'd grown of late, she hadn't realized things were quite as bad as this. They didn't know each other any more, two opposite ends of a spectrum, never designed to meet.

'I thought you'd be pleased,' she uttered, plaintively.

Freddie's look of incredulity deepened. 'Pleased you've encouraged those blasted gypsies to stay even longer and on land that was productive before they arrived to ruin it. Do you think we're made of money?'

This was too much. 'Since when has money ever been the most important thing?' she fired back.

'Since I've had this place to run,' he snapped, 'single-handed, if you ask me!'

The words, if uncomfortably too near to the truth, were unforgiveable. Mute with misery, she could only watch as he stalked past her and out, slamming the door behind him so it felt the whole house reverberated from its force. Freddie had always been hot-tempered and so had she. A pair of hotheads together, yet still loving each other desperately – or so she'd thought. Ursula took her coffee over to the table and sank down into a chair. The drink was hot and reviving and did her good but wretchedly brought another thought winging into her consciousness, doing nothing to lift her spirits. She couldn't now get her head past the cosy scene which had greeted her arrival. Pru and Freddie, heads bent together over their coffee cups, no doubt sharing a joke so Ursula had felt, immediately, she was somehow an intruder. And in her own kitchen too! She put down her cup with a trembling hand. But Freddie had been so right in many respects. Wasn't it time she faced the truth? Farming was in Pru's blood. She loved the land. She was far more proficient in the myriad of tasks about the place than Ursula and Freddie must surely know it too. She could guess exactly what he must be thinking and she could hardly blame him.

What a crying shame he hadn't married Pru instead!

Effecting a quick change from her riding gear, Hettie rushed back downstairs, leaping the bottom three stairs and catapulting into the hall, startling the two adults who stood quietly talking there. Her mother caught firm hold of her arm, frustratingly delaying her.

'There you are, Hettie!' she muttered, through gritted teeth. 'Aren't you going to say hello to General Hawker, dear?'

'Hello, General Hawker!' Hettie responded dutifully and unenthusiastically to the elderly man with the large moustache, dressed in full military uniform, who stood bristling down at her, one brow raised in amused surprise.

'You will be joining us for dinner tonight?' Bronwyn prompted.

Delay was painful. Exasperated, Hettie pulled herself free. 'Oh . . . um . . . I expect so only . . . sorry . . . I can't stop now! Grandmamma's waiting. . . .'

'Whatever are you two up to, now?' Bronwyn asked wearily, shooting her offspring a frustrated glance.

'I'm not exactly sure. It's nothing to worry about, though.' Determined not to be detained longer, Hettie spun on her heel and fled, leaving behind her only awkward explanations, something to which her mother, unfortunately, was only far too used.

'Goodness, what it is to be young!' she spluttered, rather appalled.

The General smiled easily, a charming man but one with a glint of sharp intelligence, showing him to be no one's fool. 'You mustn't worry,' he responded, gallantly. 'I do remember what it's like to be young – just! Now, we were saying . . . I need somewhere secure to lodge our paperwork. It is all rather hush-hush, this time round, I'm afraid.'

Calling a greeting to the splendidly good-looking young soldier, left standing guard outside the entrance, as always whenever the war committee convened, Hettie hurried down the steps and jumped into the Daimler, drawn up, door open, throwing herself onto the back seat next to her grandmother, who was waiting with thinly veiled impatience. Nearly exploding with happiness and the information she'd hugged to herself so joyfully since Leon, the gypsy leader, had first imparted it, Hettie turned towards her excitedly.

'Grandmamma you'll never believe what's happened. . . .'

'I'm sure I won't,' Katherine interjected, drily.

'After Naseby, you know, the battle fought all those years ago during the Civil War. . . .'

'Yes, I do know, darling. . . .'

'When Alexander Hyssop was mortally wounded, it was the gypsies who brought him home to Nell Loxley to die!'

Katherine's glance was a mixture of exasperation and amused affection. 'Goodness, child! Whatever are you going on about now?' she enquired, pleasantly enough, before leaning forwards to rap smartly on the glass partition dividing Bill Walker from the car's occupants. The engine started up and the car began to roll smoothly down the drive. Hettie's face shone with excitement.

'There was something else too, to do with that time, though I've no idea what exactly because Leon wouldn't say!'

'Leon?' Katherine was evidently growing confused.

'Leon, the gypsy leader,' Hettie explained impatiently, too late remembering then that, given how her grandmother felt about the gypsies, perhaps this wasn't the most tactful of subjects to have introduced. She smiled placatingly. Her grandmother's expression had grown worryingly severe.

'Hettie, I hope you haven't been consorting with . . . with gypsies!' She had difficulty even articulating the word so unpalatable was it on her tongue.

Hettie frowned. 'But why ever not? I can hardly ignore them when their camp is so close by. Look, what Leon's told me about Alexander. . . . Absolutely fascinating. . . .'

'Fiddlesticks! A tall tale and gypsies are full of them,' Katherine opined.

Met with such a lack of enthusiasm, it was difficult not to

feel crushed. However this was her grandmother and Hettie was too used to dealing with her to be daunted for long. 'He wasn't making it up,' she muttered, petulantly. 'He's not that kind of a man. You don't know him, Grandmamma.'

'He's a gypsy,' Katherine retorted. 'The police should have moved their caravans on when they had chance. Perhaps it's time I had a word.'

Hettie was genuinely shocked. Entirely inadvertently, not only had she landed herself in trouble again but worse even than that, it appeared she'd caused more trouble for the gypsies too, the last thing she'd intended. Her grandmother was a fearsome woman and that was a fact. A little thread of resentment rose. If, because of something that had happened many years ago, this old woman had formed a prejudice against a group of people seeming to Hettie fair-minded and decent enough, then that wasn't her, Hettie's, fault. She spoke carefully, determined, above all, not to make the situation any worse. 'Grandmamma . . . I know it was a gypsy woman who once tried to burn Loxley down but it isn't fair to blame other folk who had nothing to do with it just because they're gypsies too!'

She spoke so earnestly, the swift retort hovering on the old woman's lips died an instant death.

That she'd given her irascible relative something to think about was plain. A triumph, small as it was, giving Hettie a flash of insight into what life would be like when, wonderfully, everyone finally accepted that she'd grown up. She was getting there, slowly. She smiled, changing subjects swiftly, another sign of childhood left behind so, if she had but known it, a wave of sadness rolled over the woman sitting so stiffly upright beside her.

'Where are we going?' she enquired, for the first time, taking a note of her surroundings. The car had passed through the village, speeding out into the countryside. Rolling hills and high peaks and crags interspersed with picturesque villages, the countryside Hettie had always known and loved. 'It's something to do with

Alex Windrow, isn't it – the man who painted that portrait of Mother?' she intuited, seeing by her grandmother's expression that was it, exactly.

'What else could it be?' Katherine responded drily and putting all thoughts of her dear, darling child growing up firmly out of her head.

'You've found out who he is?' Hettie asked, eagerly.

'I said I'd make enquiries,' Katherine agreed, pleasantly. 'A man matching his description is put up at The Oak in Hingham.'

'Are we going to see him?'

'Why not?' she agreed.

They were in the tiny and remote hamlet of Hingham, sliding to a halt by a green bearing a single, massive oak tree and opposite a public house, aptly named The Oak. A few stone-built cottages and a church with a brook, overhung by trees, to the back of it, was all the place boasted. Hettie couldn't think why an internationally acclaimed painter would have the slightest desire to stay here. Perhaps this was a scene he'd wanted to paint, like he'd so obviously wanted to paint her mother? It did look rather idyllic, she supposed. Excitement bubbled inside her. Bill Walker jumped from the driving seat and walked smartly round to open the passenger door. Katherine eased herself stiffly out, Hettie scrambling quickly after her. She grinned at Bill, who winked before returning to the car to settle himself down and await their return.

'What are you going to say to Alex Windrow, Grandmamma?' she demanded, eagerly.

'We'll see,' Katherine said, heading towards the entrance porch as, at that moment, through it, a young man appeared. Dark, curly hair and a frown Hettie remembered all too well. The sight brought with it a surprising awareness of how glad she was to see him and, what's more, that she'd been hoping she might since first she'd spied Alex Windrow.

'Lewis!' she said, gratified to discover, given the broad beam plastered across his face, he was actually pleased to see her, too. 'What are you doing here?'

'Not much. I'd been thinking of coming to see you, if you must know.'

'Were you? But why didn't you? There's an absolute load to show you round at Loxley!'

'And are you going to introduce us?' Katherine enquired, pleasantly but with an edge to her voice.

Hettie blushed. 'This is Lewis Steed, Grandmother. The boy I told you about. Alex Windrow's his uncle, well his adopted uncle, really. . . .'

'And is your uncle in now?' the older woman broke in, testily.

'He's in . . . the bar,' Lewis finished lamely, to the old woman's retreating back as, dismissing him as of no consequence, brushing rudely past him, she headed off inside.

Katherine was, she discovered, more than keen to acquaint herself with a man who'd dared gain financially by painting a portrait of a family member for public display and worse, compounding the crime by not asking permission first. It wouldn't do, it simply wouldn't do! She'd always thrived on cut and thrust, the heady battle of dispute and wretchedly, since Harry's death, there'd been so little of that of late. Leaning on her stick, she stumped through into the bar, a low-ceilinged, oak-beamed room with low benches placed strategically around the wainscoted walls and where a medley of brasses hung. A pleasant and welcoming room, an oasis for guests and villagers alike to chat and enjoy a drink in congenial company. A low fire burned in the hearth, by which the single customer the room housed, sat at a table, facing outwards and nursing a pint glass. Katherine's gaze roamed over him uneasily and, just as quickly, returned. A solid, well-dressed figure, a man whose thick and unruly brown hair was peppered with grey. As if he'd been expecting her, his gaze lifted from the depths of the glass into which he'd been staring. Meeting the angry, resentful gaze she remembered too well, Katherine's heart lurched, the years falling away as if they'd never been. Her lips parted, forming the name, so astonishingly, she found there. The name belonging to George's illegitimate son, Harry's half-brother and her stepson, the man she'd hoped, prayed, had gone for good.

Instinct and upbringing, even in these dire circumstances caused her to put one foot in front of another, moving her body stiffly forwards even if a part of her, the greater part, wanted instantly to set off in the opposite direction and as fast as she could.

'Katherine Loxley. But how are you, Stepmama?' Reuben Fairfax murmured, rising to pull out a chair and smiling coldly. 'Please. . . . Do sit down. I wondered how long it would take you to find me.'

Chapter Six

The afternoon sun spun patterns on the threadbare patches in the sitting room carpet, much as Bronwyn had tried to disguise the worst of the damage by strategic placement of the furniture. If only that was all she had to worry about! With a growing unease years of training had taught her to disguise, Bronwyn took her tea and sat down next to Roland. Her attention, meanwhile, centred on Hettie, who was lolling – and there was really no other way to describe it – in a chair next to the Reverend Lawrence Payne, Loxley's vicar and eminent historian. Bronwyn had invited the elderly cleric for tea, seeing it as a good opportunity for Roland to sound him out about Loxley, for there was very little he didn't know about its history.

Since yesterday, and following Katherine's startling revelation concerning Reuben's unexpected return, this tea party had been the furthest event from Bronwyn's mind. She'd been left mulling over Katherine's dogged and perverse refusal to tell Hettie the truth about Reuben. According to Katherine, it was enough Hettie knew Alex Windrow, the painter, and Reuben Fairfax, Loxley's ex-gamekeeper were one and the same and, no matter how Bronwyn tried to persuade her otherwise, she still refused to see it any other way. The fact remained, indeed had kept Bronwyn awake half the night, that even if, as Katherine insisted on pointing out, Reuben was only Harry's half-brother, he was still Hettie's uncle, a relationship she surely had a right to know about? One look at her daughter's earnest face, lifted trustingly towards the vicar, made up Bronwyn's mind. Much as she understood Katherine's antipathy towards Reuben, it wasn't right to leave his connection to this family unacknowledged. Once Katherine had returned from yet another of the interminable committee meetings presently filling her diary, hopefully together, they'd put Hettie right.

'You're quiet today, Bron?'

Roland's voice broke into her consciousness. A distant relative he might be but did he have a right to know about Reuben too? He was watching her over his teacup, his eyes flecked with genuine concern. A kind man and one whom the more she'd got to know, the more Bronwyn had grown to like. Once again, she was forced to acknowledge the feeling making ripples in the still millpond of her life. She liked Roland and sensed that he liked her too. More than liked him if the truth be known. . . . She smiled wanly.

'I'll be glad when this War Office's convention is over, Roland. I know it doesn't seem much but. . . .'

'Soldiers crawling all over the furniture. Men in suits in awkward places and all with prodigious appetites?'

'Something like that!' She laughed.

'If there's anything I can do to help? You do look tired; understandably so when you consider all the extra work you've had of late, amongst which I include my own presence here, I'm afraid!'

'You mustn't say that. . . .' she murmured before, perhaps unforgivably, her attention drifted again, recaptured by Hettie, who was looking so very much as if she was up to something, her mother was bound to sense trouble. Hettie's slightly strident tones drifted plainly across the sitting room.

'Reverend Payne? Did you know that after the battle of Naseby, it was the gypsies who helped the wounded Alexander Hyssop return to Loxley?'

Everyone knew of Hettie's odd fancies, even the vicar. Vaguely amused, the kindly old man gave her unusual question his considered attention. 'I'm afraid I haven't heard that, Hettie! It is true,

however, that Alexander Hyssop was wounded at Naseby. . . .'
Before he could warm to his theme, however, the door opened
and Soames appeared, hurrying towards Bronwyn with an
unusual alacrity. That he was discomposed was clear.

'Your Grace, we have visitors,' he murmured, quietly.

At once, a voice rang out, mocking and familiar. 'Spit it out,
man. Even given the house is overrun by soldiers, you know me
well enough by now – or at least you ought!' That voice – that
face! Two men had followed the butler into the room, the first of
whom caused Bronwyn's heart to constrict.

She'd been expecting him. Indeed, had made up her mind: if
he hadn't turned up, then she would have gone to find him. It
was so very long since she'd seen him and yet, he hadn't changed
at all. She put down her cup and stood up, in the circumstances
holding out a hand that was remarkably steady.

'Reuben. How wonderful to see you,' she said, quietly.

Afterwards, she was unsure how matters were arranged so
satisfactorily other than that Roland must have picked up on
what could have been an awkward situation. Shortly, Hettie was
dispensed with Reuben's companion, Lewis, ostensibly to show
him round the grounds, whilst Roland and Lawrence Payne were
headed tactfully into the library, intent on seeking out manuscripts concerning the seventh Duke which Bronwyn had earlier
invited Roland to browse through at his leisure. She was left
alone with Reuben, who seated himself across from her unasked,
his fierce, inscrutable gaze fixed on hers.

'It's good to see you,' she murmured, gathering her wits.

'It's good to see you too, Bron,' he responded but with such
warmth, she was both surprised and touched. The years between
melted as if they'd never been. Reuben, with whom she'd always
felt an affinity. Kindred spirits, they'd both had their troubles
living here on the estate, their lives, down in some measure to
Katherine, made more difficult than they ought to have been.

'Katherine not in?'

'She's at a meeting.'

'She'll be sorry to have missed me.'

His tone was mocking but Bronwyn ignored it. She had too much to tell him. 'I wanted so much to let you know about Harry,' she began. 'He was your brother, after all, Reuben. You had a right to know. I'd no idea how to get in touch with you. . . .'

'His death made the papers, even in Germany. I am sorry, Bronwyn, about Harry. . . .'

'You shouldn't have had to find out like that!' she insisted, sadly, aware even now how unfair Reuben's growing-up years had been, leaving him a part of this family and yet, perversely, nothing to it at all. 'Why did you run away, Reuben? And then to stay away and never send word! You might have known we had a need of you.'

He shifted uneasily. 'I came back for the funeral. But do you imagine Katherine would have wanted to see me?'

They both knew the answer to this. Better to do what he'd done, which was to disappear quietly after it rather than, at such a time, being left to tangle with Katherine, raking over old sores thereby. With an ease which took her by surprise, he moved the conversation to safer ground. 'Your daughter's a fine lass. . . .' he said.

'Your niece, Reuben,' she urged him.

'Aye, she has a look of Harry about her.' His flashing smile, a rare happening she remembered now, too quickly faded. 'And have you told her about me?' he asked, seeing at once by her expression that was the last thing she'd done. His face clouded angrily. 'But wasn't it always thus!' he muttered. 'Family but not family, as if I'm a bad secret to be swept out of sight!'

She couldn't have summed it up better but the conversation had taken a wrong turn and in a way she'd never intended. Something else that tended to happen around Reuben, she remembered now. He'd always been a man who believed in stating fact as fact. 'I can't speak for Katherine of course but I do mean to tell her, Reuben, when the time's right. You surely must understand why?' she responded, quietly. 'Don't let's fall out over it and certainly not when you've only just got here! Tell me everything that's happened to you. . . . Hettie tells me you're a successful artist. But that's absolutely wonderful!' She was talking too quickly, trying to smooth the situation over and yet genuinely interested in how he'd managed to turn his life around. Thankfully, he'd relaxed, stretching his long legs out before him and regarding her thoughtfully.

'How do these things happen?' he mused. 'I was in the right place at the right time, I expect. After I left here, all those years after the war, I travelled. Greece, Italy, Prague, landing in Berlin when the money ran out and surviving on my wits doing odd jobs for a local artist I chanced to meet. He gave me a roof over my head and, better still as far as I was concerned, he taught me how to paint. My life . . . took off.'

He made it sound so easy and yet, how could it have been?

'And the boy with you today? He has a look of you about him, Reuben.'

Reuben shook his head. 'If so, it's accidental. He's my aunt's stepson. I stayed on in England after Harry's funeral and took the trouble to look her up, my one surviving relative from my mother's side. She'd recently lost her husband and was having trouble with the lad. I took him back to Berlin to help her out more than anything.'

Bronwyn smiled faintly. She'd never thought of Reuben as a mentor. The day continued full of surprises. 'That was good of you, Reuben,' she ventured.

'Aye, it was,' he agreed, complacent and, anger apparently forgotten, relaxed back in his chair. Some things never changed, she mused and Reuben's mercurial mood swings was one of them. A troublesome man and yet she was more pleased to see him than she would have believed. A connection with Harry even he couldn't deny. Suddenly it didn't matter what Katherine would say when she got back and found him here.

'You will stay, a while at least?' she burst out impulsively. She hardly knew what she expected in reply but she was surprised at his flashing laugh of delight.

'Aye, Bronwyn Loxley! If you want me to stay, I will and gladly. . . .'

'Did you know your uncle was once gamekeeper on this estate, Lewis?' Hettie demanded as she led the way across the bridge under which swirled the deep and omnipresent Lox. Behind them lay the New Hall, before, the crumbling ruins of the old, reaching brokenly into the slate-grey sky. The rain, which had been threatening all day, continued to hold off. She glanced up anxiously.

'I knew he'd been a gamekeeper here once,' Lewis answered carefully, remaining annoyingly unimpressed with all she'd shown him so far.

'But it's a coincidence, don't you agree?' she persisted. 'I can see now where the portrait of my mother came in but it's odd we met as we did in Venice and never realized the connection.'

'I dunno, is it?' His words were offhand but said with such a glint in his eyes, she wondered if he was teasing her. She frowned. Even knowing what she now did concerning the circumstances of Alex Windrow's portrait of her mother, there was still something about it which disturbed her.

Leaping nimbly amongst the fallen masonry, she headed them under the crumbling archway and into what once had been Loxley Old Hall's cavernous entrance; now a mass of broken and lichen-covered stone, strewn haphazardly around empty, gaping windows and doorways. An oppressive, unearthly place which should have given her the shivers and yet oddly never did. 'They used to say this place was haunted by Nell, the first Duchess of Loxley,' she said, meaning to shock him and disappointed when it elicited so little response.

'I don't believe in ghosts,' he answered, annoyingly.

Unsure why she felt the need, Hettie searched for something else with which to impress him. He unsettled her and though their acquaintance might be slight, he had from the first moment she'd ever seen him. 'You can reach the New Hall from here through a secret passageway,' she blurted out, the first thing that came into her head. 'I'll take you through it someday, if you'd like? It emerges in the fireplace in the hall, there's a concealed door here somewhere. Amazing, isn't it, to think no one knew of its existence for years and years. . . .'

For the first time since he'd arrived, Lewis appeared interested. Acknowledging it with a small stab of satisfaction, Hettie began to feel her way around the crumbling masonry surrounding the area once obviously the fireplace. 'It's here, somewhere!' she exclaimed, turning back suddenly and, Lewis meanwhile having moved closer, discovering him too near for comfort. He was invading her space, gazing down at her with his mocking gaze so she wondered what he was thinking. And then she had the most distracting thought that he was about to kiss her and wondered, vaguely, what she'd do if he did. From its vantage point in one of the gaping windows, a crow cawed mockingly.

'What are you up to?' The voice, so full of accusation and arriving so unexpectedly, exploded into Hettie's consciousness, jolting her thoughts and bringing her crashing back to reality. She blushed, stepping back quickly, as she should have done in the first place, she realized belatedly, and looked round to see Bill, framed in the doorway. He was scowling. But after the way he'd treated her of late, making it plain he preferred his new friends at college to spending time with her, he had no right to look at her the way he was looking at her right now. Her indignation grew.

'I'm not up to anything!' she responded hotly.

'Aren't you going to introduce us?' he demanded, his gaze shifting angrily to Lewis.

There was little alternative, unless she meant to be rude.

Wistfully, Hettie wished things were back to normal and she and Bill were the good friends they'd always been. She smiled doggedly.

'Oh . . . um . . . Lewis, this is my old friend, Bill; Bill, this is Lewis who works for the man who used to be the gamekeeper here, until he moved abroad and became an artist. He's painted a portrait of Mother. Oh, you ought to see it, Bill, it's simply spiffing!' She stood back, aware that, in her nervousness, she'd said more than she'd intended, relieved when, albeit ungraciously, the two boys shook hands. By common consent, the secret passageway apparently forgotten, the little party began to make its way back through the ruins towards the road and the bridge. A silence had fallen no one seemed to know how to break.

'I saw you from the road,' Bill proffered, begrudgingly, at last.

'You were coming to see me?'

'Not exactly,' he returned, colouring up, so Hettie guessed he wanted to say more and couldn't because of Lewis. Vainly, she searched for a topic that might shift the conversation onto more palatable ground.

'What do you reckon to the gypsies camping on Freddie Hamilton's land?'

'What about them? They're only gypsies after all!'

'But don't you think gypsies are fascinating and rather romantic?'

'Hardly, Het. . . .' he answered, regarding her pityingly.

'I saw their caravans when we arrived. . . . Have you been to see them yet?' Lewis asked, flashing Hettie such a warm smile, she couldn't help but smile back.

'I have, actually. . . .' she agreed happily. Lewis, it appeared, understood exactly why she should find the presence of gypsies, in such close proximity to Loxley land, so exciting. They were exotic and unpredictable and out of the ordinary to everything else that went off around the estate.

'I wouldn't mind having my fortune told!' Lewis chuckled.

'Why don't we visit their camp? Now, if you'd like?'

Someone after her own heart it appeared, unlike Bill, who stood glaring at Lewis as if he'd suggested they should fly to the moon and back. Hettie would have gone too, like a shot if only a little nagging conscience hadn't reminded her that, unfortunately, duty called. She sighed. Duty always stopped her from doing what she wanted.

'I have to go home to change for dinner or Grandmother will be after me, I'm afraid. . . .'

'After dinner, then,' he persisted.

'But it'll be dark!' she responded, indignantly.

'So?' A slow smile crossed his face and again she caught a flash of mocking humour. The most irritating boy she'd ever met and yet. . . . Hettie had never visited the gypsy camp at night and she was recalling now the oddly seductive strains of music she'd heard the night before when she'd gone to shut her bedroom window. Hearing it, so unexpectedly, throbbing into the darkness, somehow it had moved her, so she'd found her body swaying with the beat. She'd stayed listening, left wanting to hear even more.

'Alright, let's do exactly that!' she responded recklessly, ignoring Bill's snort of disbelief.

'Don't be stupid, Het,' he said, at once.

Hettie glared. Since when had Bill appointed himself her conscience? His attitude only goaded her and he should have known better. 'It isn't stupid! What's wrong with the idea?'

'Why don't you come too?' Lewis taunted, looking directly at Bill. 'You daren't, dare you! Hah! I bet you're scared!'

'Say that again, if you dare!'

Suddenly, dislike had turned to aggression. Before Hettie could stop them, the two boys were squaring up to each other so she hardly knew what would have happened if, at that moment, a car hadn't appeared from the direction of the hall and pulled up on the bridge in front of them.

Reuben Fairfax climbed out of his car, frowning at the scene confronting him, the two boys looking as if they'd like to knock seven bells out of each other and this girl here, Bronwyn's daughter, his brother's child, with obviously no idea what she ought to do to stop them.

It had been some day. The visit to the hall, his childhood haunt, worse, seeing Bronwyn again and instantly, every single emotion from which he'd run away returning with the force of a blow. He loved her; he'd always love her and what a crazy fool he'd been to imagine he'd long since put those feelings behind him. You couldn't run away from love and, as if his subconscious had been aware of it all along, he supposed that was what had eventually brought him back here, the one place in the world he should have avoided like the plague.

'What's going off?' he barked.

'Nothing,' Lewis returned, stepping back from Bill and kicking out moodily at a loose stone in the road.

'Get back in the car. . . .' Reuben's words were directed at Lewis but his gaze was still centred on Hettie, softening at the sight of her. Despite everything Bronwyn had said, he found himself longing to tell her the true nature of their relationship, that she need never worry about anything again because he'd always look out for her and keep her safe. He owed Harry that much at least! The fact she looked perfectly capable of looking after herself only somehow amused him. 'You'd best get off home,' he murmured, gently for him so, as if aware of it, she shot him a curious glance.

'I'll see you, later,' Lewis called to her, before trailing reluctantly round to the passenger side and getting into the car. Reuben climbed into the driving seat and started the car, circumnavigating the pair left on the bridge and driving quickly away. 'What was that about?' he demanded curtly.

'Something and nothing,' Lewis returned, his shoulders lifting into an indifferent shrug.

'You behave yourself, my lad or else. . . .' Reuben's voice trailed away. Why hadn't he realized he couldn't face Bron and not feel for her exactly what he'd felt before? What a blithering idiot not to realize exactly what had brought him back here!

He drove only a short distance before impulsively pulling up onto the verge which ran alongside what had once been a path leading down into the wood and was now long since overgrown.

'Wait here,' he muttered to Lewis before climbing out. His heart was hammering against its ribcage, his head full of what had happened in his past life here. Instinct led him on, beating a way through the tangle of undergrowth where once had been the path, guiding his way against the darkness of trees and tangled undergrowth, ploughing on regardless until he was out of breath. All at once, oddly shocking him, as if he'd hoped it only an obscure memory, he came upon a glade and a cottage, sadly fallen into a state of disrepair. The sight made him gasp out loud. His hand rose, massaging his chest as if against a pain. Part of the roof was fallen in, the windows were gone, dark, gaping holes mocking him, from which the swallows swooped and dived. He stopped, unsure whether to venture further forward and wondering now why he'd come here, tormenting himself. Odd to think he'd once been happy here; content to let his life drift in perfect anonymity. What had driven him to leave, worse, to spend the rest of his life running away from an emotion he couldn't outdistance, no matter how hard he tried?

He should never have come back and yet he knew he could never have kept away. The knowledge tore from him so he swung smartly round, blundering the distance back up through the trees to the car, his frown of discontent changing in its chameleon like way into one of perplexity to discover that Lewis, confound the lad, had taken advantage of his absence and disappeared.

Hettie returned to the hall in a rush. She was thrilled about the evening before her and yet she was unsure now whether Bill, who'd gone off in such an odd mood, would participate in the adventure or not. So far apart had they grown of late, she'd believe him only when he turned up; it wouldn't even surprise her if he meant to tell her mother and spoil all their plans.

As she headed upstairs, General Hawker appeared from the State Room, hastily converted by Bronwyn into a meeting place for the war committee. He was carrying a bundle of papers under his arm.

'And how's your day been, m'dear?' he asked kindly.

Pushing thoughts of Bill to the back of her mind, Hettie grinned. 'Fine and dandy, General, thanks!'

'And shall we see you at dinner tonight?'

'I expect so, General. . . .'

Aware the news had pleased him, she stood watching momentarily as the elderly military man headed off in the direction of the antelibrary, a billiard room in olden days, today a small, dark room containing only table and chairs and a number of indifferent paintings, behind one of which was the safe where Loxley's valuables and documents were kept and where, for the duration of the convention, he was intent on lodging the committee's papers. Not for the first time, Hettie wondered what the committee members could possibly discuss of such a very great importance that it had to be locked away out of sight. Grandmamma said Nazi strength and power was growing at an alarming rate and everyone should pay attention to what was happening in Europe. She said the government was trying to fit the situation into the framework of British military and diplomatic policy, whatever she meant by it. Hettie struggled to understand the biggest part of what her grandmother told her but after what she'd seen for herself in Berlin, she accepted she must at least try. It was important. She was a duchess. She should know such things.

The thought had no sooner entered her head, vaguely unsettling and disturbing as it was, than she remembered the escapade planned for tonight. An adventure and when life had been so very boring of late! A smile crossed her face, catlike in its stealth and which, if only Katherine Loxley had been around to see it, would have worried her tremendously.

She was late. She'd yet to dress for dinner. Humming happily to herself, she headed quickly upstairs.

Hettie had the uneasy feeling there was trouble brewing between her mother and grandmother but given it was a situation to which she was unfortunately all too used, the evening meal passed off credibly well, made memorable to her only for her ill-concealed impatience that it should be quickly over. At last it was done, the company decamped to the sitting room for coffee and she was free. Rushing upstairs, she effected another fast change, this time into a serviceable skirt and jumper, before making her way boldly down the main staircase and, ignoring the hum of voices emanating from the sitting room, gliding swiftly across the hall to the front doors, desperately afraid, even now, that someone would see her and demand to know what she was doing, thereby putting paid to all her plans. Heart hammering against her ribcage, she opened the doors and escaped outside.

The moon was round and full, bathing the world in a silvery glow curiously enhancing to all she hoped lay ahead. Another chance to see Leon and hear any other nugget of information concerning the long ago connection between Loxley's inhabitants and the gypsies, at which Leon had so far only hinted. Calling cheerily to the soldier on duty at the bottom of the steps, she hurried away to be quickly swallowed up into the muffled depths of darkness, cutting across the lawns to the meadows by instinct and making her way down to the bridge, her heart leaping to find Bill already there, his face looming in the moonlight. He looked anxious. She did so hope he wasn't going to spoil things. His greeting was hardly encouraging.

'This is ridiculous, Het,' he began.

'It'll be fine, you'll see. . . .' she soothed.

At that moment, there came the pad of footsteps across the bridge and Lewis appeared, his eyes glowing like a cat's in the dark. 'What are we waiting for?' he asked softly.

Lewis, at least, appeared to be entering into the spirit of adventure. Hettie grinned into the darkness, moving swiftly past him to lead the way, even so with a grave sense of Bill scowlingly bringing up the rear, which she did her best to ignore. Silently, the little party made their way up the lane towards the edges of the Loxley estate and onto Freddie Hamilton's land, reaching the drystone wall circling their neighbour's meadow without mishap and close enough now to make out the dark shapes of the caravans, lit here and there by the flickering glow of the large, communal campfire Hettie had seen from her bedroom window. A horse whinnied and, at that moment, the sound of a guitar struck up, pushing out softly against the edges of darkness and drawing them in with its wild, elusive strains. Lewis vaulted the wall and without thought, Hettie followed him, not stopping to see if Bill came after her, yet happy when he did, down towards the caravans and the lively, dancing flames around which a number of caravan people sat, amongst whom, thankfully, they could make out Leon's distinctive form.

They might as well have announced their presence with a clarion call. Abruptly the music stopped.

'We have visitors,' the gypsy leader murmured, staring with his startling, deep-set eyes towards the gap between two caravans where the little party stood. Feeling faintly alarmed, Hettie emerged into the circle of light, only too wretchedly aware of the hostile glances cast in their direction from the other gypsies. The situation could have proved awkward but Leon only smiled benignly and shifted up to make room on the rug upon which he sat.

'Make yourself at home, Your Grace,' he said pleasantly. 'You and your friends are always welcome here.'

More relieved than she would have cared to admit, Hettie,

followed by the boys, headed swiftly towards him and shortly, the little group were seated happily around the campfire, drinking a strangely bitter brew served in tiny, bone china cups by a large, plump gypsy woman with a tangle of wild hair and a wide, smiling face. Once more the music struck up and a woman's voice began to sing in accompaniment, low and soulfully, words Hettie couldn't understand and yet still touched her so it was as if she did understand them, every single word. She was soothed, amongst friends, people who would do her no harm and might even do her good.

Time passed. The music stopped and stories were told, tales passed down from generation to generation of gypsy folk, tales of charms and changelings and gypsy curses and Saint Sarah the patron saint of the Roma people. 'Tell us a tale, Leon,' a husky voice called to general approbation.

The old man turned towards Hettie, his forthright gaze bearing into hers so oddly, though she was well aware of Lewis and Bill listening with an equal intensity, it appeared to her that what followed was for her ears alone. The old man began in a low, soft voice which only added credence to his story.

'Once, many years ago, in Saxon times, when England was a wild and lawless place. . . . Edmund, the Magnificent, King and mighty warrior, took to himself a wife, a fine lady by name of Elgiva, a young woman of such very great beauty that, in his delight at the coming union, the King gave orders that a fabulous, jewel-encrusted sword should be struck in her honour. A warlike gift from a warlike man. But Queen Elgiva had other and more consistent qualities than her beauty, much as it was. A care for the poor and homeless and above all, a desire for truth and justice. A truly gentle woman who determined that her new husband must know these things too.

'They were in love. Edmund wanted to please her. And so it came about, miraculously, under Elgiva's guidance, a change came over this troubled land. King Edmund eschewed his lust for war, instead embracing statesmanship whilst his fabulous sword, Aelric, meaning "All Powerful" and more normally a symbol of war, was transformed, wonderfully, to a symbol of peace and love. And so it was passed down to their sons, Edwig All-Fair and St Edgar the Peacemaker and again, down through the royal kings of England. . . .'

An owl hooted and Leon broke off, smiling gently, aware he'd held the attention of all in that circle of fire but, most of all, Hettie, Duchess of Loxley, who sat entranced, hands clasped around her knees, hardly daring to move, so closely had she been listening. Shivers ran the length of her spine. It was a wonderful tale and she so much wanted to hear more but to her frustration, the old man clapped his hands and rose to his feet, signalling the evening was at an end. Instantly, the camp broke up, the folk around drifting away, back to their caravans to light their lamps which glowed in the darkness like fireflies. An old woman with a bent back put out the flames of the campfire, muttering to herself the while.

'It's late, Your Grace. You should go home,' Leon said, turning towards Hettie.

Though the gypsy had spoken kindly, it was still a dismissal. He left them, heading swiftly back to his caravan, and there was little else for the party to do but to scramble to their feet and troop back the way they'd come, vaulting the wall to regain the lane and the rise of the hill, where they walked quietly down to the bridge, each sunk deep in their own thoughts as if the evening had cast a spell they were loathe to break, even Bill.

Hettie needed to be alone and turned down Bill's offer to walk her home. Her thoughts were spinning; her spirits embroiled in a strange, faraway land in which a king had struck a magical sword and all for the glory of the woman he loved more than life itself. Darkness swallowed her up, only faint strains of light remaining but enough to illuminate her return through the damp, clinging meadow to the gardens beyond. By the time she'd reached the hall and assured the guard at the steps she had a right to entry, her good humour was miraculously returned, refuelled by what, after all and on reflection, had proved to be a glorious adventure and given her so much food for thought. Musing on Leon's wonderful and romantic tale, she was more convinced than ever that he'd told her for a reason, though temporarily, she'd no idea what that reason could be.

Luck was still with her. Inside, a low hum of voices issuing from the sitting room told her, miraculously, the company still lingered and only Soames, emerging from the direction of the servants' hall with a tray bearing clean glasses, was around to note her return.

His brows rose. 'It's late, Your Grace,' he murmured, in a faintly disapproving tone.

'So it is,' she answered innocently, aware she'd fooled him not one iota. She grinned and the corner of the old man's lips lifted upwards. Friends of old and she knew her secret was safe and that wild horses, or even her grandmother at her fiercest, could never have dragged it from him.

She'd no wish to hang about. 'Goodnight,' she called softly, going quickly upstairs to her room, undressing in the dark and falling into bed where, as soon as her head touched the pillow, she fell into a deep and refreshing sleep.

She woke with a start to the sound of voices downstairs. Hettie's eyes opened, a fragment of dream involving a war-like Saxon king, his beautiful, gentle queen and a fabulous jewel-encrusted sword, clinging to her senses. A thin, pale light shone through the chink in the curtains, falling onto her face so she blinked sleepily, reluctantly allowing her mind to clear. It was early yet, too early for her grandmother to be abroad and yet it was her grandmother's voice that Hettie could make out amongst an unsettling clamour deep within the heart of Loxley. Something had happened and something serious by the sounds of it. Wide awake now, she jumped out of bed, scrambling hastily into her dressing gown to make her way downstairs, guided by the voices towards the west corridor and the ante-library, where she was alarmed to discover several soldiers in full uniform and any number of tousled figures milling around. She skidded to a halt. Something serious indeed had happened to bring her grandmother out in full public view in such a state of dishabille.

'Whatever's wrong?' she called.

Seeing her, the old lady came hurrying towards her, her response so shocking, Hettie gasped out loud. 'Someone's broken into the safe,' Katherine Loxley retorted grimly. 'Soames has gone to ring the police. All the war committee's papers have been stolen, I'm afraid.'

Chapter Seven

Under the portrait of Nell, charismatic First Duchess of Loxley, General Anthony Hawker stood talking to Chief Inspector Digby of Scotland Yard, the strain of the morning's events showing clearly on both men's faces. Two uniformed members of the Chief Inspector's team, trusted men both, stood discreetly by. The General was annoyed, so much was clear.

'You've no business here,' he said curtly. 'This is an army matter! Who called you in?'

'I did,' Katherine answered, before Digby had time and arriving downstairs in time to hear this last. Swiftly, she joined the two men. The theft of the war committee's documents had shocked everyone but when action had been needed, she'd been the one to take it; hence her call to Scotland Yard. Straight to the top had always been her motto. That the Inspector had dropped everything was evident by the speed of his arrival. She nodded a greeting. 'You've helped us once before, I recollect, Inspector,' she said.

'Chief Inspector, Your Grace,' Digby interrupted, rocking complacently back on his heels. A small, shabbily dressed man with a keen intelligence lurking in the depths of his narrow, close-set eyes. A man unafraid to tread on toes, Katherine recollected, wondering now if she'd done right to call him in. But someone had to find the thief and sooner rather than later!

'A gypsy woman once tried to burn Loxley down,' she ventured, shuddering at the memory, even now. 'And as we're unfortunate enough to have a gypsy encampment not more than a mile from these premises, if you want my opinion, my good man, it's pretty clear you'll find your culprit there.'

'Early days yet, Your Grace,' he proffered.

'It's an army matter in any case.' Genial as was his usual manner, Hawker's voice was filled with suppressed anger. A man not to be crossed, Katherine sensed, elevating him in her estimation.

'The PM's asked to be kept up to date,' Digby murmured, interrupting her musings and proving, thereby, much as she liked to think it, his arrival was not just down to her manoeuvrings. 'It's a serious business, I'm afraid. We've been asked to help in any way we can.'

Hawker took a moment to consider, quickly coming to a decision. 'Very well, man. We'll join forces. You'd best see the room where the papers were locked, though there are no visible signs of a break-in. . . .'

First despatching the policemen below stairs for refreshment, he led the way along the north corridor and into the painted gallery, to the stairs at the bottom which led to the antelibrary. The soldier on duty outside the door saluted smartly before standing back to allow the little party entrance into the small, square room, the dimness of which remained unalleviated by its plain walls and wainscot and whitewashed ceiling. A second door, secreted between two inlaid bookcases, along the adjacent wall, led into the library. A number of indifferent paintings apart, a green baize table and a battered leather armchair were all the room contained.

'There's hardly anything, as you can see,' Katherine commented, nodding towards the bookcases. 'George kept his collection of equine books here. The room was his bolt-hole. . . .' Trying not to think what George would have had to say about recent events, she crossed the room to the portrait, by a local artist of the time, of her husband's hunter, Thunder, a fine beast he'd used to ride bareback around the estate. Sighing, she lifted the painting down, revealing thereby a small, green safe in which was kept all Loxley's documentation and valuables. Propping the painting on the floor against the wall, she unlocked the safe and opened the door to disclose the papers it contained, together with a cask holding the few, if infinitely valuable, pieces of family jewellery. 'Nothing else was taken,' she murmured. 'Only the war committee's papers, I'm afraid. It's clear the thief knew exactly what he was after.'

'And who knows the combination?' Digby asked, sharply.

Katherine considered. 'The General here . . . Bronwyn and myself. No one else, I can assure you . . . Inspector. I change the combination regularly and especially for the duration of the convention.'

Refusing to rise to the bait, Digby smoothed a hand over his thinning hair. 'You're sure you've told no one else?'

'I have not! I assure you. . . .'

Brave man to bait Katherine Loxley and in her own lair, too. 'And both doors to this room are kept locked?' he continued, oblivious to Katherine's affronted glare and firing questions in such a rapid succession, it gave her no chance to think. She frowned, nodding towards the interior door. 'That door's inaccessible. A bookcase was moved in front of the other side to make more room in the library. It's been so for years.'

'And there's no possibility this bookcase could have been moved?' Digby asked.

Hawker shook his head. 'We've checked already. It hasn't.'

Katherine frowned. 'The outer door's more normally kept locked. The General has the key.'

'I keep it on me,' he chimed in, backing her up. 'There's no way anyone else could have got hold of it.'

'Where is it more normally kept?'

'In my dressing table drawer. . . .' Katherine answered.

'You're sure it's the only one?'

'Of course I'm sure!' she snapped, her gaze following the Chief Inspector's towards the window. 'And that's jammed and hasn't been used for years,' she said, finishing the account of a conundrum to which, already, she'd given many a troubled thought and to which so far she'd managed to come up with no viable solution. But someone had managed to break in and steal those precious papers and she could only pray this man would quickly discover who it was.

Crossing to the window to satisfy himself as to the truth of all she'd told him, Digby swung round to face the room again. His expression was fierce and inscrutable. 'Someone's been in here as shouldn't have been but rest assured, ma'am, I'll find out who!' he muttered but with such vehemence and determination, for the first time that morning, Katherine's spirits lifted.

Standing framed in the sunlight which filtered through the morning room window, Bronwyn was trying, if failing miserably, not to dwell on the thoughts of exactly what damage the theft of the war committee's papers, shocking as it was, would do to Loxley's reputation. Rather the family jewellery had been taken than documents of such national importance; it was bound to throw them all in a bad light. Even now, she couldn't believe what had happened, finding herself wishing desperately she could simply wave a magic wand and put the situation to rights.

'Roland, that this should have happened whilst you're here,' she fretted.

Roland de Loxley sat drinking yet another cup of coffee, all they'd done all morning. 'I can't say I enjoyed Hawker's grilling but I think I passed muster. . . .' he murmured, getting up to refill Bronwyn's cup. 'Should I go home, do you think? I don't want to be under anyone's feet.'

'I'd rather you stayed. . . .' Bronwyn replied, sipping her drink meditatively and speaking only the simple truth. At the same time, she couldn't help but see the way Roland's face lit up at her words. There was trouble enough without further complications, she considered, a little sadly.

At that moment, thankfully, voices were heard in the hall, Soames and another she recognized instantly. 'Reuben's here,' she added, quietly.

'Why don't I do some work in the library?' Roland suggested tactfully, springing up at once. He saw her hesitation. 'Please . . . I'd like to.'

A shadow crossed Bronwyn's face. It was easier to give in than to tell him the truth that, for some reason, Reuben unsettled her so she feared to be left alone with him. 'I'll see what he wants. . . .' she said, deciding quickly it was expedient to do so. They'd problems enough this morning and she hated to think Reuben might cause more. She put down her cup and followed Roland out. He headed swiftly upstairs as Reuben came hurrying towards her.

'The place's crawling with police! What's happened?' he demanded, roughly.

'Will that be all, Your Grace?' Soames called, hastening after him.

'Thank you, I'll see to things now, Soames. I'll tell you,' she said to Reuben, as she led the way back into the morning room. As succinctly as she could, over fresh coffee, she told him, feeling a sense of relief to get the whole wretched debacle out of her system. 'It feels as if the world's fallen in,' she confessed, once she'd finished.

'You mustn't distress yourself,' Reuben murmured, with such a surprising gentleness, instantly and oh, so wonderfully she was reminded of Harry. If only a miracle could happen and Harry was here with her now! Bronwyn was horrified to feel tears pricking the back of her eyes. Even worse, instinctively she knew Reuben was aware of them too so she remembered then how sensitive he'd always been to her feelings. More like Harry than he knew. Valiantly, she made an effort to pull herself together. 'Reuben, I'm sorry. . . . You can't possibly want to know all this.

Is there some way I can help you?'

He looked awkward. 'I hardly like to bother you now.'

'Please, if there's anything? Whatever it is!'

'I was wondering if you'd seen anything of Lewis, then. I'm afraid he's disappeared. I know he'd fixed up some kind of a meeting with Hettie last night.'

'Oh, but Hettie had dinner with us last night. . . .' Bronwyn stopped, aware then that she'd no idea what Hettie had done with herself after dinner and, worse, given that young lady's behaviour of late, her mother could well believe she'd gone out on some escapade or other and never said a word of it to anyone. Hettie, she was afraid to say and despite all attempts to the contrary, was getting out of control. Reuben's normally ruddy colour deepened.

'The lad didn't come back last night. I haven't seen him since.' He'd no need to spell out his thoughts on the matter and she was only too relieved to put him right.

'Hettie was tucked up in bed fast asleep,' she told him, thankfully. 'I checked before I turned in. She's lending Cook a hand this morning, keeping out of the way, I presume. Why don't we go and ask her?'

Reuben put out a hand, delaying her. 'And does she know about me?' he asked.

He meant did Hettie yet know about his relationship to the family? An uncomfortable question and typically Reuben, but the wrong one and at the wrong time and she saw he knew it too.

'Reuben, there's hardly been chance. . . .'

'But you do mean to tell her?' he persisted.

He couldn't help himself and, Bronwyn conceded, if she were in his shoes, she'd feel exactly the same way too. 'She has every right to know,' she agreed, quickly. 'But only when the time's right. . . .'

'What have I a right to know?' murmured a familiar voice, behind them.

Bronwyn spun round, feeling alarmed and ridiculously guilty to see Hettie, framed in the doorway. Her heart began to thump. How much had she heard, exactly?

Hettie's stint in the kitchens had done her good. She was feeling virtuously smug; she'd been of use and, at the same time, had managed to hear the gossip in the servants' hall, rife given all that had gone off. All in all, it was turning out to be a very exciting morning. At sight of the two adult faces confronting her, however, some of her good humour vanished.

'What have I a right to know?' she persisted.

'Nothing to worry yourself over, darling. . . .' her mother answered, quickly. Far too quickly to Hettie's mind and she was growing more convinced by the moment that something was up.

An awkward silence developed and it was the man she now knew as Reuben Fairfax, his face working strangely, who broke it. 'Nothing, she says! And what do you think it might be, young lady?' he snapped, his fierce gaze turning to Hettie.

'Why, I've no idea!' she told him, defiantly.

He rocked back on his heels, an odd, cruel smile playing across his lips. What he said next shocked her to the core. 'I'll tell you then, shall I? It's only that I belong to this family! I'm your grandfather's by-blow and your uncle, my dear, your dear father's half-brother and someone should have told you long before now.' He spoke roughly, imparting the information in a way that only made it all the more alarming. Hettie's head spun as, desperately, she tried to assimilate the news. Gathering her wits, she articulated the first thought to fly into her head.

'But what on earth does Grandmamma think?' she demanded, crossly.

'It was before their marriage,' her mother chimed in, darting a look towards their visitor that, upset as she was, Hettie could only think boded ill for his future.

Reuben's eyes blazed. He bore grudges, Hettie could see.

Young as she was, even she knew old hurts lay buried deep. 'Aye! An affair with a maid, a lass he thought not good enough!' he snapped.

'But I thought you were the gamekeeper here?' she protested.

'Your grandmother took Reuben in and had him brought up here, on the estate. . . .' her mother interjected.

'Neither fish nor fowl!' The subject of the old woman's largesse frowned, angrily

'Oh . . . gosh . . . . But that was good of Grandmamma, wasn't it?' Hettie said, not quite sure what they expected from her and really, rather shocked. She stared hard at Reuben, remembering now how he'd broken up the fight between Lewis and Bill and how fiercely he'd looked at her afterwards so she'd wondered then what she'd done to deserve it. And all the while, he'd known he was her uncle! A strange, wild man and she'd thought so from the very first moment she'd met him.

'Should I be pleased?' she asked, having no idea if she should.

He stared back. 'Some wouldn't,' he answered honestly.

'You do have a look of my father about you,' she murmured, fretfully. 'I . . . I miss him.'

'We all do, lass.'

The response came quickly and was unexpectedly reassuring. She swung back towards her mother, seeking more truth. 'Why didn't you tell me? Was that down to Grandmamma too?' she asked, hitting on the truth at once. Wouldn't that just be like her? Her dear grandmother thought Hettie wasn't old enough to know anything yet!

'She does find the situation . . . difficult,' her mother agreed.

Taking everyone by surprise, even herself, suddenly Hettie grinned.

'Uncle Reuben! Who would have believed it?'

That was Hettie, a gust of fresh air blowing through Loxley's deepest, darkest corridors. Her mother smiled, a rather painful smile, and Hettie even saw amusement lurking in Reuben's eyes. It disappeared far too quickly. 'Have you seen Lewis?' he demanded, abruptly.

'Not today,' she answered guardedly, the memory of last night's escapade rushing back into her head. If anything could have put flight to the startling news she'd just learned, this was it. No one knew about the visit to the gypsies and, as far as she was concerned, that was exactly how it should remain.

'But you did see him last night?' Reuben persisted.

How much did he know? This new addition to the family wasn't the kind of man with whom you tangled, Hettie sensed. Her immediate response, to deny all knowledge, died an instant death. If the truth couldn't be avoided, it was best to confess, she summed up quickly, dreading already what her mother would say. 'I did sort of see him after dinner last night,' she began, tentatively.

'You went out?' her mother asked, sharply. 'Hettie, what have you been up to now?'

There was no hope for it. She told them. She'd gone with Bill and Lewis, to see the gypsies. They'd heard some fabulous tales, but most fabulous of all, the story Leon, the gypsy leader, had related concerning a Saxon King Edmund and his Queen, Elgiva and a fantastic sword named Aelric, forged in honour of the marriage. It had been a magical evening and it would stay with her the rest of her life. And then. . . . Well, that was it, really. She'd parted company with the boys at the bridge and they'd all gone their separate ways although she wasn't sure where Lewis had gone after that, exactly. . . . Her mother was clearly appalled. Abruptly, Hettie's unexpected euphoria at the recounting of events disappeared.

'Hettie, how could you? Anything could have happened. . . . Why don't you think?'

'But I do think, Mother!' she interjected, indignantly. 'I think more than anyone ever gives me credit for. . . .'

'Is this other lad Bill, Lizzie's lad – her first-born?' Reuben broke in, fiercely.

'His dad, Sam Tennant, owns the garage in the village,' Hettie explained, eagerly.

'Sam Tennant's still here and married to Lizzie?' He sounded surprised.

'He adopted Bill as his own. Reuben, I hardly see why you're so worried,' her mother interjected, to Hettie's relief, her attention, if only momentarily, thankfully deflected.

Uncle Reuben, as Hettie had already decided she must now think of him, sighed heavily. 'Lewis has history,' he said, managing to shock her all over again. 'He's been in trouble with the police before, I'm afraid. . . .'

Ursula hunkered down on a level with Maisie May and held up the little dress she'd just extracted from the box beside her, clothes collected over the last few days from friends and neighbours and brought with her here to Leon's comfortable and comforting little caravan. She'd worked hard, chivvying everyone she knew with children, to spare as many unwanted clothes as possible. So much wasted time, Freddie had complained, which would have been better spent on the farm.

Ursula pushed all thoughts of Freddie's vexatious temper from her mind. She didn't want to think about Freddie right now.

'Pwetty,' the little girl lisped, stroking the material, shyly.

'It is, darling, isn't it,' she agreed, brushing the little girl's cheek with her hand. She stood up, replacing the dress in the box, her ready smile fading when she saw Leon's expression. The gypsy leader looked put out and Ursula had a strong suspicion why that was. 'You don't mind, do you, Leon?' she asked.

'And would it matter if I did?' he asked, answering her question with another.

'It would be so much better if you did agree!' she returned quickly, wondering now if she'd affronted him in some way. But it was clear the old man didn't want the gypsy children to go to school. The atmosphere in the caravan bristled with his offended dignity and her own good intentions. This was going to be more difficult than she'd so blithely assumed and she should have realized. She smiled encouragement. 'It's only a few bits and bobs, clothes people no longer need, their children have grown out of. . . . And, oh, Leon, you are alright about the children going to school, aren't you?' she burst out, passionately.

'Maisie May's not old enough for school yet,' he pointed out.

'But the other children – it's such a wonderful opportunity – think of all they'll learn!'

Folding his arms, Leon stared down at her impassively so she realized anew what a strong-minded man he was, a man who, once he'd made up his mind, wouldn't be budged. She took a deep and steadying breath. 'It's only for three afternoons a week,' she persisted. 'They'll soon get into the routine.'

'We're never in a place long enough for routine, routine is anathema to us,' came the predictable answer.

'But you can't be leaving yet!'

'It wasn't so long ago you couldn't wait for us to leave.'

Ursula blushed. It was true and she couldn't deny it. Happily, she saw Leon's eyes were twinkling and at once she was filled with relief. He was teasing her. Everything was going to be alright after all!

'A trial period only, mind,' he warned, if he had but known it, echoing Cynthia Bradwell, the village school head teacher.

'That's all I ask.' She smiled.

In the distance, a police bell clanged. 'Something's going off at the hall?' the old man conjectured.

She nodded. Freddie had seen Tom Compton earlier that morning, who'd told him the news. 'They've had some kind of a break-in. You do know the war committee was meeting there this week? They've had some papers stolen, apparently, important documents and it's created no end of a stink,' she said, passing on the news and making a mental note to call round at the hall later to see if there was anything she could do to help. Nowhere seemed safe any more, even fortress Loxley! Ursula shivered, forcing her mind back to the business in hand.

At that moment, the kettle began to boil on the stove and, to her horror and without warning, Maisie May set off in determined fashion towards it. Ursula's reactions were instinctive. With a yelp of warning she dashed towards her, scooping her hastily up into her arms but only just in time. Another second. . . . Horribly aware of the tragedy with which they might have been dealing, unable to bear the thought, she clasped the little girl to her fiercely.

The colour draining from his face, Leon sank down into a chair. 'That child will be the death of me,' he muttered, at that moment, looking every one of his years, more numerous than Ursula had guessed, she thought now, shocked by it. An old man who, much as he so obviously loved Maisie May, must surely, at times, find the care of her a trial?

'Why don't I take Maisie back to the farm with me?' she proffered. She glanced down at the child, emotion shadowing her face. 'You'd like to see the baby piglets, darling, wouldn't you?'

Even Leon hadn't the heart to spoil the little girl's obvious pleasure at the idea and, in as short a time as it took to make their way from the gypsy encampment back to Merry Weather Farm, Ursula was holding her up over the side of the pen to see Sadie, the Gloucester Old Spot, and her brood of ten fine piglets, lying supine, tails curled in a milky delight. Maisie May laughed out loud to see them, a sound that did Ursula so much good to hear.

Fresh from the winter planting at which he'd been working all morning and already fed-up to the back teeth with it, Freddie Hamilton trooped wearily round the side of the barn. Up at the crack of dawn, hardly time to force down a bit of breakfast before he was out in the fields; repetitive, back-breaking work. . . . At once, he stopped, brought up short by sight of Ursula with a little girl in her arms, holding the child up so she could see into the pigsty and Sadie's new litter of pigs. The pair were so engrossed, they hadn't even heard him. Something inside the farmer tightened in pain at the sight, more so when he realized how happy Ursula looked – and how long it was since he'd seen her look that way. He'd no need to think why either for, if ever a woman was cut out for motherhood, it was his Ursula. How he railed at the fate that had denied her children! And him too, he reminded himself, for once acknowledging feelings he more normally pushed down deep inside. It hurt like hell to think there'd never be a son to whom he could pass on the farm.

Wondering whose child it was, he walked towards them. 'There you are, Ursula,' he murmured softly, miserably aware of her instinctive flinch at his words. She turned towards him so he saw now the dark circles shadowing her eyes. 'I've just finished Top Field,' he said, struggling for something to say. 'Pru's making a start on Lower Brook. . . .'

'Hah! That's good of her. . . .'

She sounded so bitter it shocked him. Was there something more than her words, seeming to him laden with a meaning of which he'd no idea? But this was what it had been like between them of late, and how he hated it! Listlessly, she put the little girl down and would have led her away if only he hadn't planted himself firmly in their path, blocking their way. 'Aren't you going to introduce us?' he asked, pleasantly he hoped.

'This is Maisie May, Leon's grandchild. . . . Leon, the gypsy leader,' she answered, confirming his suspicions and already sounding defensive. As if she imagined he was going to argue – and in front of the child, too. Freddie knew he ought to be cross; that many men would assume the child had been brought here deliberately to flout him. To both the adults' surprise, perhaps most of all to his own, he hunkered down in front of her, smiling gently.

'I bet you'd like some milk and a biscuit?' he murmured.

The little girl nodded uncertainly but nevertheless, when he stood up, allowed him to take her free hand. Across the top of her head, he flashed Ursula a warm smile, catching her surprise and taking mild satisfaction in it. It was clear their marriage was undergoing some kind of a transformation, raising all kinds of difficulties of which they'd never dreamed, but wasn't it more important how they went on from here? They had to make a start somewhere. Resolutely determined, a small flame of hope burning inside him which refused to be extinguished no matter what trials beset them, he ushered the little party back towards the house.

As she'd hoped and intended, Bronwyn managed to intercept Katherine on her return downstairs from showing Digby and Hawker the safe in the anteroom. Bronwyn had just got back from seeing Reuben to his car and after what he'd just so provokingly and prematurely revealed to Hettie about his relationship to this house, it would never do to allow Hettie to get to Katherine first. Hettie, meanwhile, she'd despatched, ears burning, back below stairs, with orders to give Cook a hand with dishing up the lunch. She'd gone so meekly her mother was already suspicious about her plans.

'Could I have a word?' she asked and, not waiting for answer, swung on her heel to lead the way through into the morning room.

'Reuben's been again, I see?' Katherine observed, following her in and not troubling to hide her annoyance. 'We saw him from the anteroom window. Bronwyn, you mustn't encourage him. Digby remembered him at once and was asking some very pertinent questions. It wouldn't surprise me if he didn't think Reuben's got something to do with this wretched business. You know his thoughts last time he was here concerning Reuben starting that wretched fire that nearly burnt the place down round our ears!'

'And he was proved wrong!' Bronwyn snapped irritably if

perhaps forgivably. 'What have you been saying this time to put him under such a cloud?'

'Nothing other than he left here years ago and he's since made another life for himself,' the older woman returned blithely. 'But it's bound to look suspicious, don't you think? All those papers going missing and Reuben just happening to turn up at the same time?'

'Katherine, for heaven's sake!'

'I'm only saying, my dear.'

'Hettie knows!' Bronwyn interrupted, hastily and, irrespective of the provocative nature of Katherine's outburst, determined to tell her. 'Everything,' she added meaningfully, making up her mind to play down Reuben's role in the matter. There was trouble enough as it was. 'Reuben and I were talking about it, unfortunately, and she caught the tail end of our conversation. I'm sorry but it left me with no other option than to tell her.'

It was a slightly distorted view of what had happened but the best she could come up with. Only her hand, tightening around the brass handle of her walking stick, gave indication of Katherine's displeasure. 'And what did the child say?' she demanded, querulously.

Bronwyn understood exactly why this proud, indomitable woman considered her husband's illegitimate child by a servant girl something she would infinitely rather keep to herself. Her expression softened. 'You know Hettie, Katherine. She took it in her stride. I told you there was no need to worry. She's young! Young people look on these things so differently.'

At once, astonishingly, Katherine deflated. Her defences were down and she was vulnerable, showing a side to her nature more normally no one was allowed to see, least of all Bronwyn. 'I hate it the child's grandfather should be shown in such a bad light,' she muttered, sadly.

Sorry as she felt for her, Bronwyn persisted. 'I do understand,' she replied, as gently as she could, 'but Reuben is still Hettie's uncle and she has a perfect right to know it; particularly now she's lost her father. Oh, Katherine, we can't deny his existence!' she burst out, passionately.

There followed an uncomfortable pause. Had she said too much – outlined a situation that Katherine, even after all these years, still felt too raw to accept? The response, when it came, brought with it a rush of relief.

'Aye, well, no doubt you're right,' the older woman muttered, albeit ungraciously.

As a concession, it failed to last. Her mother-in-law's more usually forthright gaze hardened.

'Whatever the rights and wrongs of it, it's only certain, there's nothing I can do about it now. . . .'

After a lunch for which no one appeared to have any appetite, Hettie was relieved to get away to take the dogs for their afternoon walk, away from the soldiers and the policemen and Chief Inspector Digby, whom she'd disliked on first sight, heading for Bill's instinctively, where, to her annoyance, she was cornered by Lizzie, understandably curious over the sight of both police and army crawling over the grounds and determined to prize as much from Hettie as she could.

Bill finally came to her rescue, suggesting they continue her walk together.

Dogs in tow and once out of the village, they followed the path into the wood, taking refuge in the sanctuary offered by its massive trees and rustling, reassuring presence. 'Have you seen Reuben?' she demanded, burning to tell him what she'd so startlingly just learned concerning the artist's parentage and then deciding, at the last moment, not to, after all. Once she'd have told Bill without thinking and the fact she couldn't now was a painful reminder of how far apart they'd grown of late.

'He called round before lunch, wanting to know what had happened to Lewis,' he answered.

'And did you know?' she asked. Aware of how much the two boys disliked each other, the information surprised her.

'He slept on our sofa last night. He'd missed the last bus. I could hardly leave him out in the road.'

'And then what?' she asked curiously.

Bill shrugged. 'And then he went. Before anyone else was up and about, so I've no idea where he's gone and so I told Reuben. I say, Het, that's awful what's happened at the hall. Are you all alright?'

'Of course we're alright! It's been rather exciting,' she replied, then wondering if, after all, it actually was. It was unnerving to think of someone creeping about the place whilst they'd been asleep. They could have been murdered in their beds, the place set on fire. . . . Now she thought about it, it was rather scary though she'd never have admitted it, not even to Bill. 'There are no signs of a break-in,' she told him, the one thing puzzling her more than anything else. Another and even more perplexing thought catapulted into her head. She frowned. 'When you found me with Lewis down at the Old Hall, yesterday, I was looking for the catch to the secret passage,' she murmured, remembering too, a little shamefaced, how she'd been trying to impress Lewis.

'So?' Bill could be remarkably obtuse at times.

It was too awful to say and yet she did say it because, no matter how far apart they'd grown, this was still Bill. 'I couldn't find it but. . . . Oh, Bill! What if Lewis came back alone and discovered it for himself? What if he used it to break into Loxley to steal those papers?'

'But why on earth would he?' Bill looked incredulous.

Her brows furrowed. 'I don't know. . . . He wants to sell them on and make some money? He's a spy in league with the Nazis?' It sounded ridiculous, even to her ears. The truth was, Hettie knew nothing about Lewis other than he was an unpredictable and sometimes angry young man. She could believe anything of him, she realized. 'He's been in trouble with the police before,' she said.

To her annoyance, Bill was still unimpressed. 'That doesn't mean to say he's responsible for this, Het. So he managed to secrete himself through a locked door, locate the safe and then open it? How would he know the combination? And anyhow, how do you know he's been in trouble with the police?'

If there was anything Hettie hated, it was to be disbelieved and especially when, for once, like now, she was telling the truth. 'Uncle Reuben said so . . . and Uncle Reuben knows the layout of the house, come to that,' she retorted, with more temper than tact, meanwhile acknowledging Bill's start of surprise at the term of endearment. What news! What a hoot! And how odd that after all, she'd blurted it out when she'd only just decided against telling him. Perhaps, deep down, she'd wanted to tell him and why shouldn't she when, despite their present differences, they'd known each other all their lives.

So she told him what she now knew to be true, crazy as it seemed, even to her ears. Alex Windrow, alias Reuben Fairfax, was her father's half-brother, result of a liaison between her grandfather and a maid before her grandparents had married. Reuben had been brought up here on the estate to become the gamekeeper until he'd taken it into his head to run away and become a painter instead. 'It's Grandmamma I feel sorry for,' she finished, remembering the old lady's pained face over the lunch table, so though Hettie had longed to talk to her about what she now knew, she couldn't somehow, for fear of trampling over her feelings. For once, the old lady had looked her age and vulnerable in a way to which Hettie simply wasn't used.

Whatever response she'd expected from Bill, it wasn't the one she got.

'Hah! I wouldn't worry about your grandmother. She's as tough as old boots, that one!' he snapped.

They'd reached a clearing in the wood in which stood a ramshackle, tumbledown dwelling, mildewed with rain and the years. It used to be the gamekeeper's cottage: Uncle Reuben's old house she realized. She stopped, turning quickly towards him.

'What's Grandmamma ever done to you?' she demanded, crossly.

'You'd be surprised!' he returned. Two high spots of colour stained his cheeks.

'Would I indeed! Why, exactly?'

Nothing was so certain than something was bothering him. A dull suspicion, an intuition she'd suppressed for ages, rose suddenly, alarmingly, to the surface. She was remembering now all Bill's hurtful behaviour of late, since before she'd gone on her trip round Europe, and how she'd never really been able to understand it. 'Did Grandmother warn you off me in some way?' she demanded, an outlandish idea, she knew, and yet one, as soon as she'd given it air, she knew to be true. This was terrible, worse than she'd thought. She could make a good stab at why her irascible relative might have done such a terrible thing, too – to do with the old lady's outdated ideas about their respective positions in the world. Hettie, the Duchess, Bill, the mechanic's son. . . . As far as Katherine Loxley was concerned, what possible hope could there be for a future together? Best nip it in the bud! Hettie could almost hear her now.

Bill plunged his hands in his pockets, stabbing angrily at a loose stone on the path with the toe of his shoe, so obviously confirming all she'd just said, Hettie's temper, always simmering, burst to the surface. Wait until she saw Grandmamma again! How dare she! Why, she'd a jolly good mind to go back to the hall this minute and give her a piece of her mind. . . .

She couldn't bear to think how she and Bill had been kept apart purely because someone else, even her grandmother who she loved more than anyone, had decided it should be so.

'Why didn't you tell me?' she implored, for some reason, angry with Bill now too. But he should have told her! If he'd told her, they surely could have worked something out!

Before he had a chance to answer, out of the corner of her eye, in the cottage beyond, Hettie caught sight of a movement in one of its gaping windows. A shadow moving back so quickly, at first she wondered if she'd imagined it – and yet she knew she hadn't. She gripped Bill's arm, her fingers digging in so deeply he winced.

'Someone's watching us from the cottage,' she whispered, hoarsely.

Someone silent and stealthy, keeping back and out of sight, listening to things they had no right to hear.

Chapter Eight

'Come out, whoever you are!' Hettie demanded, crossly.
A magpie flew shrieking from the treetops, disturbed from its lofty perch and fading quickly into the distance. Horribly, the silence grew. And then, to Hettie's relief, framed in the doorway of the ruins of the gamekeeper's cottage, she saw Lewis.

'Whatever are you doing here?' she scolded as he came slouching towards them. As he drew nearer, she was aware of a surprising fear lurking in his eyes so she wondered then what could have put it there. Lewis had never seemed to her the kind of boy to be frightened of anything – or anyone. 'Reuben's after you,' she warned, remembering now the fractious relationship between the pair in Berlin. Had Reuben done something to upset him? 'Why didn't you go back to your digs after we'd been to see the gypsies?' she asked. 'You've caused all sorts of trouble!'

'Hah! Why should I care? Alex . . . Reuben doesn't own me!' he snapped. His troubled gaze settled on Bill. 'What's he doing here?' he demanded, rudely.

'I presume you've heard about the burglary?' Bill returned, showing an unaccountable hostility towards someone who, after ... '... know very well.

'Yeah . . . I've heard. Leon told me. . . .'

'Bit odd, isn't it?' Bill persisted. 'You arrive and things start going missing and then . . . hey . . . we find you hiding away down here!'

'You think I'm the thief?' Lewis's voice rose and, incredibly, it appeared the two boys were shaping up for yet another fight. Hettie stepped between them.

'You've found the passageway into the hall, haven't you?' she demanded of Lewis. She frowned up at him, her every intuition telling her this was so. He was hiding from something or someone and it wasn't only Reuben. Had he any idea Reuben was really her uncle? It was hard to tell what he knew and what he didn't. 'You did find the secret passageway, didn't you?' she persisted, stubbornly.

To his credit, he never tried to deny it. 'I never got to use it,' he prevaricated before adding, alarmingly. 'Oh, Hettie, I'm in such a mess!'

'You'd better tell me what,' she said, at once.

Thankfully, his truculence had disappeared and once again, despite his faults, he was the boy she'd grown to like. 'I wanted to see you, if you must know,' he admitted, sheepishly. 'Only after I left Bill's, it was too early for visiting, of course. . . .'

'Yeah, well done for hanging around to thank my mother,' Bill cut in, sarcastically. 'She didn't have to put you up.'

'You tried sleeping on your sofa?'

'Better than sleeping rough! You could have said thank you, that's all I'm saying. . . .'

'Bill, let him talk!' Hettie laid a reassuring hand on Lewis's arm. 'Carry on,' she coaxed.

Throwing Bill a mutinous look, he ploughed on doggedly. 'I was waiting until it was decent time enough to call on you but then I saw the police crawling all over the place. It spooked me, I can tell you and, given I'd rather not have bumped into them. . . .'

'You came down here?' she prompted.

A wary look crossed his face. 'Not exactly. . . . Not at first. . . . Like I said, I wanted to see you and I happened to think of a way I might possibly get into Loxley unseen. . . .'

And how was that, exactly, she wondered, not having to think too hard. Hettie's gaze widened. 'You thought you'd use the secret passageway?' she exclaimed, seeing by his face that was it exactly. She whistled softly between her teeth. That had been one crazy idea. She was impressed.

'I was looking for the entrance, down by the ruins and then, suddenly, this door opens up in front of me and out pops a little chap I'd never seen before, like he was a ghost or something. Balding, eyes too close together. He frightened me half to death.'

'Chief Inspector Digby,' Hettie breathed, sure of it. It sounded too much like their Chief Inspector to be anyone else. Her grandmother must have told him about the existence of the secret passageway and invited him to explore. For Lewis to have bumped into him at that precise moment was just rotten bad luck. Bad luck seemed to follow Lewis round, she mused, wondering why that was.

'He said he was a copper. He wanted to know what I was up to.'

'So what did you tell him?' she asked, curious to know.

'I didn't, I ran off.'

'Idiot,' Bill interjected.

Hettie couldn't argue. 'But if he doesn't know who you are?' she coaxed.

Lewis's eyes glittered. 'You think he hasn't made it his business to find out? How suspicious do you think it looks? Stuff going missing, me with history – which I'm sure you've heard about already – and apparently with knowledge of how to get into the hall unseen. I'm not stupid. I thought I'd lay low awhile and down here seemed as good a place as any. It's a mess, Het.'

'So it is,' Bill agreed, sounding so smug even Hettie threw him a furious look.

Lewis was in trouble, so much was clear but the question was what was to be done about it?

'You have to go back,' she said, frowning. 'It'll look worse than ever if you don't. . . .'

Between them, they argued him onto a bus which passed by

the inn in which he was staying, though perhaps even Lewis, stubborn as he was, realized he couldn't lurk about in that pile of old stones forever. 'I hope he ends up where he's supposed to,' Hettie muttered as it disappeared round the corner in a cloud of exhaust fumes.

'We can't do any more, Het,' Bill complained. His gaze narrowed. 'Can we talk?' he asked.

Having a pretty good idea what it might be about, Hettie pulled a face. He wanted to talk to her about how her grandmother had tried to split them up and, worse, what they were going to do about it: the last thing she needed right now – at least, not until she'd talked to her grandmother first and given her a chance to explain what she thought she'd been playing at. Hettie had always been fair, though even she failed to see how her elderly relative could extract herself from this one.

'They'll be wondering what's happened to me. I'd better get back,' she muttered, already edging away.

'Soon then,' he said, looking put out.

'Soon,' she agreed smilingly. Before he could delay her further, she set off at a brisk pace, dogs in tow, back towards the hall.

The earlier, frenetic activity of the day was gone, replaced by a strange and unexpected stillness, shrouding Loxley as if it were a tangible entity, as if the very stone of which it was built was offended by its violation, so that it had settled itself, waiting broodingly, for whatever would be – a game of chess to which Hettie hadn't, as yet, worked out the next move. Once inside, she headed for her grandmother's sitting room, surprised to see the Reverend Lawrence Payne emerging from it and remembering then, belatedly, it was Friday, the day the elderly cleric took tea with her grandmother to discuss the week's events. It occurred to Hettie that she was glad the larger part of the war committee had packed their bags and gone so that only General Hawker and a handful of soldiers remained.

'A bad business this, Hettie,' Lawrence Payne said, waiting for her and smiling down on her kindly. 'But you're not to worry. I'm sure the police will catch whoever's responsible.' He nodded his bird-like head and would have hurried on but then delayed. 'Your mother told me you were enquiring about a King Edmund, some story that the gypsies told you?' he asked.

So much had happened since Leon had first told Hettie about King Edmund and Queen Elgiva and the fabulous sword, known as Aelric; it took Hettie a moment to recollect. She nodded uncertainly. The vicar's kindly old face filled with enthusiasm.

'I wanted to remind you about our magnificent stained glass in the west window. Perhaps its existence first sparked your interest?' Hettie might have agreed if only she'd the slightest idea what he was talking about. And then, miraculously, she remembered the interminable walks to church of her childhood, every Sunday morning, accompanied by Dizzy and passing under that very window. In her, as then, childish way, preoccupied as she would have been with whatever her father might have planned for afterwards – Hettie's particular Sunday treat to which she used to look forward all week – she'd been captivated by the vibrant colouring of the glass and the figures depicted within it. It was a wonder for poor Dizzy had despaired over her lack of attention to detail. She'd never paid attention to anything Dizzy had pointed out, Hettie realized now, feeling faintly ashamed.

Her face cleared. 'You're talking about the stained-glass window which depicts the Kings of England!' She beamed happily.

'That's the one!' the vicar agreed. 'But you'll know a medieval chapel once stood on the very spot where our dear church stands now? The Kings depicted, for the most part, are Saxon Kings and for that very reason, I suspect.'

'And is King Edmund amongst them?' she demanded, eagerly.

'Next to Edward "The Martyr" and over Ethelred "The Unready!"' he said, chuckling at her ignorance. Despite the wild ways for which she was unfortunately renowned, Loxley's vicar had always been fond of Hettie. 'You're very young, Hettie, and as Loxley's present incumbent, there's so much you have to learn. You must visit the church soon and I shall tell you all!' So saying, he put on his hat and was gone; on to his next call of duty, for everyone knew the Reverend Payne for a man who took his duties seriously. Unlike Hettie, who didn't, she fretted, making a mental note to try harder in the future. The vicar's intervention had deflected her and she remembered now, with a little rush of annoyance, what had brought her hurrying back to the hall in the first place.

Her grandmother stood by the window, framed in the sunlight which fell directly onto her face, highlighting every line and wrinkle and so much showing her age, it brought Hettie up with a start. Hettie had never much considered her grandmother's age before, she realized, with an odd stab of pain and considering it now. At once, the bigger part of her anger disappeared. Whatever this old lady had done, wrongheaded and interfering as it was, Hettie had no need to remind herself, it was because she loved her dearly, just as Hettie loved her back in return. She frowned, wondering how best to begin what was, after all, bound to be an awkward conversation. There was no way, she decided quickly, other than to come right out with it. But not angrily, she realized. When anger stirred, nothing was ever resolved.

Belatedly aware of her presence, Katherine started, turning towards her.

'Hettie! I was wondering where you'd got to.'

'I've been to see Bill,' she replied, carefully.

'Hah! Have you!'

Indignation lent wings to the young girl's tongue. 'Grand-mamma, I know you went to see him before I went on the Europe trip. You made him feel he wasn't good enough so he pretended he was fed up with me and didn't want to see me any more.'

'He told you, did he?' Katherine Loxley demanded, her tone suggesting that by it, somehow, Bill had managed to fall even further in her estimation. It clearly wasn't fair. Forgetting her resolution, Hettie's temper flared.

'Bill didn't tell me, I worked it out for myself!' she answered, hotly. 'I think I always knew, deep down, you must have said something – or how else explain his behaviour of late!'

'He's not good enough for you, child,' came the calm response.

Hettie gasped. 'But I'm not a child, Grandmamma, I'm seventeen! You simply can't tell me who I can and can't see!' she retorted, indignantly. 'Oh, can't you see! You have to let me live my own life. . . .'

Her voice trailed to a halt, all too aware now of the full weight of her grandmother's gaze upon her, so resolute and unbending; so sure that by sheer force of will, she could beat her down to her way of thinking. But she had seen sense, that was the point. She was thinking of Reuben, the man she now knew as her uncle and how she'd so wanted to talk to her grandmother about him, only she'd been put off, scared of hurting the old woman's feelings and making a difficult situation even worse. Experiencing one of the sudden and blinding flashes of insight to which she was increasingly prone, Hettie realized her grandmother didn't like being told things any more than she did and that this was the biggest part of the problem between them. They were too much alike, the only difference being, given their disparity in ages, experience had taught her grandmother to suppress her emotions, a genie in a bottle she didn't dare to let out for fear of what she might find. Odd to think of her grandmother's actions fuelled by fear, Hettie mused, a thought which filled her with determination. Hard as it was, harder than even she had anticipated, they should get this out into the open! She took a deep and steadying breath.

'Grandmamma, I wanted to say, what happened with Uncle Reuben, all those years ago must have been really hard for you.

It was good of you to take him in like you did. You didn't have to. . . .' Amazed by her own courage, she laid a tentative hand on the arm of the woman standing so resolutely before her, surprised to find it was trembling. Had she said too much? Offended her irreparably? She swallowed hard, waiting for the heavens to fall.

Katherine Loxley's gaze roamed fiercely over the dearly loved face. And then, oddly, as if she was still alone in this room, her thoughts drifted, the years falling like leaves to reveal the young woman she'd always been, deep inside. A young woman, much like this one, she thought, wryly. One prepared to forgive any transgressions if only to keep the man she loved!

'He was a rogue, your grandfather, my dear,' she murmured. 'Larger than life and determined to live it to the full. I loved him, don't you see? I did it for him. I would have done anything for him.' Her voice was querulous, an old lady's voice, shocking to her now. She smiled, ruefully. Her gaze softened, saying then a thing which made everything so clear, it caused Hettie to rush straight into her arms and hug her tight. 'Oh, don't you see, my dear?' she said, quietly. 'I want, one day, that you should know a love like that too. . . .'

The after-lunch bell clanged, summoning the children who, moments before, had been tearing joyfully around the playground. Obediently, they formed into a thin crocodile and filed back into school. In some trepidation, Ursula ushered the little group of gypsy children into Cynthia Bardwell's more-than-capable hands.

'They'll be fine, don't worry.' Cynthia smiled. A strong-minded, efficient woman and Ursula had every confidence that she would do her very best for the gypsy children. Taking tight hold of Maisie May's hand, she stood with the other Romani mothers until the last child had disappeared inside the building. The door swung to. They were gone.

She looked thoughtfully down at Maisie, it occurring to her then how long it might be before this little girl had chance to go to school or, indeed, if she ever would. Life wasn't fair and Ursula knew that as well as any. Deep in thought, she walked back to the camp with the other women; surprisingly touched that they should chatter away to her so pleasantly about everyday things around the camp that she soon felt as if she belonged.

Leon was sitting at his little table in the caravan, whittling pegs. Maisie May ran straight to him, climbing up onto his lap to wrap her arms around his neck.

'Are you alright? You do look a little tired, Leon, if you don't mind me saying,' Ursula observed.

'The Devil makes work for idle hands. I'm fine, as you see.' The gypsy leader smiled ruefully, yet willingly abandoning his work to see to the child and settle her more comfortably on his knee. Ursula was dismissed; there was nothing else to do but return to the farm, where she determined to make a start on the mess that was her kitchen and which, in her eagerness to help take the children to school, she'd left behind her. As she was washing the pots, through the window over the sink she saw Freddie, talking to Pru. Things had been better between her and Freddie of late. They were both making an effort and yet, oddly, something about the way he stood, surely far closer to Pru than necessary, began to undo some of the good they'd achieved so far. Ursula dunked a cup under the soap suds, lifting it so suddenly it cracked against the tap. She stood, staring down stupidly at the jagged red line, oozing blood, on the ball of her thumb.

At that moment, Freddie came into the kitchen. 'What have you done now?' he demanded, crossly, moving swiftly towards her. Ursula frowned, put out when he insisted on fetching the first-aid tin from the sideboard and tending to the wound himself and yet, perversely, despite her ill mood, enjoying the attention. They'd used to be so good together, she remembered wanly, before life with all its setbacks had got in the way.

'Why aren't you more careful?' he scolded, fastening the bandage and neatly tying the ends.

'I was watching you talking to Pru, if you must know. I can't help thinking how good she is around the farm!' she blurted out, instantly wishing the words unsaid. She was jealous and it was unworthy of her but her resentment towards dear, amiable Pru had been growing of late.

'Pru loves farming,' Freddie agreed, looking surprised.

'More than me, certainly,' she admitted, quietly. Some of her temper deflated.

She'd only succeeded in deepening his confusion.

'I've never, ever compared you with Pru, darling. . . .'

He was kidding himself and it was time he faced reality.

'You mean to say, you've never given a single thought to what your life might have been like married to someone like Pru?' she demanded, instantly aware that her words had shocked him.

'But Ursula, I wouldn't ever want to be with anyone but you!' he protested, at once.

The words, spoken so sincerely, should have been balm to her soul and yet somehow, even they weren't enough. What was wrong with her? Why couldn't she accept what he said? If she kept pushing him away like this, one day he wouldn't come back. She took a deep breath, making a conscious effort to be fair and to try and see things from Freddie's point of view. Poor Freddie, immersed in the farm and landed with a wife who was anything but a farmer's wife. Hence her absorption in the gypsy children, she realized now.

'Freddie, I'm sorry,' she said.

'For being you? Don't be.' He smiled and immediately some of the tension in the room lifted. His relief was palpable. He changed the subject onto safer ground. 'Did the children get off okay? I thought you might have brought Maisie May home with you.'

Ursula busied herself returning plasters and creams to the

medicine tin, finally shutting the lid. 'I'm picking her up from Leon's later. I'm longing to get back to ask Cynthia how everyone's getting on. Freddie, I know I haven't said as much but. . . . It was good of you not to have involved the police again over the gypsies.'

At her words, a mixture of weary resignation flickered across her husband's face. A sore, moreover costly admission, even Ursula had to admit. 'How could I? Think how it would scare little Maisie,' he returned, looking pensive. 'Ursula. . . . You're not getting too fond of Maisie? I know she's a grand little girl but she's not ours, remember?'

Recognizing a truth of which she'd had to remind herself many times already, Ursula nodded uneasily, telling him then about the incident back in Leon's caravan when the little girl might so easily have scalded herself. 'I only got to her in the nick of time. When I think what might have happened. . . .'

'Don't think it, then. . . .'

'It's just I'm worried. . . .'

Freddie frowned. 'I understand, love, of course you're worried,' he murmured gently. 'But it's really not your problem. Try and not get so involved. Promise me?'

He meant it for her own good, but was he right? Ursula's mind shifted uneasily. The fact that she remembered, only too well, the transient nature of Maisie's presence in their life suggested something else too, leading her to recollect a conversation with her mother, of which she'd been too immersed in self-pity, at the time, to take much note. A natural progression from helping the Romani children to a realization there were other children out there, desperate for a chance in life. She looked up quickly and, for the first time in too long, a burning hope flickered into strong and vibrant life.

'Freddie . . . have you ever given any thought to adoption?' she asked.

*

Chief Inspector Digby stood in the bar of Hingham's The Oak, watching Reuben pensively. The ex-gamekeeper, now artist of international renown, was drinking tea, his large hands with their long, sensitive fingers cradling his mug, his long legs stretched out under the table at which he sat. He flashed the inspector a spiteful glance.

'Sit down, man. You're making me nervous,' he muttered moodily.

They were alone in the bar.

'I prefer to stand, if you don't mind, sir. Now then . . . Her Grace informs me, you used to be her gamekeeper?' the policeman began, introducing a topic Reuben had been expecting. That Katherine Loxley would have been too proud to reveal anything else concerning their relationship, he also knew. His lip curled and yet something about this little man warned him he was no one's fool and that he should tread carefully. He would make it his business to find out about his parentage, prizing it from Katherine whether she liked it or not. A terrier of a man whose bark would never be as painful as his bite.

'You must know the place inside out – together with the secret passageway I've been hearing so much about.' The inspector rocked back on his heels, his smile beguilingly pleasant.

'I know it as well as any,' Reuben answered, uneasily.

'And you lived here until you upped sticks and settled in Berlin . . . where you took to . . . painting?'

His tone was offensive but Reuben was both old and wise enough to know that it didn't do to rile the police unnecessarily. Even so, he hung onto his temper with difficulty. 'I travelled around Europe first but, yes, after I settled in Berlin, I "took" to painting,' he answered.

Digby's brows rose. 'The National Socialists have taken firm hold there, I understand? We shall have Mr Hitler to deal with soon if I'm not very much mistaken. . . .'

Disliking more than ever the turn the conversation had taken, at last Reuben allowed his real feelings to show. 'I'm too busy with my work to worry overmuch about politics and I suggest you do the same, man!' he snapped. Realizing he may have gone too far, he took a deep and steadying breath and found a smile, cold and angry as it was. 'But I'm forgetting my manners. You'll take some tea?'

As a deflection technique, it failed, miserably. 'I had mine earlier,' Digby replied easily, his voice taking on a sharper edge. 'Bad business this at the hall, don't you agree? Secret papers of national importance, whisked away in the wink of an eye and no one appears to have any idea how it could have happened. You'll understand I have to ask everyone. . . . Where were you, exactly, last night?'

Reuben shifted uneasily. That he was a suspect was clear, not only because of his past at Loxley, wretched as it was, but also because of his recent residence in Berlin where he could so easily have come into contact with people keen to get their hands on papers belonging to Britain's war committee. His gaze hardened into two flints of ice. 'I was here. Ask the innkeeper,' he said, flatly.

'All night?'

'Certainly! That is. . . .' He crashed to a halt, chewing his lip, unable to reveal, without landing Lewis in a heap of trouble, that he'd been out half the night looking for him. His gaze flickered upwards; relieved his charge had returned, if sullen as ever, at least safely ensconced in his room until his employer told him otherwise. 'I went for a walk before I turned in,' he confessed.

'Where did you go?'

'Here and there. I just walked.'

There was a pause during which Digby contemplated and Reuben stared him out. All at once, the little man grabbed his hat from the table where he'd laid it. 'That will be all . . . for now. You'll be staying here for a while, I'm assuming?'

'For a while,' Reuben returned quickly, thinking inconsequentially of Bronwyn. Bronwyn, who was never far from his thoughts and who'd asked him to stick around. That being so, the hounds of hell couldn't prize him from the place.

Thoughts of Bronwyn warmed him through. The policeman turned to go but then retreated.

'You have a boy called Lewis Steed working for you?'

Katherine, it appeared, had been in an uncommonly communicative mood and Reuben cursed her for it. The lie tripped easily from his lips. 'He's running an errand for me at the moment,' he said.

'He's been in trouble with the police before. . . .'

Reuben's scowl deepened. The old curmudgeon had been busy. 'Something and nothing, little more than stupid, boyish pranks. He has nothing to do with this other business; I can assure you of that, Chief Inspector.'

'All the same . . . I'll need to talk to him sometime soon. I'll be back.' And with that warning, he was gone, leaving Reuben staring fretfully after him. He finished his tea quickly, staring moodily down into the dregs. So, both he and Lewis were under suspicion, a knowledge causing him again to regret the crazy impulse that had driven him from the comfortable life he'd made for himself in Berlin, bringing him back here to Loxley. Loxley, where his life had always gone wrong!

He rose to his feet, sighing heavily. But there, even he had to accept, given the swift rise of the Nazis in Germany, there was nothing so sure but that he would have had to come home sometime.

Her mother and Roland de Loxley had taken the car to see Hyssop Manor, the childhood home of the parliamentarian, Rufus Hyssop, Nell's husband. Hettie wasn't sure when the idea had first occurred to her that she and Bill should take tea with her grandmother in the meantime but fuelled by the certainty that it was important to maintain the momentum of everything they'd achieved so far, she'd inveigled her curmudgeonly relative into issuing the invitation for Bill to join them whether she'd liked it or not.

At the bottom of the stone steps, under the imperious glare of the two stone lions standing either side, Bill hung back awkwardly. 'Are you sure your grandmother really doesn't mind me joining you for tea?' he asked, for the umpteenth time since Hettie had pressed him into this visit.

She grinned. 'She's absolutely furious but now she's admitted what she's been up to, she could hardly say no. We've got to go for it, Bill! She can't be allowed to get away with the havoc she's wrought. Besides, I've told you, she's sorry about it now. . . .'

'But, Het . . . I can understand why she did what she did and exactly why she thought I wasn't good enough for you. There are so many differences between us, socially speaking; I'm surprised sometimes you even give me the time of day. . . .'

Appalled to find not only was he having such thoughts but, worse, was actually prepared to give them air, Hettie treated him to a withering stare. She hated the idea he could think such rubbish. That he had no idea how to handle her grandmother was patently clear but, there again, he wasn't on his own there. Much as she loved her, even Hettie had to concede her elderly relative was the most awkward old curmudgeon possible. She could hardly blame him for that.

Some of her tension relaxed. At once, Bill grinned.

'Oh, Hettie, I have missed you. . . .'

'Why, and I've missed you, too,' she returned sweetly, perfectly aware he wanted to kiss her again. Before he should have chance, she put herself out of the way, turning quickly and bounding up the steps and inside and into the hall. Of course she knew it was wonderful they were back together again, she'd missed him like anything; but there was no denying, her trip to Europe had changed things. She'd tasted freedom and discovered she loved it and it was influencing her thoughts on what she wanted to do with the rest of her life. Inside, a battle was raging and she wasn't yet sure of its outcome, only that Loxley was and would always be a huge part of her life. She led the way into the sitting room, her mind still churning over the facts. Bill somehow complicated matters and in a way she wasn't quite ready for yet.

Soames had just taken in the tea and sandwiches and cakes, always served in the hall at this time to fill the gap between lunch and dinner, smiling fondly at Hettie as they passed and closing the door softly behind them. Katherine Loxley put down the plate of sandwiches she'd just helped herself to and sank down into the chair.

'There you are,' she said, stiffly, her voice full of reproof.

Belatedly, Hettie realized that bringing Bill here and so quickly after their clear-the-air conversation, might appear, conceivably as if she was crowing. Why hadn't she thought! The situation could have proved awkward if Bill hadn't, unexpectedly, discovered his courage.

'Please don't mind me, Your Grace. Hettie's invited me for tea but I won't stay if you'd rather not,' he said, stepping forward with his usual diffident manner but speaking with such a quiet dignity, Hettie could see that it had impressed even her grandmother. Instantly, some of the room's tension was diffused. Graciously Katherine inclined her head and, from that point on, things might have gone swimmingly if only, just as they'd settled down and were tucking into what was proving a splendid tea, the door hadn't opened to reveal Inspector Digby. He stood, hovering impatiently, his face alive with a barely suppressed excitement. That he had news of some importance to impart was clear.

'I'm sorry to disturb Your Grace but, if you've a moment, there's something I'd like to show you.'

'Can't it wait?' Katherine enquired, snappishly and yet curious despite herself. 'Oh, very well, if I must. . . .' Sighing pointedly, she got up and followed him out. Determined not to miss out, Hettie took hold of Bill's arm and hustled them out after her, intrigued to see the little Inspector lead the way up the main

156

staircase before heading, in some determination, towards the antelibrary.

Inside, he made straight for the bookcase to the left of the door.

'I did wonder how our burglar got in,' he muttered, almost to himself, and, as his increasingly intrigued audience hovered nearby, extracted a penknife from a clutter of string and keys he pulled from his jacket pocket. Ramming the rest back into his pocket, he opened the knife, and then kneeling in front of the bookcase worked with it at the inlaid panel of wood nearest the door, prizing away a rough square of wood. He leaned forwards, slightly red-faced, to reach inside the aperture it surprisingly revealed. 'You'd never know there was a catch here, unless you were looking for it . . . voila!' he cried and, much like a conjuror revealing a magical trick, leapt up and back as, to their general astonishment, with much creaking and groaning, the bookcase slid away from the wall. A contraption working pretty much the same as the one downstairs in the fireplace in the main hall, Hettie imagined, if only they'd realized its existence! Katherine gasped out loud. An opening, barely wide enough for a slim person to pass through, lay revealed.

'Well, I never!' she murmured, clearly shocked.

Hettie blew out her cheeks. 'Gosh! How did you find it?' she demanded, impressed.

Digby nodded happily. 'Once I heard about the first passageway, it seemed obvious there might be another . . . and it was only a matter of time before I found it.' He smiled complacently. 'The walls in this place must be of an incredible thickness. There's a passageway between the wall cavities, leading to an almost vertical descent to the lower floor. I've followed it through, right out of the hall and down to the ruins! It joins the secret passageway between the New and Old Halls through a concealed door more or less undetectable from the other side, unless you knew it was there, of course. No wonder, even after the initial find, you never discovered it. Loxley is more of a laby-rinth than anyone realized.'

'Oh, gosh, I shall have to see it for myself!' Hettie murmured, excitedly.

'Henrietta Arabella, you'll do no such thing!' Katherine warned.

It was too late and Hettie was too impetuous. Blatantly ignoring her grandmother's orders to the contrary, she ran swiftly to light the lamp on the table nearby and, lifting it, beckoning to Bill to follow her, returned to squeeze through the opening. Inside, holding up the lamp, she whistled softly, alarmed to find she was in an unbearably claustrophobic corridor, so narrow it felt as if the walls were pressing in on her, hemming her in. Lamplight cast grotesque shadows on the walls and the smell of mould and mildew was overpowering. But how could this passageway exist when she'd imagined, in her innocence, she knew every twist and turn that Loxley had to offer!

Breathing out slowly and deliberately, she stifled a rising tide of panic.

'Gosh, it stinks,' Bill said, the light mooning his face as, with difficulty, he squeezed through after her. Hettie smiled a reas-surance she was far from feeling. There was no way to go, only forwards. 'Ever onwards,' she whispered, her voice hoarse with excitement. Holding the lamp up, leaving Bill with no option other than to follow her, she made her way boldly into the looming darkness, a journey that seemed to go on forever but, in reality, was only a few short minutes. All at once, she catapulted to a halt to stare down in a blind panic at the yawning chasm which had opened up at her feet. Cursing softly, Bill bumped into her.

'Whatever now?' he snapped peevishly.

'There's a vertical drop, that's what!'

'For heaven's sake be careful, Het. . . .'

He'd no need to tell her! They'd come upon the impossibly

narrow, winding steps the inspector had warned them about, plunging down into blackness so any unwary traveller would have been bound to have fallen head first, no doubt breaking their neck in the process. Visibly shuddering, Hettie held up the lamp, illumining the walls around. Suddenly she gasped out loud.

A draught flared the light upwards, drawing her attention to the wall directly above, where she was astonished to see intricately scrolled lettering chiselled into the stonework.

But surely Digby must have seen this too? If he had, he'd failed to recognize its importance, unlike Hettie who did, at once. She held the lamp higher, peering up at it, her heart thumping so loudly she was sure even Bill must hear it.

'Let's get back, Het. Leave those steps for another time. It's dreadful in here. . . .' he implored.

'Listen to this,' she said, sharply, ignoring his complaints. She began to read out loud, her voice trembling with excitement, strange words of which she couldn't, as yet, make the slightest sense:

When Aranrhod in her greatest power
Burnishes the Angel Bright
Then shall mighty Aelric strike and
Great Glory come to Loxley again. . . .

'Whatever does it mean, Bill?' she exclaimed, swinging back towards him in great animation.

'Why? What do you think? Nothing at all – only the work of a deranged madman with nothing better to do – probably one of your ancestors! The Lord knows you have enough of them! I bet these old passageways are full of such rubbish,' he returned, scathingly.

He didn't understand. Seizing his arm, Hettie shook it roughly.

'Aelric is the sword Leon told us all about!' she implored. 'Oh, for goodness' sake, Bill – don't you realize what it means even now? It's absolutely wonderful, it means Leon's tale was true and I always thought it was. This is exactly the proof I've been looking for . . . Aelric really does exist!'

Chapter Nine

Hyssop Manor was a low, half-timbered manor house, nestled deep in the valley. If, on numerous occasions, Bronwyn had driven past it about her daily business, it was a while since she'd stopped. She'd been with Reuben at the time, on the way back from Lawrence Payne's old house where they'd viewed a couple of paintings the vicar owned of Nell, the First Duchess. She'd been pregnant with Hettie at the time, she remembered, and, just as now, desperate to get away from the hall.

The day was waning, bringing with it the first hint of autumn's chill, reminding her how quickly time was passing. Unsurprisingly, given the theft of General Hawker's secret papers and the trouble it had brought crashing down on the innocent heads of Loxley's occupants, she'd neglected Roland too much of late. She leaned back against the car, smiling across at him. 'I thought you'd like to see where our illustrious Nell's husband grew up,' she murmured, happily.

'The Duchess who married one Hyssop and yet loved another?'

'She was an ardent Royalist despite her husband,' she reminded him.

Roland nodded, thoughtfully. 'I'm not being critical. I admire her and why wouldn't I? During the Civil War, my side of the family fled to France whilst Nell, brave woman that she was, had the heart and courage to stay and fight. It couldn't have been easy for a woman alone. But I wonder how Rufus felt, his brother slain, fighting for the wrong side, so to speak?'

Bronwyn's face suffused with the enthusiasm that had seen her suggest this visit in the first place. 'They were troubled times, Roland, pitting family members against each other. I can't think now why I've never tried to find out more. It's not as if I've never had chance! We could do some delving together, if you'd like but I . . . I suppose you have to go home?' This last slipped out. Bronwyn was unsure why Roland's imminent return was such anathema to her and yet, it was. A shrug of his shoulders warned her she might not like what she was about to hear.

'I can't put it off much longer, I'm afraid. And yet, I hardly like to leave you with all this trouble?'

'You mean about the stolen papers? Having you here has helped,' she admitted and then worried that had made her sound too needy. Well, she *was* needy and there was no disguising it and, after all, unattached as she was, what possible harm could there be? If her relationship with Roland deepened into something they both apparently lacked in their lives, then so be it. Companionship, warmth, a shoulder to lean on . . . Roland de Loxley was an attractive man and she liked him very much, just as she knew he liked her too. At the same time, Bronwyn was wise enough to know she was still grieving over Harry and was subsequently vulnerable. She'd hate to cause herself even more pain and, in the process, cause this man pain too when she'd little idea what other troubles he might have in his life.

'I've really enjoyed getting to know you, Bron,' he murmured, moving close enough so that his breath fanned her face, and her nostrils became keen to the first faint scent of his cologne. They were alone and, for once, far from prying eyes. It was a surprise, all the same, when he bent his head and kissed her, lightly, on the lips, a kiss that lasted only seconds before he pulled away, his eyes on hers, gauging her response. Enjoyable, certainly, a pleasurable kiss but did she, should she, want to repeat the experience? Unsure what she'd started, she stepped back and out of harm's way, aware too that much as he tried to disguise it,

Roland was annoyed at her reticence.

It was a relief to get back in the car and drive home, enduring – and there was no other word to describe it – a strangely muted conversation during which time neither quite dared to say what was on their minds. Should they have kissed? Were they truly ready for the heavy baggage which came along with a physical relationship? Bronwyn sensed that, whatever his past, Roland was ready, that as far as he was concerned, that was what this afternoon's visit had been about.

'I've so much enjoyed this afternoon,' he murmured, thereby proving her conjectures. They'd parked up and were walking back towards the hall. He was flirting with her and his expression left her with no room for doubt. He'd enjoyed their embrace and imagined she had too. Had she then, let things go too far, giving impression of something on offer when she wasn't sure it was? She hated to think she was being unfair.

For a moment, the hall appeared a sanctuary and if only, once inside, the feeling had endured but no sooner had they got through the door than Hettie, Bill in tow, came rushing down the great staircase towards them. More trouble, Bronwyn thought wearily, reading it in her daughter's face, currently flushed with overexcitement. Not now, Hettie, she wailed inwardly, but had no chance to stop the deluge that was her daughter before she launched in.

'Mother! You'll never believe it!'

'I won't, darling, if you don't tell me.' Gathering her wits, clinging onto her patience only with difficulty, Bronwyn passed her coat to Soames, who, as was his wont, materialized as if by osmosis.

Hettie was unstoppable. 'We've found another secret passageway!' she cried out. 'Chief Inspector Digby says it joins up with the one leading down to the ruins. There's some sort of a riddle on the wall above the stairs and, oh boy, didn't I just know it, it proves Aelric really does exist . . . or did once, at any rate, just like Leon told me. . . .'

Bronwyn hadn't the slightest idea what her daughter was talking about and it was suddenly too much. The afternoon, Roland's move on her and now Hettie, hardly giving her a chance to draw breath.

'Aelric? Hettie, whatever are you on about now? You're not making the slightest sense!' she retorted, sharply, for her.

Hettie exhaled slowly and made a visible effort to calm down and marshal her thoughts into some semblance of coherence. She started again, elucidating clearly this time. Chief Inspector Digby's discovery of yet another secret passageway, this one behind the bookcase in the anteroom, so the canny little man had a pretty strong suspicion now how the thief had managed to get past a locked door to steal the war committee's secret papers. 'He says the country's rife with spies! They're simply everywhere and it could be someone from the village or even one of the servants living here in the Hall!' she burst out, before the unlikelihood of this preposterousness penetrated even her consciousness. She grinned, sheepishly.

'It must at least be someone with a pretty strong knowledge of the hall?' Roland chipped in, eagerly. Bronwyn nodded uncertainly.

'But what's this about a riddle?' she demanded. Eagerly, Hettie explained about the writing she'd discovered carved into the wall over the secret stairwell and the reference it contained to Aelric, King Edmund's fabulous and legendary sword, struck in honour of his beautiful bride Elgiva, whose tale had first been recounted by Leon, the gypsy leader. 'You're not still going on about the gypsies?' Bronwyn groaned, longing for a good soak in the bath where at least there'd be chance of a little peace and quiet.

Katherine had joined them in time to hear this last.

'Stuff and nonsense!' she boomed. 'Take no notice of the child, Bronwyn. It might be helpful to know how the thief got in and stole those papers but as for the rest. . . . A few odd words written so many centuries ago, we'll never understand their meaning now.' The full force of her gaze came to rest on her unfortunate granddaughter. 'Haven't I told you already, young lady? Gypsies are full of wild tales and you're not to believe a word they say!' she finished, icily.

Hettie flared up. 'Well, I jolly well do believe it!' And, what's more she was going to prove it no matter what anyone said, even her grandmother! Glowering round at the assembled company, Hettie thought it absolutely typical. No one believed her, no matter how much she tried to convince them. 'I'll walk home with you, Bill,' she muttered huffily and not even waiting to see if he followed her, marched swiftly out.

Outside, at the bottom of the steps, she swung round, angrily. 'Wouldn't you just know it! You might have stuck up for me in there, Bill!'

'I suppose your grandmother does have a point, Het,' he muttered, uncomfortably.

'But you can't side with her, too?' she wailed. 'Bill, you were there when Leon told us about Aelric. You know how convincing he was!' Another thought catapulted into her head, one that determined her on action. Her eyes flashed in triumph. 'Leon doesn't know about the riddle yet. We'll tell him what we've discovered and see what he thinks. . . .'

'What, now?' Bill complained, too late. Even if she had heard him, she wouldn't have taken any notice, he conceded, miserably. As far as Hettie was concerned, impulse always followed far too quickly on from thought, sometimes even on no thought at all. He ran after her, such being her impatience to get to the gypsy encampment to talk to Leon, even then he struggled to keep up. Shortly, they'd passed the boundaries of Loxley's estate to reach Freddie Hamilton's land and the meadow on which the Romani folk were camped. The aroma of burning cedar assailed their nostrils, a thin spiral of hazy, grey smoke, wisping up into the air, announcing the gypsies' presence. It was a different world up here, wild and untrammelled and Hettie realized now that was why she loved it so. The afternoon was fading, the sun sinking like a ball of fire over the horizon. For once oblivious to it and to the small knot of gypsy women by the communal fire, in process of preparing the evening meal, she marched boldly up to Leon's gaily decorated caravan and made to knock on the door. Before she'd chance, however, it opened and the gypsy leader himself appeared, looking as if he'd been expecting her, Hettie thought, which couldn't possibly be true.

'Your Grace. . . . Bill. . . . Please, come in and make yourself at home,' he murmured, moving aside to let them step past him. Inside, they discovered Maisie May sitting at the table, swinging her legs on a chair much too big for her and munching on a slice of bread and jam obviously meant to tide her over until supper time. She smiled stickily. Hettie tousled her head fondly.

'Hello, little one,' she murmured, removing a battered rag dolly from the sofa under the window before sinking down next to Bill, where she sat, looking about her in some surprise. For once, Leon's normally neat living quarters appeared in disarray, dirty pots and clothes scattered everywhere. A basket of pegs the old man had been in the process of sorting, lay spilled on the table and floor where they'd fallen.

'This isn't a social visit, I take it?' Leon intuited, settling his long frame on the chair across from his visitors. He looked tired, Hettie thought, experiencing a pang of guilt for disturbing him. Too quickly it disappeared, submerged in everything she had to tell him about what had happened that day and to which he listened intently, particularly when she reached the part about the riddle in the secret passageway.

'What did it say exactly?' he interrupted eagerly.

Doing her best to recollect, Hettie screwed her eyes shut. 'It was something about Aranrhod in her greatest power. . .? When Aranrhod burnishes the angel bright, then shall mighty Aelric strike and great glory come to Loxley again. . .?' A shiver raced the length of her spine and her eyes flew open, shining with excitement. 'Oh, Leon, what on earth could it mean, do you think? Whoever left it?'

'Nell, undoubtedly,' the gypsy answered, gravely.

This was so obviously true, Hettie couldn't think now why it hadn't occurred to her already.

'Oh, but of course it must be Nell!' she exclaimed. 'There must be loads of secret passageways we know absolutely nothing about. I bet the old place is riddled with them!'

Leon ran his hand through his mane of white hair. 'Aranrhod was a legendary heroine from antiquity. Some worshipped her as goddess of the moon.'

'I see,' said Bill, who obviously didn't. Hettie, who didn't either, threw him a look of affection. He might think this was a wild goose chase but he was still here, by her side and, after the way she'd been disbelieved by her nearest and dearest, it meant a lot.

'It proves Aelric's existence though, doesn't it,' she asserted, the one thing closest to her heart.

Leon's eyes twinkled. 'As far as we gypsies are concerned, there was never any doubt.'

'But what had your people to do with it?' Bill demanded.

Leon was clearly enjoying his tale. He leaned forwards, settling his hands, with their long fingers, on his bony knees. 'The sword Aelric was passed down through the royal line until it came into the hands of Charles, the Stuart King who secreted it, with other of his treasures, in a monastery, in the heart of the Midlands. Times were tough; the royal court full of intrigue and double-dealing and there were those about the King he didn't trust. It was deemed wise to spread his wealth around.'

'And?' prompted Bill, failing to see the relevance of this.

Leon frowned. 'And when his forces looked to be defeated, Alexander, his trusted lieutenant, was despatched to take care of it before it should fall into enemy hands. The poor young man was wounded as he left the scene of battle. . . .'

'But then what happened?' Hettie chipped in, wondering how Leon could possibly know all this.

Leon, she thought, knew everything. His gaze glittered and grew distant, as if he could hear both sound and smell of battle and the cries of the wounded and dying, both horses and men. 'Grievously injured as Alexander was, in flight from the parliamentary forces who hunted him down, it was a sacred trust he determined to carry out before he died. His strength was dwindling but still he managed to ride on to the monastery and relieve the monks there of their duty in the care of Aelric. The question then must have been what to do next. Cut off from his comrades, the country swarming with enemy soldiers, weak as he was, he headed for the one place he knew both he and Aelric would be safe. . . .'

'Loxley. . . .' Hettie breathed, entranced.

Leon nodded gravely. 'Alas, the poor young man was too weak, his injuries too deep. Luckily for him, our people found him and took him in, hiding him when Cromwell's forces left no stone unturned in hunting him down. . . .'

'The gypsies took him to Nell?' Bill asked, looking plainly disbelieving.

Leon nodded. 'So our legend has it. Tales passed down to while away a winter's evening. Having no liking for the stern faced Parliamentarians who hated the gypsy folk, our people were Royalist to a man.'

'But then what happened?' Hettie implored, desperate now to hear the rest. 'I mean after Alexander died. Nell was left with Aelric?'

Leon shrugged. 'I presume so. Our people only knew, having delivered both Royalist and sword into Nell's safe hands, neither was ever heard of again.'

There was a silence whilst Hettie considered this. She was

shocked, certainly, but above all, it seemed to her, a wonderful tale and already her head was spinning with its implications.

'But what could have happened to it? I mean, we know what happened to Alexander. He died and Nell had him secretly interred. She might have buried Aelric with him.' She frowned. That patently hadn't happened or the sword would have been discovered when Alexander's mortal remains were found, now reburied in Loxley's churchyard, next to Nell and Alexander's brother, Rufus. 'Leon. . . . Do you think Aelric might be buried in some secret place in, or near to, Loxley?' she asked, an enquiry too much for Bill, who snorted in amusement, receiving a furious look from both Hettie and Leon for his pains.

'Who knows, Your Grace,' the old man said, stiffly and clearly offended, rising quickly to his feet.

Their visit was too obviously over. 'He might have told us more if only you hadn't been so rude,' Hettie spluttered indignantly, once they were safely outside. Bill's expression was so dismissive, she could have shaken him.

'You surely never believed him, Het? It's all so much bunkum!' He was as bad as everyone else, after all. 'Those words in the secret passageway aren't bunkum,' she responded, indignantly.

'No, but. . . .'

'No buts, Bill! Oh, can't you see? There is something in it and whatever it is, I'm not resting until I find out!' she interjected. Frustrated, she swung away, heading swiftly towards Loxley and away from the curiously endearing little cluster of gaily decorated vans where, already, lamps were set to the windows, soft, warm globes of flickering orange-yellow light, pushing out against the encroaching darkness.

'Sorry,' Bill said contritely when, at last, he'd managed to catch her up. Out of breath, he reached for her hand. So surprised was Hettie by this, she let him take it, wondering then, too late, whether she really ought. Her apparent acquiescence must have emboldened him. Taking her further by surprise, he stopped and, in one action, pulled her towards him and kissed her firmly on the lips. A warm glow suffused her. It was so unlike him and, for a moment, her reaction was only one of pleasure and admiration for his bravado. And then reality set in. 'Bill!' she cried, outraged. Alarmed by his expression, she sprang back. 'Don't do it again,' she warned.

'Alright,' he agreed but still looking so inordinately pleased with himself she guessed now he'd planned it all along. Her hand moved to her lips, touching the spot where he'd kissed her and wondering how she felt about it. She thought she'd enjoyed it but it had been over so quickly, it was difficult to tell. Perhaps she should let him kiss her again? What message would that convey? The fact she was confused didn't necessarily bode well for Bill's obvious and growing desire to move their relationship forwards. She did like him though; she liked him a lot . . . even if he was, well . . . more like a brother? She marched on, thoughtfully, darting quick glances his way and feeling a little cross now, as if her confusion was his fault.

'You'd no right to do that,' she admonished him, determining to keep space between them this time, at least until she'd sorted out her feelings.

Three days later

'You look pleased!' Freddie pushed a cup of tea across the table towards Ursula, who'd just returned from the village school to see how the Romani children were faring. None of her business of course but she'd felt compelled, if only to set her mind at rest she'd done right in enrolling them there in the first place. Fortunately, Cynthia Bardwell had been pleased to see her, allowing her access to the classroom so she could see for herself the cluster of heads bent so assiduously over their desks and happily absorbed in their work.

'As you can see, we're all doing very nicely, thank you. . . .' the older woman had retorted, sounding rather surprised, as well she might. It had been hard to refrain from saying, 'I told you so.' Quickly, Ursula filled Freddie in on the visit. 'I bumped into Bronwyn Loxley on the way back,' she finished. 'You'll never believe it, Freddie. They've stumbled across yet another secret passageway in the hall! Just imagine. . . . Living in a place all these long years and it can still take you by surprise!' She took her cup, sipping her tea appreciatively and chuckling quietly. 'She's had me in stitches about Hettie and some notion the girl has there's a fabulous sword hidden at Loxley that'll make all their fortunes if only she can find it! Poor Bronwyn, she's got her hands full with that young lady. . . .'

Entertaining as had been the conversation, there had been something else, of even greater importance than Hettie Loxley's over-excitable imagination. Ursula's laughter quickly disappeared. She sat down, cupping her hands around her tea and regarding Freddie meditatively. Despite more pressing concerns, a warm glow was bubbling away inside her. There was no doubting, she and Freddie had turned some sort of a corner of late, particularly after their heart-to-heart about adoption, something for which they'd discovered, wonderfully, they both longed in equal measure.

'I called in to see Leon, too,' she said, abruptly.

'Ah. . . . Did you, indeed?' Freddie murmured, shooting her a wary glance.

'Only to tell him how well the children were doing. . . .'

'But?' he prompted, seeing that there was something on her mind and that she was struggling to tell him what it was.

She took a deep breath. 'It must be too much for Leon, looking after Maisie May and then having all his gypsy council work on top. He said as much, in fact. . . .' she told him, remembering vividly the scene in Leon's caravan. There'd nearly been another calamity when the little girl had reached up for the knife on the table with which her grandfather, only moments before, had been whittling pegs. Thankfully, Leon had seen her in time, hastily whisking the offending article out of harm's way. Had it been Ursula's imagination that the place had been particularly untidy and lacking in its normal state of cleanliness? There'd been no mistaking what Leon had said as he'd so thankfully clutched Maisie to him. 'This little girl needs more than I can give her. If only she had loving parents around her, Ursula! Younger folk who can give her what she needs. I'm too old. I must do something. . . .' he'd exclaimed, looking so sad, meanwhile, Ursula's heart had gone out to him. He was doing his best in a difficult situation but even she saw how impossible it was. What other impression should Ursula draw than Leon recognized it too and was already making plans for Maisie's future?

She took a swallow of tea to steady her nerves. 'I think he realizes Maisie's getting too much for him,' she said, hesitantly, then quickly seizing her courage. 'Oh Freddie! He more or less said he's thinking of finding someone else to look after her. And, if that is the case, then. . . . Why not us? Why can't we look after her? Surely we're as good as anyone?'

Freddie frowned. 'What are you trying to say?' he demanded sharply.

'I think we ought to offer to take her in,' she blurted out quickly, hardly daring to look at him then, in case, in one stroke, he destroyed the worlds she'd been building, all the way home.

'Adopt her, you mean?'

Ursula's heart leapt up, brimming with frustrated love. 'Yes! Why not!'

'Ursy, but what a crazy idea. . . .'

'But think of the life we could offer her, Freddie, the opportunities we'd put her way. The farm, a proper and loving home, a sense of belonging. . . .'

'Leon loves her. He'd never agree.'

'I know he loves her enough to put her welfare first! And we'd make sure he saw her, lots, whenever he wanted. We could even find him a cottage close by. He'd still be her grandfather. . . .'

Freddie reached for his wife's hand, rocking it gently between his own and even then, hating to disappoint her. 'Darling, I do understand but you must know this is only a pipe dream.'

He spoke so reasonably but what had reason to do with this? 'We could at least ask him!' she implored.

'Love, I can't bear you should be hurt!'

'You mean you wouldn't want to adopt her?' Even Ursula couldn't believe this. Freddie's gaze, that could still turn her insides to water, met hers, reassuringly steadily. He shook his head.

'Of course I'd love that to happen. She's a grand little girl.'

He was weakening and they both knew it. Had she swept him along with her plans? She'd used to, once upon a time, before her hold on him had been loosened by his other mistress, the farm. But he must agree to this – he simply had to! She jumped up quickly. 'I could go now and at least broach the subject? Before he has chance to make other arrangements!'

'I don't know, love. . . . You can't just charge in!'

It was too late. Ursula was too fired up, too determined to carry all before her with the force of her argument. 'I'd be very tactful. Just to see if he really was thinking that way. I needn't necessarily say anything about us; just see how the conversation goes – test the water, if you like?'

Put like that, it was hard to disagree. Freddie stood up, what he said next bringing a wild joy springing into Ursula's heart. 'I'd better come with you, then,' he murmured. 'But you must promise me, Ursula. . . . You mustn't get your hopes up. This is only a preliminary enquiry. We can't exactly come right out with it, yet.'

There was a world of promise in that 'yet'. But that he was right, she knew. She nodded eagerly. It was enough he'd agreed, that he wanted to go with her, if only to shield her from hurt. 'I have to at least try, Freddie' she admitted quietly. 'And now. . . .

Before it's too late. But I do accept what you mean, I promise. It's just. . . .'

'It's just you're you and impulsive as ever?'

He sounded resigned and yet there was a hope, too, lurking in his eyes which told her so much more than he'd ever admit. He'd love it too, if they could adopt Maisie May. She took his hand and squeezed it, her heart beating rapidly as they went outside, through the yard and up towards the hill and the meadow where the gypsies were camped. Now the miracle had happened and she'd actually got Freddie to fall in with her plans, Ursula's mind was full of misgivings. What would Leon say? Had she imagined his intentions? Pushing aside her doubts, she opened the gate to the meadow and led the way through it towards Leon, who was outside his caravan talking to another man. A youngish man, slim and wiry, with dark, curly hair, his gaze betraying a flicker of interest at their approach. Wound up as Ursula was, there was still something about him that was disturbingly familiar.

'Leon,' she called, both gratified and soothed by the old man's quick smile of welcome.

'Ursula . . . and Freddie too. But what a lovely surprise! You're welcome here, both of you. You've arrived just at the right time. . . .' So saying, he turned to the man beside him, saying a thing then, so shocking to all Ursula's impossible plans and dreams, that instantly they collapsed into trembling disarray.

Clearly having no idea of the wound he was about to inflict, Leon smiled widely. 'Porter, these are the neighbours I was telling you about, Ursula and Freddie Hamilton, who own this land. Ursula, Freddie, I'd like you to meet Porter, my son-in-law and Maisie May's father. Isn't it wonderful? He's returned to accept his responsibilities. He's going to look after Maisie at last!'

In her comforting and comfortable little kitchen, Mary Compton busied herself refilling the teapot and stoking up the fire for her visitor. The afternoon had grown cold in that dreary way of early autumn, giving a hint of the winter to come. 'Reuben, it is good to see you,' she murmured, finding, delightfully, it to be perfectly true. 'Tom's gone to the wholesaler. He'll be sorry to have missed you.'

'I'm not here to see Tom,' Reuben muttered, forthright as ever and accepting his tea as of right, complete with the two sugars she remembered he'd always taken, stretching out his legs towards the fire and sipping it moodily. He'd obviously something on his mind but then, so had she.

'I've had the Inspector round here,' she told him, getting in first.

'Digby?' A faint alarm registered on Reuben's face which, despite the passage of years, she acknowledged was still a handsome one.

'That's the one,' she agreed. 'And asking a lot of awkward questions about you and the lad . . . Lewis, isn't it? I thought you might have brought him with you.'

'He's gone to the hall to see Hettie,' he informed her, sharply. 'What did he want to know?'

'How long you've known him. What he does in your employ, exactly. . . .'

'Blasted man, did he indeed,' he muttered, looking displeased.

'He asked about you too. What you used to do here, that sort of thing.'

'You told him, of course!' he snapped, irritably.

'As little as I could,' Mary agreed, equably and refusing to be rattled. For all his fine clothes and fancy manners, it was clear beneath the thin veneer, the same Reuben lurked, prickly as a room full of porcupines! The thought made her smile, for which she received another furious stare. 'Give over, lad. You're amongst friends here, remember?' she said.

Her words soothed him and she blessed the deity that had put them there, ready on her tongue when needed. He finished his tea and put down his cup.

'What do you know about this Roland de Loxley?' he asked, abruptly.

Mary had known this was no impromptu visit and realized now what it was about. Her old friend was here to quiz her about Roland because, like everyone else, he sensed there was something going on between him and Bronwyn. Reuben had always liked Bronwyn, more than liked her if he'd ever admit it. Her heart filled with pity but, despite it, she told him all she knew. It was little enough and only what she'd been able to glean from Bronwyn herself. 'I thought he'd have gone home long before now. There must be something – or someone keeping him here,' she finished quietly.

'Bronwyn, you mean?' he demanded, his eyes filling with a pain he couldn't quite disguise. She'd always been able to read him like the proverbial book, closed to most folk but never to her. Her answer would give him more pain but it seemed kindest, in the long run.

'They spend an inordinate amount of time together,' she answered, carefully. 'Though it's hardly surprising, given, as I say, he's only recently discovered he's from the same branch of the family.'

'Family – the same as me?' demanded this most passionate and impetuous of men.

Mary nodded uncertainly, unable to stop the thought rising that any relationship with a man like Reuben, no matter how loving, would be as being caught up in a maelstrom. No! Reuben was the last person Bronwyn needed in her life right now, particularly when the poor lass was so badly in need of peace and quiet.

It was time for straight talking. 'You still have feelings for her, don't you?' she demanded.

Suddenly, the years rolled away and he was as ever, the same lad who'd used to take refuge in her kitchen to pour out his woes. 'I love her. I always have and always will,' he admitted, as if owning to a crime instead of the most natural feeling in the world. Sadly, Mary shook her head. Given he'd used to be the gamekeeper round here and Bronwyn, despite her lowly origins, was still mother to Hettie, the present Duchess of Loxley, as far as she, Mary, could see, the poor man was headed for trouble.

Still she struggled for the right words to say what she believed badly needed saying.

'Reuben. . . . You don't think you're, well, reaching above yourself?'

That was putting it mildly and yet, even so, she saw that she'd offended him. As far as Reuben was concerned, he was as good as any man on God's earth and who could deny him? He was a grand man, a passionate man, if one who sometimes took some understanding. But there! He'd had much to put up with in his life and that was the truth. He sat, struggling to express his frustration so she wished now desperately she'd kept her observations to herself. She reached over awkwardly and patted his hand, all the while restraining the impulse to throw her arms around him and assure him everything would turn out right because, after all, it generally did . . . didn't it?

Suddenly, her heart full of misgivings, Mary wasn't so sure.

After she'd discovered him hiding away in Reuben's cottage, Hettie had never since clapped eyes on Lewis so she was only too happy when that afternoon, he'd turned up unexpectedly at the hall. He'd made his peace with Reuben, he said, and he was presently keeping a low profile and doing what Reuben told him, which was to avoid the police. Circumnavigating Soames, who appeared intent on ushering them into the sitting room, Hettie had dragged him straight up to the anteroom and into the secret tunnel to show him the words carved into the stonework and to ask him what he thought.

Lamplight flickered, flaming grotesque shadows on the walls.

'I knew you'd want to see it,' she said, leading the way out again and back into the anteroom whilst inwardly owning to a sense of disappointment Lewis hadn't appeared all that impressed.

'This tunnel links up with the other, you say?' he asked, dusting a cobweb from his sleeve.

She darted him a curious glance, wondering now if, subconsciously, she'd meant it as some kind of a test. 'You really didn't know, did you?'

'For goodness' sake, don't start that again!' he snapped, clearly offended.

Hettie was at once contrite. 'I'm sorry, that was thoughtless. It's just, what with the war committee papers being stolen and suspicion falling on everyone, it's been so difficult round here of late.'

'Hah! Tell me about it. . . .'

He must be the prickliest boy in the world. Doing her best to put his rudeness aside, Hettie concentrated instead on the matter in hand. 'What do you make of the riddle?' she asked.

'Dunno, something and nothing, I expect.' He shrugged. Her face fell. She'd thought Lewis at least would have understood. 'No one will believe me!' she entreated. 'But I'm sure Aelric is hidden somewhere near here. Nell Loxley was a Royalist at heart. She'd have kept it safely against the King's return, above all.'

'You shouldn't believe everything Leon tells you,' Lewis muttered, looking amused. 'Oh, Hettie, you know what gypsies are like!'

'Folk, the same as any other folk,' she argued.

He smiled suddenly, a rare smile, transforming his face so she saw how good-looking he really was, so much so, for a moment she wondered. . . . Bill's face loomed large. Hastily, she pushed the thought aside. Any relationship with Lewis would bring trouble, she knew.

He was evidently prepared to humour her. 'Say Nell did hide this . . . Aelric . . . whatever it's called,' he mused, looking thoughtful, 'and she left the riddle as a way of explaining?

It doesn't exactly make much sense. I mean, who or what is Aranrhod, for heaven's sake?'

'Leon says she's the goddess of the moon. . . .' Hettie stopped, her expression suddenly changing. 'But I know who'd tell us – the Reverend Payne! Why ever didn't I think? We'll go and ask him.'

'What, now?' Lewis demanded, too late for she was already heading for the door, leaving him no option but to follow her.

Downstairs, Hettie crossed the hall and flung open the front door. And then she froze, looking in shocked surprise at the man she'd discovered on the doorstep, his large bulk looming before her and his hand raised to pull the bell. A man with presence and breeding, immaculately dressed if exuding the faintly menacing air she'd always found so disconcerting. A man she'd assumed she'd never see again! Whatever would her mother say now? Crazily, it flitted into her mind that Dizzy, at least, would be pleased.

Fully cognizant of her surprise, Count Charles Dresler smiled, revealing thereby small and perfectly even teeth. 'Hettie, my dear,' he murmured. 'You did say I must come and look you up?'

Chapter Ten

Bronwyn Loxley helped herself to a glass of wine from the drinks tray, thanking Soames politely before turning her attention back to the company assembled in the sitting room, prior to the evening meal, a company comprising mostly family, which included Roland, plus Dizzy Pettigrew, hastily summoned from her home in the village to make up the numbers. Count Dresler's arrival had thrown them all into a spin, Bronwyn in particular, left with the headache of what to do with him. She was still vexed with Hettie, presently chatting animatedly to her grandmother about goodness alone knew what, Bronwyn fretted, a little peevishly. Her troubled gaze roamed around the room, landing on the convivial figure of the Count, who stood, glass in hand, holding forth to Dizzy, who gazed up at him adoringly. Taken with the idea of Loxley's former governess harbouring romantic feelings for anyone, and such a distinguished man to boot, Bronwyn's gaze lingered. There was no doubt, the Count was a charismatic, distinguished figure and she could well see why Dizzy was so smitten. Another time, perhaps when she hadn't been so preoccupied with Roland, his company might even have been welcome?

Her gaze shifted again, this time to Roland, who stood by the French windows, sipping a glass of sherry. Remembering their embrace that afternoon, not for the first time Bronwyn wondered where their relationship was headed, or, indeed, if it was headed anywhere.

'You look pensive,' he observed, aware of her perusal and moving swiftly to join her.

She smiled, playing for time and not fooling him one iota.

'I'm alright, really I am, Roland. And you?'

'I'm not sorry for this afternoon if that's what you imagine,' he murmured. His gaze softened, his eyes flashing hidden depths so for a moment, she felt herself sucked into the invitation she read there. 'You're not having second thoughts, Bron?' He frowned.

'No, of course not . . . that is. . . .'

'You're not exactly sure?' he probed, gently.

That was Roland, a man who believed in going straight to the heart of a matter. He deserved honesty if nothing else. Her hand was trembling. Confused, she put her drink down on the table beside her and took a deep breath. 'There's never been any one else since Harry and even thoughts of starting another relationship scares me. I just feel that . . . events this afternoon have moved things along a little too fast. Does that make sense? That's not to say I don't like you,' she concluded hastily. Having got all this out, jumbled as it was, Bronwyn immediately felt better. She smiled up at him, relieved when he smiled back, albeit ruefully.

'I do know what loss feels like, Bron. . . .' he murmured, his ready smile falling away so she was reminded again of the troubled past at which he'd so far only hinted and had yet to confide. He'd told her so little about his past, she realized, determining to ask him now.

'You must have your problems, too, Roland?' she prompted.

Clearly uncomfortable, he took a gulp of his wine. 'We can't be our ages and not carry some sort of baggage, I expect,' he replied. 'There was someone once, if you must know, someone I probably should have got over long before now but . . . well. . . . You know how it is?'

She did know, exactly. 'I wish you'd tell me, that's all. I can't help otherwise.'

'Her name was Lilli,' he began, still reluctantly. 'I've known her forever, since I was a boy. Our families were close; we used to spend our holidays together. We were friends long before we fell in love though things went much deeper with me, I'm afraid. I sometimes think . . . I wish I'd never met her. I've never really got over her.'

'It didn't work out?'

'No, not really. Something happened – something bad. It's like . . . she's a part of me I can't quite shake off. I can't forget her and I don't even know if I want to. . . .'

'I do understand. . . .' she answered when it appeared nothing else was forthcoming. But she did understand and hadn't only been speaking empty words meant to placate. In an odd way, what Roland was describing were exactly her feelings for Harry. She'd never really got over Harry and she knew that now.

Frustratingly, at that moment, the Count detached himself from Dizzy and joined them.

'I've been meaning to thank you for putting me up at such short notice, Your Grace,' he began suavely, in his almost impeccable English. So saying, he took her hand, kissing it so gallantly, she blushed. There was no mistaking the look in his eyes. Despite a faint and instinctive aversion towards him, she couldn't help but be flattered. He was a handsome man and no wonder Dizzy was so smitten.

'You're planning to stay a while?' she asked him.

'I'm over here on business,' he agreed, pleasantly. 'After your daughter's most kind invitation, it seemed too good a chance to miss. But I'd hate to think I was putting you out.'

Bronwyn's smile was genuine. Poor man, so far from home and with the sensitivity to know he might be in the way. 'Nonsense Count, of course you're not putting us out in any way. Please. . . . You must let me introduce you to Roland de Loxley, who's visiting us from France. . . .'

The Count clicked his heels and shook hands formally, gazing into Roland's face searchingly before letting go his hand and returning his attention to Bronwyn. 'We must talk business soon.'

'Please, feel free now, if you'd like? Roland is family.' She smiled, feeling good giving air to such a truth, or as good as family, she conceded, no matter how tenuous the connection between their two distinctive branches of the Loxley line. The Count nodded, agreeably.

'I've always been wary of the maxim against mixing business with pleasure. So much more palatable, don't you agree, to manage a little business and yet enjoy oneself too? So, my dear, your daughter tells me you have items of historical interest you may wish to sell?'

Even if Hettie hadn't already warned Bronwyn about the reason for the Count's visit, she was still wary. She didn't know this man; though Dizzy had assured her that he was perfectly genuine. Aware of her reluctance, the Count took a card from the top pocket of his jacket and presented it.

'I'd be perfectly willing to value any article you wished to show me and guide you through the market. Difficult as things are back home presently – politically I mean – I still have many contacts.'

'Blasted Nazis,' Roland muttered, under his breath.

The Count's brows arched in surprise. 'You're no friend to the Nazis, Mr de Loxley? But I can assure you they do much good. Our country was left in such turmoil after the war. People starving, so few jobs. . . . We needed a strong party to pull us together.'

Roland shook his head, too vehemently for politeness' sake, Bronwyn thought, if privately agreeing with him. She threw him a worried glance. Aware of it, he apologized at once. 'I'm sorry, Count. It's just I can't say I like the way things are going in Germany. In my humble opinion, Herr Hitler has much to answer for.'

'There's much change afoot,' the Count agreed, amiably, returning his attention to Bronwyn, who found herself pinned under the intensity of those cool blue eyes. 'Now – how about you show me round tomorrow but only if you've time, of course?'

He was charming and affable and, given their current financial plight, it surely couldn't do any harm to have expert opinion on any Loxley valuables that might prove saleable? Quickly, Bronwyn made up her mind. 'Tomorrow will be fine,' she agreed.

Her grandmother had gone to talk to Dizzy. Hettie stood, thoughtlessly twirling her hair round one finger and regarding her mother quizzically. She'd been worried what her mother would say about the Count's unexpected arrival but really, there'd been no need. Any frustration she felt at discovering him on the doorstep and having to cancel her planned visit to Lawrence Payne was long forgotten. In any case, she'd already sorted out another time. . . .

'Hettie!' her mother called, catching her gaze. 'I'm just promising to show the Count round tomorrow. You'll be joining us, I presume?'

Hettie nodded uneasily. 'It'll have to be later though; I've arranged to see the vicar with Lewis, first thing. We want to ask him about that riddle in the secret passageway. Have you heard about that yet, Count Dresler?' If he hadn't, she was only too happy to tell him. She moved closer, her expression bubbling over with excitement. 'It's to do with a sword, named Aelric. A fabulous jewel-covered sword, worth an absolute fortune, I should think. I'm positive it must be hidden round here somewhere, if only I'd a clue where exactly!'

'Darling, don't bother our guest with all that now,' Bronwyn interrupted, forestalling the gleam of interest shadowing the Count's face.

All Hettie's good humour vanished instantly. Trust her mother to put a spanner in the works! But Aelric did exist and, what's more, it was hidden here, at Loxley, she was sure of it. She frowned. Some day, she would find it and then everyone would be sorry! She launched in again.

'Have you caught up with Reuben Fairfax yet, Count? Oh, but I forgot . . . you know him best as Alex Windrow. You do realize that he grew up here on the estate and that he used to be our gamekeeper?' The silence greeting this little volley of information told her, belatedly, she'd somehow blundered again. She stood, chewing her lip and wishing, too late now, she'd kept the information to herself. But surely, the Count knew all this already?

'Alex . . . Reuben has told me a little of his history,' the Count returned, smoothly. 'I knew he planned a visit. He's still in the area, I believe? It will be good to see him again. . . .'

The conversation moved onto safer ground but it was still a relief once they'd gone in to dinner and then, after another interminable interlude, when the evening was finally over and she could escape upstairs to bed where, tired out by the day's events, she immediately fell asleep. In the morning, after an early and hasty breakfast eaten alone, everyone else still being in bed, she went down to the bridge to meet Lewis, as they'd prearranged.

'Trouble?' he asked, taking one look at her face and grinning.

Thinking of the Count's unexpected arrival, the gaffes she'd made, one after another, Hettie didn't know quite where to start. 'And some,' she said, grinning back. 'Shall we go and find Bill?' Bill, she'd decided, should be in on this too, even if, as she'd expected, some of Lewis's good humour instantly disappeared at the news.

'If we must,' he agreed, heavily.

Fortunately, Bill was up and, always an early riser, breakfasted and working at home rather than at college. To his mother's obvious frustration, he was only too keen to desert his books.

'You do know this is a wild goose chase?' he observed good-naturedly as they set off towards the vicarage, situated next door to the church and where Lawrence Payne had moved once he'd taken up the role of Loxley's vicar permanently. Hettie was aware of the two boys exchanging amused glances and annoyed by it, marched on in front.

Lawrence Payne himself answered the door, his kindly old face breaking into a smile of greeting when he saw the young people grouped in the rectory porch. 'You're here to find out more about the church, Your Grace?' he enquired, referring to his earlier invitation for Hettie to drop in any time she wished.

'The great west window, at least, vicar,' she agreed, stepping aside as he pulled the door closed behind him and following him with the others, back through the churchyard. She was thinking of the lecture he'd earlier imparted concerning the history of the church, built by Nell Loxley and according to records, replacing the crumbling ruin, all that had remained of the building from Saxon times. Surprised by it, Hettie was aware of a quickening interest.

Inside the church, she stood gazing up admiringly at the combination of columns and arches and then, as usually happened once inside these dusty old stones, her cares simply drifted away, leaving in their place a feeling of connection with the past and all its many traditions, as if generations of Loxleys, long since gone, were reaching out to claim her as one of their own. She'd never told anyone she felt like this. They'd think her fanciful but here, more than anywhere, even Loxley, she understood the importance of her position on this estate.

'The place seems different from Sunday,' Bill observed, shooting her a puzzled look.

'God's house has many guises, my boy,' Lawrence Payne responded quietly, leading the way past the font to the church's famous west window, where the young people clustered round him, emitting exclamations of approval. But it was a wonderful sight, a Gothic arch, its stained glass divided into sections by vertical shafts and tracery of stone.

'Why, it's beautiful,' Hettie said, as if she was seeing it – really seeing it – for the very first time.

'You've only just noticed?' the kindly old cleric remonstrated, unable to keep the hint of reproof from his voice. His face alive with a sudden enthusiasm, he stood gazing up at it as if he too was seeing it for the first time. 'Church windows of the period were mostly thematic,' he mused. 'Stained glass as an art form was used to educate a largely illiterate population. The technique itself was developed in Saxon times. . . .'

'And these folk depicted were actually Saxon kings?' Lewis asked, sounding impressed.

Lawrence Payne nodded. 'Egbert, King of Wessex, Alfred the Great, Edward the Elder. . . . And here is your Edmund . . . Edmund the Magnificent, born in 922, a canny statesman as well as warrior king.' He indicated a pane of glass, three rows down the perpendicular, of a particularly striking and vibrant hue, depicting a fair-haired youth on whose head a jewelled crown sat easily, his hand extended towards a young girl with luxurious golden hair, kneeling at his feet and gazing up at him in clear adoration.

'Queen Elgiva?' Bill whispered.

'Mother of Edmund's sons, Edwig All Fair and St Edgar the Peacemaker,' the vicar agreed, amiably. 'But other than she was a woman of great compassion, we know little about her. Truly, she was an angel and blessed by God. After her death, it was reported many desperately ill folk journeyed to her place of burial, praying to be healed of their complaints, many successfully, it has to be said. In some places, she's still revered as a saint. . . .'

'Gosh,' Hettie muttered, impressed.

He shot her a curious glance. 'You seem interested, Hettie?'

This dear old man didn't know the half of it and it was about time she told him. Quickly, as succinctly as she could, she told him again about Leon's captivating tale and her unshakeable belief in Aelric and the riddle in the secret passageway, surely verifying its existence.

The vicar's bony fingers clasped together. 'Your mother's told me about the riddle, too,' he said, sonorously. 'She's also told me she's worried about you, Hettie. . . .'

'Well I can assure you, she's no need, vicar,' she declared, loftily.

He was amused. 'Why don't I come up to the hall and take a look?' he proffered.

He could do no more, even Hettie had to admit, but at that moment, the church door opened and a man appeared, walking quickly towards them. Instantly, Hettie's hackles rose.

'Chief Inspector Digby,' she said, coldly.

Ignoring her, the inspector's gaze settled on Lewis, who paled visibly. 'Well, well, Lewis Steed, we meet up at last,' he said pleasantly. 'You come along to the station with me, young man. I've some questions wanting answers to and they'd better be good 'uns, or you're in a whole heap of trouble, I'll tell you that now!'

Halting the tractor outside the gate leading to the gypsies' encampment, Freddie Hamilton leapt down nimbly, his nostrils at once assailed by the sweet aroma of burning cedar, telling him that not only had the blighters helped themselves to a once productive patch of land, but in addition, were now helping themselves to wood from the trees at the bottom of it, too. Something about the scene before him, however, rested easily on his gaze, quickly quenching his resentment. He came to a halt, resting his arms on the gate to look down at the women sitting around the campfire against the backdrop of the brightly coloured vardoes. They were chatting, peeling vegetables and throwing them into the steaming pot as a plume of blue-grey smoke rose lazily into a crisp blue sky. It was the sort of autumnal morning the farmer had always loved. Children ran, unkempt and carefree, laughing and hollering, whilst mongrel dogs, weaving in between the melee, barked frenziedly, announcing his arrival; and yet the whole picture was pervaded with such an atmosphere of peace and contentment, Freddie was more attracted to it than he could ever have believed. Had these people got it right? This was the way life should be lived? Who was he to say ought against them!

A tall, white-haired figure detached himself from a group of men standing idly by and, stretching out a hand of greeting, glided swiftly towards him.

'Farmer Hamilton! You're welcome here,' Leon said.

Freddie suppressed a wry smile. Aye, welcome on his own land and he supposed he ought to be grateful for it, too. The gypsy leader's gaze rested on him thoughtfully.

'Is Ursula . . . Mrs Hamilton alright? She appeared upset yesterday,' he prompted.

Freddie winced. Somehow he'd got Ursula away from the encampment before her overwhelming disappointment at the appearance of Porter, Maisie May's father, had seen her break down completely. Leon unsurprisingly had noticed it too. Freddie sensed this man missed nothing of importance.

'She'll be alright, given time,' he said, not troubling to deny it and filled with an unaccountable desire to unburden himself. As if this strange, proud man would understand the trouble he and Ursula were going through and would be able to help them. 'How's Maisie May?' he asked, removing temptation and quickly changing subject. 'You must be relieved her father's returned to look after her?'

'I'd long since given up hope of it,' Leon agreed.

'But he's back for good now? He will care for her properly?' he demanded, discovering, to his surprise, he needed to know, not just for Ursula but for himself too. He cared about Maisie May. He wanted her to have a good life. To his relief, Leon nodded.

'He was too young when Maisie May was born, he and my daughter both,' he replied. 'My unfortunate daughter died giving birth. The poor young man was distraught. Grief makes us do wrong things but at least he's finally owned up to his responsibilities. There's much truth in the maxim, blood's thicker than water. He will make a good and loving father to Maisie, I think.'

One look at the old man's benign countenance verified the truth of this and instantly, Freddie relaxed. 'You look as if you've made your home here,' he said, finding, oddly, a thing once unbelievable, he was resigned to the gypsies' presence here. Leon glanced quickly back across the field, towards the turrets and battlements of Loxley rising so proudly into the sky. His next words surprised his visitor more than anything he'd said so far.

'Our time here is nearly done,' he murmured, his gaze narrowing. 'Mayhap you'll miss us when we're gone. You're a busy man, Farmer Hamilton, but make sure and find time for that wife of yours.' It appeared the interview was over. With a quick smile of farewell, Leon returned to his men.

From anyone else, such a rebuke would have brought a sharp retort tumbling to Freddie's lips but oddly he knew the gypsy leader could say far worse to him and he would still demur. Deep in thought, he returned to his tractor and climbed aboard. The old man was right, in any case. He couldn't argue. He hadn't been there for Ursula when he should have been, something he cursed himself for now. He drove back to the farm, jumping quickly down and heading straight for the kitchen, so great was his sudden and urgent need to see Ursula and tell her. . . . What exactly? That he loved her? That everything would be alright so long as they worked through this together? She knew that already.

She stood at the table pummelling dough, stopping to brush a weight of hair from her face with the back of a floured hand, losing herself in work because, as she'd told him at breakfast, no matter how bad they felt, they mustn't give in to this. Something about the sight of her as he came through the door caused his heart to lurch. He drew to a halt in front of her, searching her face for any sign she'd meant what she'd said earlier, that in an odd kind of way, Porter's return had brought things to a head. . . .

'Ursula, you really are alright about Maisie May, aren't you?' he asked.

'Shouldn't I be?' she returned, shooting him a quizzical glance.

'Freddie, you must stop worrying about me. I'm fine, really I am. I know yesterday was a huge disappointment but surely it's better to know? There's nothing worse than false hope. . . .'

'Leon says Porter will take care of Maisie May. She'll have a good life.'

'Leon wouldn't let her go to him otherwise. He loves her too much.' She nodded, thoughtfully. 'I've been chasing after dreams, Freddie but. . . . No more!'

At these wise words, a tiny flame of hope sprang up into Freddie's heart, burning there steadily. Perhaps they didn't say these things often enough but, if so, he meant to redress the balance.

'I just wanted to tell you, Ursy, I . . . I do love you,' he said.

A gleam of the impish humour he'd always known and loved, reminding him of the young girl with whom, all those years ago, he'd first fallen so headlong in love, sprang up into her eyes.

'You'd better or else, Hamilton,' she murmured softly. That said she leaned across the table to drop a light and floury kiss on his cheek, only to spring back laughing when his natural reaction was to reach out and pull her into his arms.

Hettie sat drinking tea in the sitting room, meanwhile mulling over the scene with the young police constable she'd earlier harangued over Lewis's continued incarceration at the police station.

'Sorry, miss. He's in police custody pending further investigation. Matters of high security,' he'd muttered belligerently, if from behind the safety of his desk. Given the fact even Reuben's furious response had been unable to elicit Lewis's release, it was no more than she should have expected, she conceded miserably. Even worse, on the way out of the police station, she'd bumped into Chief Inspector Digby, whose smugness over what he obviously perceived as case solved had been so odious, she'd simply had to give him a piece of her mind. He'd listened patiently – and then taken not the slightest scrap of notice. Still fuming, she finished

191

her tea, returning her cup and saucer to the side table with such a clatter, her grandmother jumped, nearly out of her chair.

'Really, darling,' she remonstrated.

'I'm worried about Lewis!' she wailed, bouncing up from her chair.

'The law will take its own course,' came the sanguine response, as if Lewis's arrest mattered not one jot when, despite what everyone said, even Bill, Hettie was absolutely certain he was innocent.

'What evidence have they got?' she fumed.

'He's been in trouble with the police before,' Katherine pointed out. 'Darling, I know you're upset. You think this boy is your friend. . . .'

'He *is* my friend,' she protested, thinking then how unbearable he'd find it to be locked up and the key thrown away. It wasn't right. Her grandmother's expression, meanwhile, had grown worryingly severe. Clearly she was running out of patience.

'It's good the police have someone for stealing the war committee papers,' she commented waspishly before biting, with relish, into a buttered scone.

'But surely it has to be the real culprit!' Hettie responded, indignantly. Vainly, she searched for anything else with which she might obtain her objective, namely persuading this stubborn old woman that she, Hettie, was right. There was a long shot, worth a try. 'Grandmamma . . . you know the Chief Constable. I mean in a friendly way. Couldn't you . . . I mean wouldn't you have a word with him?' she wheedled.

'I'd never dream of taking advantage of my position. . . .'

'I wasn't asking that!'

'Weren't you?' the old lady countered sweetly.

It was hopeless. No one would listen. Disconsolate, not sure where to go, nor what to do with herself, Hettie drifted out into the hall. Something was niggling away at her even above and beyond Lewis, bad as that was.

'Are you alright, my dear?' She looked up, startled to find the Count, intent on the sitting room and tea with her grandmother, watching her curiously.

She scowled. It was their second encounter of the day. Shocking as had been Lewis's arrest, her mother had still insisted they show their visitor around the hall, listening carefully the while to his considered opinions on family valuables which, worryingly, had turned out not so valuable after all. 'No one ever listens to me!' she moaned, suddenly so miserable she couldn't care less this man was, to all intents and purposes, a stranger.

'You're worried about Lewis?' he commiserated, with a soothing sympathy springing into his gaze, like balm to her soul.

'But you know Lewis, Count! You've employed him. You surely never believe him guilty?'

'Of course not, the police have clearly got it wrong,' the German agreed, hearteningly quickly.

For the first time, Hettie began to appreciate how much she liked this man.

'You're the first to say so!' she responded heatedly. He smiled wanly.

'My dear young lady, you mustn't trouble yourself,' he soothed, a glimmer of interest showing in his pale blue eyes. 'And now. . . . What's this you've been telling me about some fabulous sword, about to make your fortune?'

He was clearly changing subject to steer her from the worrying subject of Lewis and Hettie flashed him a grateful smile. And then, her expression altered alarmingly as, unasked, the solution to the knotty problem, so painfully niggling away at her since Lewis's arrest, even before it, she realized now, catapulted into her head.

The Count might never have spoken, indeed, might never have existed. 'But that's it!' she muttered, if to herself. Unmindful of just how rude this must appear to the Count, whose brows rose in startled surprise, she spun on her heel and headed swiftly outside.

The great front door slammed behind her, leaving Loxley rocking in her wake, one thought and one thought alone hammering in her head.

She had to find Bill.

She ran all the way down to the village to Bill's cottage, scarcely waiting for Lizzie, who'd answered her impatient knock, to invite her inside, before rushing rudely past her, through into the small back room where Bill, apparently oblivious to the noise and uproar of his siblings at their varying activities, sat at the table working at his books. He looked up, his expression changing to one of pleasurable surprise.

'Het! I wasn't expecting you,' he said, springing up.

She took a moment to catch her breath. 'Bill, I know what the riddle means,' she gasped.

Too many ears were listening avidly, eyes peeled as to what the young couple would say and do next. Bill sprang up, seizing Hettie by the arm and hustling her quickly back outside, drawing her to a halt outside the garage forecourt. 'Would you like to start from the beginning?' he asked but so gently, she almost, if not quite, forgave him for not believing Lewis was innocent.

'It was something the vicar said,' she told him, more calmly now. 'About Queen Elgiva and her being so good, she was more like an angel.'

'So?' he demanded, still uncomprehending.

'So don't you see?' she demanded impatiently, resisting the urge to shake him. 'Nell built the church and if Leon's right and she wrote the riddle too. . . . Can't you see the connection? Nell . . . Queen Elvira . . . Aelric. . .? When Aranrhod is at her greatest power – well, that's the moon, obviously – burnishes the angel bright – and then shall mighty Aelric strike.'

Bill's look of incomprehension only deepened. 'I haven't a clue what you're talking about.'

She spoke slowly, as if to a child. 'It means when the moon's full and shines on the angel, otherwise Queen Elgiva, as depicted in the stained glass window of Loxley's church, then . . . then. . . .'

'Then what?' he demanded, roughly.

She shook her head, having no clear idea what would happen next or how to answer him. 'I don't know yet. But I will – and soon! At the next full moon, we have to be there, in the church, to find out!'

Happily they hadn't long to wait. A consultation of her diary showed Hettie, for once, their luck was in and only two nights later there would be a full moon. Once she'd made this delicious discovery, she waited with a thinly veiled impatience. Two long days to get through but somehow she did get through them, arriving on the given date in a flurry of nervous anticipation in which she longed for the night-time but oddly, dreaded it, too. How could she bear it if she was wrong? Now, more than ever, she found herself wishing Lewis was here, too. If responding to the prospect of being alone with her at the dead of night with an alarming alacrity, Bill was so amused at the whole idea, she could have shaken him. Lewis, meanwhile, was still in the hands of the police with no prospect yet of release. Agonizingly, the day passed. She rode Tallow, dutifully took tea with her grandmother and sat through an interminable dinner in which the Count held forth on his travels in Europe. Unbelievably, at last it was time for bed. Changing quickly into trousers and the thickest, warmest jumper in her wardrobe, she forced herself to lie down on the bed and wait whilst the house settled. At last, thankfully, she discerned every goodnight had been uttered and the last, lingering footsteps echoed tiredly towards the servants' quarters. Moonlight shone, pale and ghostly, through her bedroom window. Groping for the torch, which she'd had the forethought to smuggle into her room earlier and hidden under the bed, she crept downstairs, expecting at any moment for her mother, or worse, her grandmother to appear and demand to know what she was up to at such an ungodly hour.

She was going to find Aelric and make people sorry they'd ever doubted her!

By the front door, she froze, sure she'd heard footsteps padding stealthily behind her so that she whipped round scarcely reassured to see only the humped shapes of ordinary things normally she'd never give thought to: a vase of dried flowers, a heavy mahogany chair, the suit of armour by the stairs, faintly menacing to her now. But everywhere looked so different in the dark!

Bill was waiting on the bridge, lolling against the low wall overlooking the water, flicking his torch on and off and holding it up against his chin and pulling faces.

'This isn't a joke,' she told him, sharply. This was an adventure and one, no matter what the outcome, they'd never forget for the rest of their lives. Both more nervous than they cared to admit, they set off through the darkness, padding swiftly villagewards, their progress illumined here and there by an occasional light spilling from the window of a house they passed and indicative only of the insomnia of its occupant. Soon they'd reached the perimeter of the churchyard with its spiked, iron railings encasing the church spire, a solemn sentry against a star-spangled sky. Once inside consecrated ground, the full moon they'd been so grateful for proved a double-edged sword, casting light on the gravestones which reared, some tilted at odd angles, ivy-strewn and mildewed with age, silent and accusing against the interlopers who had no right to be here and surely would have been better tucked up in bed. Hettie shivered, averting her gaze and leading the way hurriedly along the path to the sanctuary of the porch where, to her relief, the iron handle on the church door turned readily to her pressure. She pushed open the door, which creaked in protest, loud enough – to her guilty ears – to raise the dead. Thankfully, she led the way inside. Haunting, mournful shapes that in light barely touched her, in darkness took her breath.

'Now what do we do?' Bill whispered.

'I don't know,' she said, realizing she really didn't. 'Wait, I suppose?'

What else could they do but for how long and for what, was anyone's guess. Until the moon was at its highest, she expected, peering towards the stained-glass window which glowed out of the darkness towards them, a brilliant mosaic of dazzling, vibrant colour. It seemed crazy to her now they were actually here, as if they were chasing a fantasy no one in their right mind would have given second thought to. Perhaps she really was crazy and imagined all this? Time passed, minutes which passed like hours and in which, oddly, Hettie found comfort in the saint-like features of Queen Elgiva, smiling benignly from her vantage point in the great west window. Why had she never taken notice of her before? Why had she never realized what a beautiful window this was? Queen Elgiva would want them to find Aelric and do some good with it, surely. . . .

It felt as if the church were closing in around her, a kind of smothering hush charged with expectation and seeming, to her heated imagination, as if, from their ancient and crumbling places of rest, all Loxley's many and distinguished ancestors were rising up, urging them to success.

The moon shone, round and full, peering down at them with a warm benevolence. If anything was to happen, it must be now. . . . Her heart thumped, gaining in rapidity, as if it would burst right out of her chest. 'Bill, look. . .' she whispered hoarsely, grabbing at his arm, her fingers digging in so tightly, he winced. But before her startled gaze, a miracle was happening. Elgiva's face was filled with a shimmering light, highlighting her benignity of expression before expanding outwards and shattering into a myriad of tiny flashing lights. And then, and most wonderful of all, a shaft of pure white light hurtled past the two young people watching on in such amazement, its objective the narthex of the church and the ancient memorial built into a recess in the far wall, of the Duke, Nell's father. A dramatic contrast of marble and alabaster, his austere figure lay, hands folded in prayer, a stone lion beneath his feet. The light hit at the point of his sword lying by his side, glowing fiercely before all too quickly extinguishing. As of one, Hettie and Bill rushed forwards, Hettie to throw herself to her knees to search frantically around the spot until, all at once, miraculously, she felt something give beneath her fingers. To their general astonishment, under the shaky beam of Bill's torchlight and with a grating and jarring of stone against stone, the bottom panel of the plinth, on which the Duke slept his long repose, rattled forwards. Bill whistled out loud. Pressing her face up against cold marble, Hettie scrabbled, one-handed inside the aperture just so tantalizingly revealed, seeking that which now she was absolutely certain she would find there. Wonderfully, her hand brushed against cloth. Stretching her hand out to its limit, she clawed it eagerly towards her to discover a length of material wrapped around . . . what exactly?

She knew – of course she knew! So great was her excitement, she wanted to scream it out loud. Instead, she knelt, her knees pressing into the cold-flagged floor and with a heartfelt prayer on her lips. Please, God, let it be what she thought. . . . With trembling fingers, she began to unwrap that which Nell, Duchess of Loxley, her illustrious ancestor, had concealed and which had not seen the light of day for centuries.

She gasped out loud. Revealed before their startled gaze lay a magnificent two-handed broadsword, a dazzling glory of intricately wrought gold, encrusted with rubies, opals and diamonds, shimmering and winking in Bill's torchlight.

'Aelric,' Hettie breathed, even now scarcely able to believe it.

Awestruck, Bill sank to his knees besides her.

'It's true, then,' he whispered.

'So it appears!' came a disembodied voice from behind.

Hettie jumped, scrambling quickly to her feet as Bill swung

his torch up, revealing, shockingly, Count Charles Dresler and the Luger pistol in his hand, which, for the moment and to the horror of both young people, was directed straight at Hettie's heart.

Chapter Eleven

Her heart was thudding a tattoo against her ribcage. Bewildered, Hettie scrambled to her feet, her horrified gaze centred on the Luger pistol in the Count's hand, pointed at her with an ease suggesting he was only too used to firearms. Only now did the dim certainty raise itself: other than that she had visited his art gallery in Berlin, she knew nothing about this man. With a coolness that said much for her nerves, she took in their predicament. They were unarmed. The Count obviously meant trouble. Worse, no one knew they were here.

'But I don't understand!' she wailed.

'Don't even try, my dear,' he responded calmly, his gaze flickering towards Bill and onwards again, greedily, to Aelric, so newly reborn, glinting in the moonlight like a thousand twinkling stars. His eyes widened. Momentarily, his attention was deflected, so he didn't see, as did Hettie, out of the darkness of the narthex, a man's form come creeping, gathering itself as it moved closer. Suddenly, startlingly, the figure sprang towards the Count and with such a force, the gun was knocked from his hand and the two men sent crashing to the floor. Shocked, Bill dropped the torch, plunging the scene into darkness. Undeterred, clasped in a deadly embrace, the two figures rolled over and over. Instinctively, Bill and Hettie dropped to their knees and began to scrabble round after the torch.

'Got it!' Bill muttered, closing his fingers around cold metal so a wavering light once again illuminated the scene. Hettie scrambled to her feet, much of her fear dissipated to find the Count sitting on the floor and Roland de Loxley, for it was the Frenchman who'd arrived just in time to save them, standing triumphantly over his adversary, pointing the gun to his head.

'You followed us!' Bill said, shocked.

Roland glared grimly down at his captive. 'I wasn't the only one. Are you alright?'

'Only thanks to you,' Hettie chimed in, glowering at the man who'd so recently held them to ransom. That he'd meant to rob them of Aelric was clear but had he meant to shoot them too? The thought made her cold all over.

The Count sat nursing his head. A trickle of blood ran down his forehead.

'Get up!' Roland snapped.

The man's head jerked up as, inexplicably, he barked a volley of German towards Roland, at which the Frenchman's expression faltered. He looked about him nervously.

'What's he saying?' Hettie demanded, too late cursing the lack of attention to which she'd treated German lessons at school. Horrified, she watched as Roland lowered the gun and helped the Count up, meanwhile, returning the conversation in German so once again, she was left agonizing over what had been said. She didn't even know Roland spoke the language and so fluently too. He must know neither she nor Bill understood enough to follow a conversation!

Suddenly, the outpouring ceased, replaced by a silence, more terrible than anything so far.

Hettie's hackles rose, every sense telling her that something was badly wrong.

They were in trouble again. Roland's gun hand shifted. 'I'm sorry,' he muttered, pointing the gun towards a shocked Hettie, his gaze sliding away as if he couldn't even bear to look at her now.

Hettie regarded him in blank incomprehension. But this

couldn't be happening! Why would he save them from the Count and then threaten them himself? Stifling a cry of fear, she stepped back. 'Roland? But what are you doing? Have you gone crazy. . . ?'

Mutely, he shook his head. Dreadfully, it was the Count who broke the silence, chuckling quietly to himself and causing a shiver of dread to race the length of Hettie's spine so she couldn't think now how she'd ever once liked the man. That Roland was in some kind of a thrall to him was obvious.

'I was merely pointing out to our friend here our connections. . . .' the German said smoothly.

'Connections?' Bill interrupted, as bewildered as Hettie.

'With the fatherland of course!' their captor stated gloatingly.

None of this was making sense. 'Germany, you mean?' Hettie demanded.

'He's helped our party in the past,' the Count concurred, agreeably.

Bill's eyes blazed with belated comprehension. 'You're a blasted Nazi, aren't you?'

'Politically speaking, I'm a member of the National Socialist party. . . .'

He spoke so pleasantly, as if he were talking about the weather instead of the horror that even Hettie knew was invading every part of Germany.

'Roland, what's this about?' she implored, swinging back towards him, her fears only fuelled to see the Frenchman's hand tighten around the gun. 'Roland . . . you aren't a Nazi, are you? For heaven's sake. . . .'

The Frenchman shook his head. 'I never realized . . . things I passed on. . . . But I was left with no option, don't you see? I only had a contact number. How was I to know it was this man I was reporting back to?'

It was so much garbled nonsense and yet, underneath, there ran a dreadful sense. Suddenly, to Hettie, consumed by a burning sense of injustice, everything became dreadfully clear. Roland, for some reason yet unknown, had been passing information to the Nazis, probably to this man here, a self-confessed and fully paid-up member of the party. A bunch of thugs if everything her grandmother told her was true. Abruptly, the Count's smile disappeared and she saw the ruthlessness hidden beneath the affable veneer.

'Give me the gun, Loxley!' he barked.

To her dismay, appearing a broken man, Roland tamely handed the weapon over and with it, the Count motioned the little party, Roland included, towards the dim interior of the church, illumined still by moonlight, shining benignly now through the great west window.

Filled with dread, casting a lingering glance back towards Aelric, lying discarded on the floor, Hettie was left with no option but to do as she was bidden, heading back down the aisles and in the direction of the chancel. Once there, the German pointed with the gun towards the sacristy, the small side room where Lawrence Payne kept his books and vestments.

'Get in,' he barked, tersely. 'And get a move on!'

They trooped inside, the burly figure of the Count momentarily framed in the doorway before, with one swift movement, he slammed the door shut behind them and they heard the sound of the key grating in the lock. They were trapped.

Four square walls with a single, high window, too small even for Hettie to squeeze through. The Count's footsteps faded quickly away, on his way no doubt to pick up Aelric before making good his escape. Furious now, Hettie ran to the door and rattled the handle but to no avail. There was no escape and she knew exactly who to blame.

'How could you! I can't believe it, Roland! You! A spy?' she spat, rounding on Roland de Loxley angrily and yet still with the wits to take satisfaction in the fact he was as trapped as they. Serve him right too!

Three things happened then. The Frenchman's face crumpled, the light went out and Bill swore violently, under his breath.

'The battery's gone,' he muttered, shaking the torch.

No one appeared to know quite what to do other than to wait disconsolately for their eyes to refocus. Muffled shapes and strange shadows and, hanging on the far wall, a little bright cross belonging to Lawrence Payne, from which a strange lustre emanated, somehow giving Hettie strength.

'We only need to wait for morning,' she said, forcing a note of encouragement into her voice.

'We might as well make ourselves comfy, then,' Bill grumbled, settling himself back against the wall. Hettie flung herself down beside him.

'Are you going to tell us what's going on?' she demanded of Roland, aware of his bulk settling down against the wall opposite. He sighed heavily. All the spirit had gone out of him.

'You'll think badly of me. . . .' he answered, wretchedly.

'Too right we will,' Bill butted in.

'Let him talk,' Hettie hissed, despite her anger, acknowledging her growing curiosity as to what could have induced this man to present himself as their friend when, in reality, he was nothing but a blasted spy. Suspicion rose, rearing its ugly head. 'You stole General Hawker's papers and let Lewis take the blame for it!' she burst out, the enormity of this crime, to Hettie, worse than anything so far.

The Frenchman's voice was full of remorse. 'I couldn't help it. I had to!'

'I bet,' Bill interjected, furiously.

'Bill!' Hettie warned, alarmed, when they were in trouble enough, that a fight would develop. 'Go on,' she encouraged and feeling rather than seeing Roland's nod of complicity.

'I did it for the woman I love, desperately, a German by nationality. We met . . . oh, so long ago I can scarcely remember it now.'

'So what?' Bill demanded, failing to see the relevance of this.

'She hated the way things were going in her country and got involved with the wrong people, that's what. They were careless, leaving too many clues as to their identity. They were denounced and she was taken prisoner by the Nazis. People will say anything under torture. It wouldn't have taken them long to find out every single thing about her and about me. So they got at me through her – that's how the Nazis operate. They told me if I didn't do as they said, it would fall harshly on her. Oh, but how could I bear the thought of that!' he burst out, miserably.

'I see,' said Hettie, who suddenly did.

Like a dam burst, now he'd started, Roland de Loxley was only too eager to continue. 'I often travel on business to England and the Nazis knew it. They asked me only little things at first, to note the layout of places, factories, military establishments, that kind of thing. . . .'

'And you told them, of course!' Bill snapped.

'But what else could I do?' the Frenchman implored. 'What would you do if you loved someone and you knew they'd be for it if you didn't do what you were told?'

'I wouldn't betray my country. . . .'

'England isn't my country!'

'It isn't,' Hettie murmured, conceding this too.

His eyes glittered, like cat's eyes burning through the darkness. 'It was my rotten luck there was all that business in the papers about Alexander Hyssop's tomb. It must have jogged someone's mind high up in the Nazi hierarchy.'

'Dresler,' Bill growled.

'I swear I never knew he was my contact. I was as shocked as you. I followed him tonight to help you, remember?'

Did that excuse the rest of his behaviour? Hettie thought not. Her temper, always simmering, rose up in protest. 'You came here professing kinship when, all along, you were only interested in getting your hands on papers for your Nazi spymasters. You found out about the safe and then discovered the second secret tunnel into the room where it was kept!'

'I didn't, actually,' Roland interrupted, so vehemently, Hettie could have no doubt but that he spoke the truth. 'I found out about the safe from your grandmother. The first time I stayed, I had a snoop round and discovered the key in her bureau. It was easy enough to take an impression. The discovery of the tunnel at a later date was just an odd coincidence. The Nazis already knew about the war committee's meetings, that's why they wanted me here, I suspect. It hardly took a genius to know I'd find out something of importance, enough to keep them quiet and bring my Lilli back to me.'

'But how did you get into the safe when Grandmother changes the combination so often?' Hettie demanded indignantly. Roland laughed bitterly.

'I worked in espionage in the war – who better after all? Spending so much time in Germany with Lilli, in my youth, I speak the language fluently. A safe like your grandmother's is nothing to me.'

'A double agent!' Despite Hettie's revulsion, it was hard not to be impressed how easily his object had been achieved and how little they'd been aware of it. 'But how come you turned up here tonight just when Dresler had us at his mercy?'

Irony tinged his voice. 'Simple good fortune – or bad, as it turned out for me. I let the Nazis know about the possibility of the sword being here. Acting on that knowledge, I suspect that was why Dresler appeared. With his love of antiquity, how could he keep away! He heard you go out tonight and simply followed you. I just happened to hear him leave his room. I was curious what he was up to, that was all. I'm here to spy. I'm meant to take note and report back and the more I tell them, the more chance I'll have of getting my Lilli back. But there was something about Dresler I didn't trust. Intuition, I suppose, but doing what I do, I've developed a nose for it. I simply followed him.'

'He was following us and you followed him. . . ?'

For a moment, Hettie was lost for words. Abruptly, her anger disappeared. If she was pushed, she'd even have to admit to a surprising sympathy for this man who, after all, had only been acting in a misguided attempt to help the woman he loved. Pushed into a corner, he'd seen no other way out. She was upset, distraught even but at least now, she understood.

The problem was how long it would be before they could get out of here. She sighed heavily, stretching out her legs and settling herself back more comfortably, longing now for the morning to arrive and for Lawrence Payne to open up the church.

Katherine was sitting at her dressing table, brushing hair which, despite her age, was still luxuriant, roused from her reverie by an urgent knocking on her bedroom door. Always an early riser, she was already dressed. She got up to discover an anxious-looking Bronwyn outside in the corridor.

'Hettie's bed's not been slept in. . . .' she burst out.

'Whatever's the girl up to now?'

They were about to find out. Urgent voices from the ground floor, one distinctly Hettie's, brought both women hurrying downstairs to the hall to discover a bewildered Soames doing his best to pacify a little knot of folk comprising Lawrence Payne, Hettie and Bill. Both young people were clearly distraught.

'Whatever now?' Katherine demanded, gliding towards them.

Hettie swung towards her grandmother, eagerly. 'We've found Aelric, Grandmamma, it really does exist! We've been locked up in the church all night. . . . Count Dresler and Roland are spies and the Count's run off with Aelric. The Reverend's let us out and he's called the police and they've taken Roland into custody!'

It was too much and she wasn't making the slightest sense. Ordering her, sharply, to calm down, Katherine ushered them all into the morning room, where one of the maids had already lit the fire. Over the tea Soames had brought, in growing astonishment, the two women began to make sense of the garbled tale; it appeared to be a story lifted from a book. Hearing of Roland's involvement, Bronwyn was aware of a sharp stab of pain.

'I can't believe Roland's a traitor!' she implored, looking round in desperation for someone to disabuse her of the notion.

'I'm afraid, it's true, every word,' Lawrence Payne murmured. 'You can imagine my shock to discover Bill and Hettie locked up in my sacristy. To do de Loxley credit, he never tried to run away whilst I called the police. No point, I suppose, now his cover's blown.'

'The Nazis have the woman he loves.' Hettie threw her mother an uneasy glance. 'But he's still been spying, Mother. And it's terrible that he's the one who stole those papers and allowed Lewis to take the blame. Whatever will General Hawker say?'

The sick feeling of dread, stirring in the pit of Bronwyn's stomach, rose up, threatening to engulf her. Miserably, she acknowledged the truth. The man with whom she'd nearly fallen in love, perhaps *had* fallen in love, was a traitor, a man who'd taken advantage of her generosity. Suddenly, inactivity was a painful thing. She sprang up, looking towards Bill and Hettie. 'Go and have some breakfast and Hettie, after it, you're to have a lie-down. No arguments, darling. You must be in shock.'

'So must you, Bronwyn,' Katherine interjected, perceptively. Her grip tightened around the handle of her walking stick. 'Dresler is one thing but to think Roland took us all in. . . .' Her gaze narrowed. 'Blast Dresler for taking our property!'

'Do you mean Aelric, Grandmamma?' Hettie interjected, her face alive with excitement. 'Theoretically, it was King Charles' property so, really, it doesn't belong to us. Oh, but if only you could have seen it! It's wonderful beyond words and to think it's been hidden away here all these years! And now it's lost and we'll probably never, ever see it again. . . .'

Dumbfounded, as he usually was in the presence of Katherine Loxley, Bill spoke up.

'The police will find Dresler, Het. He won't get out of the country.'

They all prayed he was right. 'I'll ring Digby,' Bronwyn said, her mind, meantime, working furiously. 'I'll have to let Reuben know what's happened. He's been so worried about Lewis. The poor boy's innocent, after all.'

Lawrence Payne stood up. 'And I must go. After they'd taken de Loxley into custody, the police left a constable guarding the church. I'd better see if he wants a cup of tea. You'll let me know if there's news?'

'Of course, Reverend!'

They left the room, Bronwyn to spend the next half-hour engaged on the telephone, first to the Chief Inspector to furnish him with the little she knew of Dresler and then to Reuben, discovering an odd comfort to hear his voice. She was surprised to learn how much he already knew.

'I've had a call from the police to pick up Lewis,' he said, his voice ringing with relief.

Feeling anew the enormity of everything that had happened, as much as she was able, she filled in the gaps, sensing his shock even over the airwaves. 'Would you mind if I came with you?' she asked. 'They won't let you see him, Bron,' he murmured, intuiting it was Roland she wanted to see.

She flushed. Did everyone know of their relationship? Miserably, she stared at a portrait of the eighth Duke, hanging over the telephone table, which had miraculously survived that terrible fire all those years before. 'I have to talk to him, Reuben,' she muttered, already dreading it.

Reuben's next words brought a rush of relief. 'I'll call and pick you up,' he said, at once.

'Eat up, Bill, we've things to do,' Hettie said, having left the biggest part of her breakfast uneaten. Her appetite had deserted her, her thoughts were chaotic, each thread of the tangle that had been her life of late vying for attention so she didn't know what to think first. The shock of finding Aelric, the Count's wickedness and Roland's duplicity and now the overwhelming disappointment of Aelric's disappearance, the Count with it, so there was little chance of the police finding either again. She was alone with Bill; after consuming a hearty breakfast, her grandmother had disappeared upstairs whilst her mother had gone with Reuben to pick up Lewis. Hettie had wanted to go too but hadn't been allowed and she'd been too tired to argue.

'I thought your mother told you to have a lie-down?' Bill frowned, biting with relish into a slice of toast thickly smeared with marmalade.

'Are you joking? This situation is all my fault, Bill,' she said fervently. 'I have to do something. I was the one who invited Dresler here.'

'No one blames you, Het, he and de Loxley took everyone in. . . .' Bill paused, his gaze holding hers and emotion shadowing across his face so, with a heavy heart, Hettie guessed what might be coming next. 'Hettie, I know this isn't the right time to talk about this, exactly,' he began. 'But last night, holed up in the church, got me to thinking . . . where you and I are going, exactly.' This last came out in a rush. He stopped, looking wretched.

'Where we usually go, I expect?' she answered, callously flippant, trying to head him off and yet despising herself for it. It was no good. He'd embarked upon this conversation and was determined to continue it, no matter what she wanted.

'You do know . . . I love you, Het?'

Three little words, hanging in the air between them. With a quick frown, Hettie got up, crossing the room to the window to stand, arms folded, staring out into the garden. She'd put off this conversation too long and it wasn't fair. 'I love you too,' she said as he joined her, hating then that what she said next, was bound to hurt him. She turned towards him.

'Of course we love each other, Bill. We've known each other

for ever but don't you see. . . ? That's the problem.'

'But why should it be a problem? I'll never love anyone but you, Het. You know that's true.'

'That's what you think now,' she answered, patiently.

'You've been listening to your grandmother again!'

She shook her head, determined, for both their sakes, he had to hear this out. 'I've been thinking too, Bill, a lot, if you must know. Oh, but so much of what Grandmamma says is right! We are too young. We need to live a little, first. . . .'

Would he understand? But he must feel it too! She was talking about life and that they had to live it to the full, seizing it by the throat if necessary. Relationships now, at their young age, would only complicate matters. He started to protest but she reached up, laying a finger to his lips. She was right; he knew it and she saw that he did. Suddenly, inaction was anathema.

'We ought to tell Leon about Aelric,' she murmured, changing subject quickly.

Bill's face worked. 'You're right, I expect. You usually are,' he admitted.

The thorny subject between them settled, for now, at least, they fetched their coats and went outside, heading off quickly towards the gypsies' encampment, it seeming to Hettie that the Romani people had a right to know what had happened to the sword that once, centuries ago, they had delivered here, in all good faith, to Loxley. They were lucky. Leon was in his caravan, sitting with his bony fingers resting on his knees, to listen gravely to all they had to say.

'Wait here,' he commanded when finally, Hettie ran out of steam. He rose quickly, leaving them alone but returning shortly, his lean features swirling with an emotion at which Hettie could only guess. For a moment, it crossed her mind she wouldn't care to get the wrong side of this man.

'I've put the word out amongst our people. Let's pray we're not too late,' he said.

'About Dresler?' she demanded.

The gypsy's eyes flashed. 'We Romanies hear things others might not. Our people will get to know . . . wherever Dresler is. Don't worry; there's a chance we'll apprehend him yet.'

'Are you alright?' Reuben demanded roughly, of the woman sitting so self-contained in the passenger seat beside him. His grip on the steering wheel tightened, a searing pain, almost physical, assailing him, long suppressed, threatening to overwhelm him, so it was all he could do not to slam on the brakes and tell her how he felt. How much he loved her. How he'd always love her. How she could count on him at any time and no matter what.

He'd willingly give his life for her.

With effort, he dragged his mind back to the road and the task ahead. Now wasn't the time to lay his undying devotion before Bronwyn Loxley and he was beginning to doubt if that particular situation would ever present itself.

'I'm afraid I'm not alright,' Bronwyn answered. She shot him a wary glance, one acknowledging how far back they went and how, in a way she was yet to understand, he was wrapped up in her deep and sincerely held belief in Loxley. She frowned. 'It's not been much of a homecoming for you, Reuben.'

'Ah . . . home,' he muttered but in such a tone, her frown deepened.

'Are you planning on staying?' she asked.

'Would you like me to?' he fired back, waiting for the answer with bated breath and yet all the while aware she couldn't have the slightest idea of how important her answer was.

'You're family,' she said, simply. 'Of course I want you to stay.'

'I'll stay then,' he said. It was enough, more than he'd hoped, no matter what his familial connection; he'd once been the game-keeper here. It was food for thought, most of it indigestible. He was glad when they'd reached the bleak, slate-roofed building, centred in the middle of the thriving industrial town of Cossethay and serving as its police station. They discovered Lewis inside it, sitting in the main foyer, slouched in a chair across from the desk sergeant and unable to disguise his relief when they walked through the door.

'I thought you'd never get here,' he muttered, ungraciously.

Beneath the surface bravado he'd been badly frightened and Bronwyn's heart went out to him. Already she was having second thoughts. Could she really bear seeing Roland again? How could she forgive him after everything he'd done! Despite all her misgivings, instinct drove her on, making her only too aware that if she didn't come to terms with everything that had happened, it would eventually drive her mad.

'We'll soon have you home, lad. Any news on Dresler, yet?' Reuben asked, addressing this last to the desk sergeant, a grizzled, middle-aged man watching on with interest.

He shook his head. 'I don't believe there is, sir. But we'll catch him, you mark my words.'

Bronwyn frowned. 'Would it be possible to see Mr de Loxley?' she demanded quickly.

'I'm sorry, Your Grace. I'm not exactly sure it would,' the policeman returned, awkwardly. And then, seemingly from nowhere and to their immense relief, Digby appeared.

'I'll take over, Carter,' he said, crisply, his gaze settling on Bronwyn. 'This is highly irregular, Your Grace. Mr de Loxley's still under interrogation. Hawker's on his way over. It's a serious business, I'm afraid.'

'She only wants five minutes, man,' Reuben intervened.

There was a pause whilst the police inspector considered but to their relief, he gave in graciously.

'Five minutes, then!'

'I'll wait outside with Lewis,' Reuben murmured and, in a gesture of support of which Bronwyn was only dimly aware, his hand brushed her arm. Throwing him a grateful smile, she followed the Chief Inspector, alarmed to discover, when he'd ushered her through to the rear of the building, how much she wanted to turn back, to Reuben and to safety. And then, suddenly, as was so often the case when she thought of Reuben, she was thinking of Harry, so fiercely this time, his presence was almost tangible, as if he was beside her, giving her strength, allowing her to walk steadily down numerous steps and along twisting corridors and finally through a door, deep within the bowels of the building, which Digby carefully unlocked with keys he took from his pocket.

'There you go, Your Grace,' he muttered, throwing the door wide and waiting for her to pass through before closing it, softly, behind her. His footsteps receded.

Bronwyn braced herself. Roland was sitting with his head buried in his hands, an empty coffee cup and a packet of cigarettes, unopened, on the table in front of him. He looked up eagerly as she came in so, for a moment, Bronwyn saw, with a twist of her heart, a glimpse of the man with whom she'd so very nearly fallen in love. Perhaps she had loved him. How could she ever know now! This man had turned her thoughts from Harry and given her the belief she could be happy again. Wearily, she sank into the vacant chair. All she'd rehearsed saying the way over here, spilling out her anger and her pain, flew from her head.

'I thought I'd never see you again,' he said, breaking the silence if only because one of them must.

'How could you, Roland? I . . . we . . . trusted you,' she said, brokenly.

His head bowed. 'What I did was unforgiveable but I did have good reason. You have to believe me, Bron, hard as it is to understand.'

'Hettie told me . . . about Lilli. You must love her very much.' There, it was out! The one thing that hurt above all and at least he didn't deny it.

'I didn't know what else to do.'

'You led me on. You made me think you were free to love me

when all the while . . . you loved someone else. How could you do that to me, Roland?'

'It was unforgiveable and saying I'm sorry doesn't begin to address it. . . .'

'At least you admit it.' How difficult it was to keep reproach from her voice. He heard it and flushed.

'But I do have feelings for you, Bron! It wasn't all show. I'd never have hurt you, willingly. Any other time . . . given different circumstances. . . . I wanted to tell you about Lilli. It was on the tip of my tongue, so many times and yet, how could I?'

'You could have trusted me. You could have tried, Roland.' The tears she'd determined not to let fall, stung the back of Bronwyn's eyes. Wretchedly, already, the door was opening and Digby's head appearing around it.

'Time's up, Your Grace,' he murmured but with a gentleness in his voice which, even in her dismay, surprised her. She stood up, seeing before her now only a weak man. A man who'd done a bad thing in a futile effort to put right a wrong, not of his making. The evil reach of the Nazis was stretching far and wide. There were troubled times ahead and she knew that now.

After all, her overriding emotion was one of pity. 'I'll do what I can to help you,' she said.

Two days later, in a local garage in Fernley Appleton, a busy market town nestled on the edges of Dartmoor, a well-dressed man entered the premises, treating with indifference the bedraggled tinker dozing gently on its forecourt, taking shelter against the slanting rain which had been falling all morning. The place was surprisingly busy, happening to run as a thriving side business, even at this poor time of year, cycle and car hire for passing trade and holidaymakers. Patiently, the man waited his turn to be served and, when it arrived, with his old world manner and good humour, easily charmed the middle-aged lady behind the counter. Several minutes later, the key to a motor clutched in one elegant hand, his imposing figure re-emerged to stand and look around him in evident satisfaction – a man happy with his lot and inordinately pleased with life. Abruptly, the tinker at his feet stirred and woke up, a bundle of rags, shifting to pathetic life.

'Spare a few coppers, mister?' he called, tremulously.

Struck by the disparity of their circumstances, confident he'd be out of the country within the next few days and thinking nothing of it, Dresler reached into his pocket, idly flicking a coin towards the eager, grasping hand, before striding briskly away.

The driving rain which had beset them these last three days splattered relentlessly against the morning room window. Staring out bleakly into the tangled remains of a garden once so redolent of summer, Hettie wondered if, in all her short life, she'd ever felt quite so frustrated. Despite their recent ordeal at the hands of Count Dresler, Bill had still had to go into college. Lewis meanwhile, since his release from prison, had been proving curiously evasive. Even Reuben had no idea where the young man had hidden himself away. Gone to ground to lick his wounds, Hettie suspected, cross at him because of it when she'd so much to tell him. Frowning, she turned away from the window as Soames, followed by her mother, came in bearing a tray laden with tea things. Katherine Loxley was at a meeting of the Women's Institute. No matter what calamitous events beset its occupants, Loxley's life ground inexorably on. As usual, any dissatisfaction Hettie was happening to feel was written plainly on her face.

'Hettie, please cheer up!' her mother ordered, once Soames had gone. She poured tea, handing a cup to Hettie before taking hers over to the hearth to drink, where a cheerful fire burned. She was pale, Hettie saw, at last waking up to the fact, the last few days hadn't been easy for her mother, either.

'There's no news of that wretch, Dresler, yet, I take it?' she demanded, crossly.

Regrettably, her mother shook her head. 'General Hawker

rang. They still have a watch on the coast and the airports but it looks as if he's slipped the net, I'm afraid.'

'But it's so unfair!' Hettie bridled. 'You do realize, if we could only find Aelric, all our financial worries would be solved?'

Bronwyn, as ever, was philosophical. 'It'll end up in the hands of a private collector, I expect, and our Count will make himself a lot of money. I would have liked to have seen it, all the same. . . .'

There was something else Hettie needed to know, though it was an awkward subject. 'Did the General happen to say what will happen to Roland?' she asked, quietly. The business with Roland had hurt her mother badly and Hettie could have killed him for it.

'He'll go to prison,' she admitted. 'Though the General tells me, hopefully, he may be able to negotiate Lilli's release through an exchange. She'll hardly be of much use to the Nazis now they have no use for Roland.' A shaft of sunlight in a gloom of general adversity and Hettie was only too aware that, if this situation could be achieved, her mother, such a forgiving woman, would take great comfort from it.

At that moment, the door reopened and Soames reappeared to usher in the Chief Inspector, who hurried towards them, smiling, unusually for him who found so little to smile at in life. 'I thought you'd want to know, we've found that villain Dresler!' he burst out at once, news as surprising as it was welcome and Hettie's heart filled with joy. A wrong righted and a bad man exactly where he should be, safe in the hands of the British police!

'We acted on a tip-off from a gypsy. He was holed up on Dartmoor,' Digby went on happily. 'We surrounded the cottage he'd rented at first light this morning.'

'Chief Inspector, that's wonderful,' Bronwyn enthused.

'Aye, he'll have more than a few questions to answer, that one! A tricky customer, our Count. . . .'

'And Aelric? You have found Aelric, too?' Hettie demanded,

impatiently. It was wonderful news of course but unfortunately, the Count's capture wasn't the only issue at stake here. She saw at once by the little man's face that there might be a problem and her heart sank.

The Chief Inspector removed his hat, smoothing the brim with his sleeve.

'Unfortunately not, though we've turned the place upside-down.'

'But I don't understand! He must have had it with him . . . hidden it somewhere?' Hettie wailed.

Digby shook his head. 'He swore he'd put it under his bed for safe keeping and appears as mystified as anyone where it's disappeared. I have to admit, on this occasion, I happen to believe him. Your fabled sword's gone, I'm afraid. Vamoosed, vanished and only the good Lord knows where. . . .'

It was so jolly unfair and so Hettie announced, at dinner that night, to everyone gathered round the table. 'Where can it be?' she fumed.

'It's no good moaning, Hettie. We have to get on with it,' Katherine Loxley responded, tartly, throwing a discontented look meanwhile towards Bill and Reuben, their dinner guests, invited at the last minute by Bronwyn to liven up the party. Hettie had asked Lewis too but the young man had declined. Hurt by it, Hettie had arrived at the not unnatural conclusion he was deliberately avoiding her and that she must in some way have offended him.

'You mustn't worry,' Reuben said, his stern gaze settling on her mother as if it were to her alone to whom he addressed himself. Chewing thoughtfully on a stick of celery, Hettie frowned. It was ridiculous of course, but she'd got to wondering of late if her newly discovered uncle didn't feel more for her mother than he actually ought. Thoughts of her portrait in Berlin only added fuel to the suspicion.

This business was going to her head, she mused. The lamps were lit, the firelight flickered, chasing a rainbow of sparkling colour across the chandelier hanging low over the table. At once and to everyone's surprise, the door burst open and a tall, imposing figure strode into the room. It was Leon. Soames hurried after him.

'Madam, I'm sorry,' the elderly butler spluttered, full of a righteous indignation.

'It's alright, Soames,' Bronwyn answered, half-rising in her seat.

'Leon!' Hettie beamed, happily.

'A fitting return,' the gypsy leader murmured enigmatically, standing to gaze about him. With his long, flowing white locks and cloak, fastened with a jewelled pin winking in the glittering light, he looked a throwback to ancient times, a magnificent and medieval Saxon king. All at once, he tossed back his cloak to reveal the bundle he carried under one arm and which, with one bright and swift movement, he threw to the floor, the material around it unravelling as it fell so a dazzling brightness clattered on the flagstones. A ringing of ancient times, glittering and glistening gold, beset with sparkling jewels, rubies, emeralds and amethysts. But then, so much more than this, its real worth, a thing intangible.

Hettie's heart exploded in happiness and joy. Aelric was home.

In great reverence, they carried the sword to the anteroom, laying it in state on the green baize table there, where, willingly, the servants took it in turns to sit up to keep watch until an expert should be summoned from London to give it proper valuation.

'It is crown property,' Katherine mused, still clearly shocked by events.

'But it belongs here!' Hettie retorted, so adamantly, the elderly lady smiled.

They were due a hefty remuneration whatever the outcome,

wrong as it felt to value in purely monetary terms a work of art so clearly beyond value.

It was breakfast the following morning, Leon had long since departed but not before enthralling the company with the tale of how his people had tracked Dresler to his hide-out, stealing in to remove Aelric to safety before denouncing him to the police. 'It was long our trust to bring Aelric home,' he'd finished, his words ringing with pride that once, long ago, Romani people had been able to do the embattled Stuart King a good turn.

Munching on a slice of toast, Hettie was interrupted from her reverie by Soames. 'A visitor, Your Grace,' he murmured. 'I've put him in the morning room. . . .'

Half-guessing who it would be, at once she threw down her serviette and hurried through, both relieved and delighted to find Lewis waiting, the first time she'd seen him since his release from prison. Her pleasure unfortunately was of a short duration.

'I'm here to say goodbye, Het. I couldn't go without seeing you again,' he said, in one breath taking all pleasure from his visit.

'But you can't go now!' she wailed. 'Where are you going?'

'I'm going to travel; I want to see the world whilst I'm still young enough to enjoy it.'

Hettie had no idea why she was instantly so against the idea. And yet it would be good for him, she acknowledged inwardly, a chance to put all his recent troubles behind him.

'I've got something to show you,' she said, mastering both her confusion and disappointment together, taking his hand and dragging him upstairs to the anteroom. Loftily dismissing the servant keeping watch, she brought him to the table where Aelric lay in state, the morning's pale light shifting over its brilliance, catching at its myriad of jewels so even she marvelled at it anew. A veil of centuries torn away, bringing to mind another young couple who'd shared a deep and joyful union. A love Hettie knew instinctively she'd yet to find.

Lewis stood beside her. 'It's breathtaking, Het,' he murmured.

'I wish you didn't have to go' she said, helplessly and, turning towards him, remembering now how much they'd been through together.

'I'll be back. Someday,' he muttered. Before she could stop him, not even sure if she wanted to, he drew her towards him, kissing her gently and, oh so sweetly. And then he was gone, his footsteps clattering swiftly downstairs, leaving her staring after him, her gaze full of wonder and her fingers rising to trace his kiss on her lips.

Epilogue

Autumn was underway, the leaves in the churchyard drifting to join their compatriots, a riot of rich, bright colour, carpeting the floor around. Arranging the rusty-gold dahlias in the pot over her grandpa's grave, Ursula Hamilton rocked back on her heels, looking past the weathered headstone to the stained glass in the church beyond, upon which the morning's sun shimmered and gleamed, sparkling bright jewels over Queen Elgiva and Edmund, her King. And yet he was a mortal man whom Elgiva had loved with the same intensity as Ursula loved her Freddie, she mused. What affinity she felt to this Saxon Queen, who smiled so benignly on one and all.

The wind whistled, a windblown choir, a refrain of heavenly voices, rustling high up into the empyrean. Instinctively, Ursula's hand fell to her stomach, feeling its flatness and yet, too, the life so miraculously quickening there. The music in her heart rose to a crescendo, a miracle, an answer to her prayers to this sainted lady to whom those in trouble had long since prayed.

'You'll be a great-grandfather, Ned,' she whispered, hearing the old man's chortle of delight as clearly as if he were standing here beside her. Doctors weren't always right and Ned would have told her exactly as much. Smiling, she rose to her feet, quickly dusting down her knees. There was nothing to do now, only go home and tell Freddie.

Miracles happened all the time. All you had to do was believe. . . .